LACHLAN'S
PR⊕TÉGÉ

LACHLAN'S PROTÉGÉ

V. F. MASON

Edited by Hot Tree Editing

Cover Design: Sommer Stein

Photographer: Wander Aguiar

Cover Model: Colton Benson

To the power of love.

PROLOGUE

Valencia

My eyes snap open. I look straight ahead and take a deep breath, then step into a pose. I'm illuminated by the moonlight shining brightly into the room from the glass-like ceiling above me. This silent space is filled with a mysterious atmosphere, creating an almost-perfect setting for a romantic evening.

The familiar first notes of Tchaikovsky's *Swan Lake* echo through the room, and I assume the position, rising on my toes and swaying from side to side while slowly moving to the corner. I hop on my toes again, owning the stage as if nothing matters, blocking the outside world away.

To each dramatic note, I perform with my hands and facial expressions, giving away all the hopelessness of the swan, the beautiful young woman Odette, who's been captured by the dark sorcerer and can't be reunited with her lover.

The pain and heartache fuel her desire to fight against him, so she feeds on them even if they threaten to destroy her.

I swirl and swirl, rising up and down, up and down, and then a cry of pain slips past my lips as my feet land on glass. I halt my movements, barely breathing from the glass digging into my skin.

I glance down to see my white pointe shoes slowly coating in blood from all the scattered glass covering the floor; if one is careful enough to avoid it, he is a master.

My feet agonizingly throb. I can barely stand on them. My rasping breaths help me to concentrate on something other than the pain.

I've been doing nothing but dancing for the last hour. I've never performed for this long without a break in my life.

The sound of the lighter flicking fills the space as he lights up his cigarette, takes a deep breath, and exhales it in my direction while resting comfortably on the chair right in front of me. "Ah, Valencia. You know the rules. Never stop." His deep, dangerous voice raises goose bumps on my skin, reminding me once again that the monster never sleeps.

He just feeds on my misery.

He tugs on the rope wrapped tightly around my waist and I stumble forward. I can't help the groan of pain when he directs me onto the big pile of glass. The air freezes in my lungs while I pray for the hurt to pass so I can continue.

But I can't.

Instead, fear unlike anything before spreads through me. Injuries like this may ruin a dancer's career forever, and if I don't have dancing, I won't have anything in this life.

But he knows that.

Another tug. This time, I can't keep up. I land on my knees, biting my lip hard so I won't groan when the bare skin on my palms and knees land on the glass.

"Get up," he orders, but I don't.

He can dish any punishment he wants. God knows the cuts and throbbing skin are an indication of that. But I won't let him taint the one thing in my life that I love the most.

He's already taken everything else; he doesn't get to have ballet too.

He exhales heavily at my disobedience and rises, straightening his perfectly ironed three-piece suit, then walks to me as his expensive Italian leather shoes make an unmistakable sound against the floor.

With each step he takes, my heartbeat speeds up faster and faster to the point of feeling it in my throat. He places the metal head of his cane under my chin and lifts it up.

I meet his stare head on. I hate everything about this man.

Or at least I hope it's hate.

"So that's your choice?" he asks as his lazy gaze roams over me, but I say nothing.

I won't give him the last part of me that matters.

Even if it seals my death tonight.

CHAPTER ONE

Somewhere in the world...
Fall 2018

*V*alencia
      Breathing heavily, I close my eyes, hoping the agonizing pain traveling from my stomach to my head will pass, but I still the moan threatening to spill past my lips.

The white gown I'm wearing is coated in sweat as goose bumps break out on my heated skin. I try to raise my hand to find some solution or shift on the bed, but my wrist is pulled back, because the tight handcuffs don't give me freedom to move.

The metal bruises my flesh, disturbing the already-festered skin, and I hate the tears rolling down my cheeks, as they speak about my weakness. "I'm so sorry," I whisper into the space, tasting the salt on my tongue.

I can't be weak; I have to survive this, no matter what the cost.

The room's white color disturbs my eyes, because with all the harsh light shining from the ceiling, it's too bright. It has nothing but a single bed in the middle with a table behind me and the AC running in front of me that hits me directly in the face. It's a wonder I don't have a fever at this point. The walls are soundproof with an additional layer of white velvet covering them, which suffocates me even more, because no matter how much I will cry out, no one will hear me in this place.

The "punishment room," as *he* calls it.

He doesn't much like my disobedience, which pretty much means I've spent more time in here than anywhere else. Although the caged space downstairs can barely count as anything better, at least there the cameras in the corners above me do not monitor my every move.

In a second, the door opens and the woman walks in, void of any emotion as she holds a notepad in her hand. She then shifts to the table, where she breaks a few ampules and mixes something into the IV bag.

Probably vitamins that keep me alive despite *his* starving me.

I don't bother begging or asking for help, because it's useless. I found out the hard way these past few months that most people stay numb to everyone's problem as long as they are not affected by them.

A humorless chuckle escapes me, and although my whole body freezes in a cramp from the action, I can't stop it.

My naivety has to be seen to be believed. The woman turns around, frowning as she picks up the bag and walks to me, placing it on the table next to the bed. She opens her mouth to say something but quickly snaps it shut, her lips thinning into a line as if she barely keeps herself from giving me a piece of her mind.

Right. No matter how much she wants me to act normal and agreeable, he doesn't pay them to lecture me.

He pays them to keep me alive to play his twisted, disgusting games.

"You are a disgrace as a woman, you know that?" I croak through my dry throat, and her hands on the IV drip still as she sends daggers my way, but I meet her stare head on. "How you sleep at night, I don't know." Instead of responding to my jab, not that I expect it, she inserts the needle into my vein and I don't even flinch, considering they've poked holes almost everywhere.

She is quickly done with her stuff then adjusts the dosage and leans forward behind the headboard of the bed, probably to lift one of the

Newton's Cradle balls. In a second, the sound of them hitting against each other echoes through the space as she walks out, leaving me alone once again while the sound drives me insane, grating on my nerves, and reminding me this nightmare never ends no matter how much I wish it was just a dream.

But I know that's what he wants, for me to go insane, so he can attack, because he only feeds on the weak victims who he can break and destroy.

I can't give him the satisfaction. I can't let him win this time.

Snapping my eyes shut, I transfer myself to the ballet stage as the classical music fills my mind and takes me away from this place that threatens to strip me from myself once and for all.

And while I do this, the images of the last year play in my head like a colorful, horrifying movie that I know will end badly, but one I can't look away from.

I always knew monsters existed in this world.

But I didn't know they had the tendency to hide behind masks of good people.

CHAPTER TWO

New York, New York
January 2018

*L*achlan
        Whistling loudly, I put on black leather gloves and smile at the whimper that erupts from the man currently pinned to the wall by several coach bolts located in his palms, feet, and thighs.

Not that the cuts are deep, but the specific places work well on the nerves, sending signals to the head, which mix with fear and create this suffocating feeling inside one's body that he or she can never escape.

I should know, considering I've mastered and refined the craft since the age of fourteen.

"Please let me go," the man begs, but I ignore him, putting the drill together and pressing the button so the *trrr* sound fills the space. The man gasps in shock. "What are you going to do with it?"

The funniest part about humankind I've discovered during torture is everyone asks and says the same shit, no matter their circumstances or society.

I would have covered their mouths with tape just to not listen to those annoying fucking words, but then I love their screams too much to pass up an opportunity.

Spinning around, I face my victim—or teaching example, as I like to call them—and study him from every angle, displeasure speeding through me.

Sweat is coating his clothes. He breathes heavily, barely standing in place while blood slips to the floor from his wounds. The front of his pants is wet, and by the disgusting smell, I conclude it's urine.

Frowning, I check his file one more time and shake my head at the fact that this man is a preacher.

Where is his faith now?

I snap my fingers and raise them up, and in a second, classical music by Mozart blasts from the speakers. I crack my neck from side to side, basking in the energy of it.

Showtime.

Without further ado, I drill the bolts firmly into his arms and arteries, and his scream awakens the monster in me. I chuckle then shift to the other side and drill a bit more. It oozes so much blood, but he still stays alive and barely manages to rasp something under his breath—not that I care to listen.

My intention is not to kill him. Well... not yet.

First, he has to suffer. Has to experience the pain and desperation that forever coat the walls of my room, so he will know what it's like to be in the position where, no matter how much you beg, the evil person will never stop.

He'll just increase his actions, laughing at your pleadings.

So I go back to my weapons table, shaking my finger in the air and enjoying the particularly high note of the music while I scan my blade collection. The finest of silver glistens in the light and I finally choose a three-inch blade with the sharpest tip.

Walking back to him, I graze his skin from his cheek to his neck as the pulse under it speeds up, and his eyes snap open, with fear and agony permanently settled there. And then I stab him in his side. I take out the knife—he doesn't even have time to catch his breath—and I repeat the action on the other side and then right in the middle of his abdomen. He whimpers, obviously having no strength left for anything else.

I leave the knife in his gut, because I don't need him bleeding to death yet. I set the timer on the table clock, because in exactly twelve minutes, he will die as the blood drains from his severed arteries and damaged internal organs, and his body will shut down completely.

After all, I didn't get my medical degree for nothing.

Grabbing the pliers, I free his hand from the bolt nail and raise it as I lean closer to his face. I know he can hear me even if he is barely holding on to his body's last resources. "Preacher Cane," I say, and his eyelashes barely move, but it's there, so I lower my voice, because what I have to say is for his ears only. "Remember how you used to say boys who point their fingers and accuse others are sinners fit for hell?" He meets my gaze, recognition settling in his eyes. But I don't let him dwell on it for long. "Welcome to my hell," I mutter, and cut off his fingers one by one while he thrashes, but I don't give a fuck.

The minute I'm done with his last finger, I check the time and see I have five minutes left. Stepping on and cursing the fingers on the floor for good measure, I prop his eyes open with toothpicks, not letting them close, while his tainted blood almost sullies my suit. Then I turn on the video on the screen located directly across on the opposite wall.

Screams and begging erupts from the screen, and even though I have him in this position, which doesn't change any fucking thing, it still gives me satisfaction. Before he succumbs to death, I proclaim, "Your son is next." And then add, *Bon voyage* to hell, Pastor." And he freezes, appearing pitiful with everything I've done to him.

Just as his last breath leaves his body, the music of *Symphony No. 40* ends.

I turn to the window behind me and bow as applause erupts from my protégés as they watch my victim with awe, murmuring excitedly to each other—probably commenting on my technique.

Ah, the young minds who get off on just a single thought about torture.

My favorite students, they are always filled with so much hope and naivety.

Not really knowing that it's easy to dream about hurting someone, but it's hard to actually do—and control your desires, to make them work for you and not be their prisoner.

I'm always there to crush their hopes and introduce them to the world full of gore, darkness, and power that shakes your body to the point of insanity, as nothing compares to the high of taking a life.

The smell of a fresh kill.

Torture is an art form I've learned through the years, mastered for decades, and explored in different variations with anyone who I found fit.

Most people will say I'm a monster or a psycho.

However, in life, nothing is ever that simple, as evil and goodness are in the eyes of the beholder.

*V*alencia

The music of Tchaikovsky speeds up, sending swiping drums and piano mixed with violin echoing through the space and across the stage as I start to do pique turns. Swirling effortlessly on my pointed shoes, my arms meeting and separating, bringing attention to the gracefulness of each movement. The lacy white tutu stays unmovable, drawing attention to the movements of my legs as I give all of myself to the dance of the Sugar Plum Fairy.

Time and time again, I swirl on the stage as the music becomes louder and faster, pitching higher and higher, when it finally ends on the soft *dzing*. I freeze in position with one leg pointed on the floor, my body slightly leaning to the side and one arm lifted while the other is just straight by my side. I almost exhale a sigh of relief, because I've managed to handle this dance without a single mistake.

Loud applause erupts as I return to first position, taking deep graceful bows while they still cheer and applaud. I keep the wide smile on my face intact, although it takes enormous effort to do so.

Then I take a few steps forward and repeat the action, showing everyone that I have nothing but deep love for their attention and appreciation for this beautiful and mesmerizing art.

Finally, with one last bow, I dance off in the direction of the curtains and quickly end up backstage where the AC hits me from all corners, instantly creating goose bumps on my heated skin, and I shiver slightly.

Who thinks it's a good idea to blast it on max for when sweaty dancers come back? We will catch colds at this rate!

Instantly, Nora, the backstage manager, places an opened bottle of water in my hand, and orders, "Drink, we need to get you ready for Act III. Do you want to grab a bite?"

I shake my head, greedily pouring the water down my throat, and almost moan from the cooling sensations it brings me. The costume is stuck to my sweaty body, and I hate the tulle digging into my skin. It'll leave irritated spots that will last for days.

It's all worth it though as long as I have the opportunity to perform.

"Okay then." She shrugs and whistles, calling, "Jane, Valencia will be by your side in a minute. Get her ready for the next act." Then she grins at me. "Dreams come true."

Yeah, my friend is right about that. She always wanted to be a manager in the ballet, handling all the madness behind the curtains, because she had a deep love for the art but zero talent—or interest for that matter—for the stage.

I had the exact opposite feelings.

I could live inside these walls and never ask for anything more, but all this organizing crap scared the shit out of me. "You are kickass, boss lady." I salute her with my bottle.

She laughs and walks to another dancer who just finished his part, but not before pointing at the vase of white-as-snow peonies in the corner. "These came for you. Max sure is a keeper, since he showers you with attention every single performance," she jokes, and shifts her focus to Jim, not seeing how her words practically glue me to my spot while my eyes widen with the new information.

Max has been on a business trip in Paris these past few weeks, and although we messaged each other often—more like *he* did—I made it very clear I wanted him to stop sending me various gifts. I see no point on wasting beautiful flowers for them to die behind stage, mostly forgotten as the chaos after the dance rarely allows me to take care of them.

I grit my teeth as anger rushes through me, and I sigh heavily, because once again he ignored my wishes and chose his selfish desires. He has been doing it a lot lately, which only proves that taking things further with him will not happen.

Then another thought strikes me.

Max's favorite flowers are red roses, so he only sends them to me. He doesn't care I prefer other flowers, that in fact peonies are my favorite. I don't think he even bothered to ask or that I mentioned it.

Max is very anal about his behavior, so there is no way these are from him.

Furrowing my brows, I pick up the card attached to the top of the stick, open it, and blink in surprise.

Once upon a time, there was a dancing angel who gave all to her art. She never knew nightmares. Until the monster destroyed her carefully placed façade.

"*V*alencia?" Jane practically screams into my ear and snaps me out of my stupor, as I re-read the note again and again, trying to make sense of it and failing. "We need to go." I still don't move; I just shake my head in disbelief, wondering who played a prank like this on me. "You all right?" she asks, worry lacing her tone.

I finally raise my gaze to her and nod. "Yeah, sorry. Just zoned out. Are there any more notes?"

"Nope, just this one. You have more peonies in your dressing room though. They smell divine, but they are going to give me a headache." She continues to chat all the way to the dressing room while only two thoughts play in my head.

Who sent me a note that implied harm? And more importantly... what does it mean?

Lachlan

Closing the door behind me, I remove my shirt and throw it on the floor. Cracking my neck from side to side, hoping to release some tension, I freeze for a second as the old wound on my shoulder throbs more than usual.

Maybe I shouldn't have spent so much time on chopping the fucker's body apart piece by piece, but I quickly wave away the thought.

What would be the fun in that? As much as the thrill rushed through me at the idea of him being six feet under, I don't do this just for some sense of rightness.

No, killing is very much a sport for me. And like exercise, if you don't practice it enough, you get out of shape. But muscles will never forget any of it.

Smirking, I grab the vodka bottle from the bar, flick it open, and gulp greedily as the burning liquid spreads through my system.

My eyes land on the framed picture on the table, displaying the most beautiful creature the universe has ever created, and all amusement leaves me.

Instead, deep and uncontrollable rage fills me.

I step onto the balcony and assess my huge mansion. Several lights showcase the carefully crafted alcoves with roses planted in them; beautiful perfectly cut green grass spreads in different shapes and forms, sort of creating a labyrinth in the garden with various escape routes. Several roses are scattered around the place, giving it a romantic yet mysterious look that makes you fall in love in the garden if you are not careful enough.

Recently, I added a bush of white peonies to it, and they bloom spectacularly.

Narrow concrete paths lead to several fountains, which pour water generously, the sound soothing and attracting doves that rest there peacefully.

All in all, one might think it's a perfect garden for an expensive two-level house that is located on the outskirts of the city. It's surrounded by acres of land with huge iron gates so no outsiders will ever enter without my permission.

In truth though?

It's my hunting ground and only the strongest can escape me, but then that person needs to outsmart me.

And that never happens. That's why it's always amusing to watch them try.

Although, I've never challenged an angel before.

A brown-haired woman swirling in a circle on the stage completely engrossed in her dance flashes in my mind, her chocolate eyes sparkling with passion as she floats around the stage as if it belongs to her. How her graceful body is so in tune with the music that it's almost impossible to separate the two.

Whenever she performs, there is complete silence, because even the slightest breath can break the magic and bring us all back to the mortal world.

Gripping the balcony railing tighter, I allow the memories to wash over me like an ocean wave, reminding me once again of *her*.

An angel.

The time has come though to clip those wings of hers and bring her not to mortals, but underground to the depths of hell so I can taint her light with my darkness and prove that no matter where you come from, you are never immune to it.

With that thought, I lean toward the chessboard placed on the balcony table and move a pawn on the right.

Our game has officially begun.

CHAPTER THREE

New York, New York
Christmas 1998

*V*alencia, 5 years old

I glance at the clock and squeal. It's twenty past five and I jump from bed, running downstairs with all my might, my feet thumping on the wooden floor.

"Valencia!" I hear Mommy shout, but it doesn't deter me from my purpose, and in seconds, I end up in the living room. I gasp in awe, covering my mouth with my hands while my eyes are glued to the huge Christmas tree. Its tip touches the ceiling, the colorful lights emphasizing its power and beauty. It took me and Mommy hours to put it all together, but the result had to be perfect.

Santa wouldn't have visited us otherwise.

Then my eyes land on the boxes and boxes wrapped in red paper and I spring to them, grabbing one with desire and laughter while Mommy speaks from *behind me. "Valencia, a little bit of patience." But once again, I don't stop. I tear the wrap quickly and blink as I find the book in there.*

The Holy Bible.

Raising my eyes to Mommy, I whine. "I already have one." Daddy always uses the wisdom of the book whenever people come to him for advice or with their pain. He also has his favorite copy from which he preaches during Sunday services. And although I love the book as much as he does, I expected something else for Christmas.

Before she can answer, Daddy comes inside with a warm smile on his face as he joins me on the floor—while I frown.

Why did Santa send such a gift to me? I was a good girl through the entire year, and I even shared my lunches with everyone. My eyes water and I hiccup. "It's so unfair, Daddy." Immediately, his arm wraps around my shoulders as he hugs me closer, and nothing brings me more comfort than his arms.

Daddy is the only one who can give me an answer as to why Santa made such a choice.

And it's not as if I asked for much, just shiny pink pointe shoes so I can finally join the ballet class and dance like all those beautiful ladies on TV in colorful tutus. I can never take my eyes away from them when they are on.

They are simply magnificent.

Mommy and Daddy aren't sure it's for me though, so I hoped a gift from Santa would be a sign for them to agree, because it would be divine intervention, right? I don't understand the concept much, but Daddy says this plays a big role in faith.

He is the only one I really need to convince anyway. Mommy just follows him.

So I prayed and prayed and wrote a letter. Why wasn't divine intervention helping me?

"I think it's beautiful. This is a reminder to you that not everyone is as lucky as you on this day." Instantly, guilt sweeps through me when I remember we are very fortunate to live in a house and have all these gifts, when a lot of people have to live on the street and starve. Daddy takes me to shelters often, so I'll appreciate what we have and not nag. "Always keep it with you," he murmurs. I nod, and then he points his finger to the big pile. "Now check your other gifts. I'm sure Santa didn't forget about your request... like pink shoes."

My eyes light up with happiness, and I squeal and go searching for it.

My daddy is the best in the whole wide world.

New York, New York
January 2018

Valencia

"This is truly an amazing dress, Valencia," Becky says. "Where did you get it?" With envy, she scans my strapless navy blue dress that emphasizes my waistline but at the same time is loose enough at the feet that I can move freely in it. The back has a deep V that reaches the end of my spine and opens up a view of my pale skin. The silky texture creates a mixed aura of secrecy and seduction but simultaneously gives me a look of innocence.

Or that's what the designer claimed anyway when Mom dragged me to the store insisting we find the perfect attire for tonight. Why she bothered, I have no clue. The charity event is nothing special. We've done this every year for the last seven years. Rarely anyone pays attention to me.

"The designer is not well known yet. Her name is Frankie." But with the selection she has, I'm sure she'll go places.

She winks at me. "Bet Max can't wait to rip it off you tonight, huh?" She casts her eyes to the far corner of the room where the man in question stands, in deep conversation with my stepfather. "He is so hot," she mutters, and I just roll my eyes, although a slight chuckle slips past my lips.

Almost no one can resist Max's appeal.

He is tall, around six foot one with a lean body that he likes clothed in expensive Italian suits that emphasize his status as the oil heir in society. His dark hair is neatly styled, while his expressive brown eyes constantly display the drive and happiness that is so addictive whenever you are in his company.

And yet my heart feels nothing.

If it weren't for my parents, this relationship would have ended a long time ago, but the constant guilt has made me stay and pretend everything is dandy.

I can no longer do that though, and it has exhausted me to no end to always play a role in this one-actor theater that no one knows about.

Apparently my silence serves as encouragement to Becky, as she continues, "I'm so happy for your stepdad sealing the deal with the company. If everything goes smoothly, he can run for mayor." Something flashes in her eyes, as she adds, "Who would have thought you'd have it all, huh?" She's joking, but I don't miss the jab in her words.

Thinking back at it though, the jab has always been present since my mom remarried and brought us into this elite world of luxury.

We've been the four musketeers, Becky, Nora, Bella, and I, who entered the dancing world with our eyes wide open and hearts full of dreams. We'd promised ourselves to always follow our path and perform on worldwide stages, earning praises along the way, so one day we could open a dance school with famous ballerinas as teachers.

Life had other plans for all of us though, and we barely stayed in touch. As I discovered in the following years, ballet is a lonely sport on most days, especially if you are talented and the teachers pay more attention to you. The minute you take a break, everything changes.

Especially the people around you.

Since the charity event is one of the yearly assurances that my family is known for, Victor rented an exclusive mansion on the outskirts of the city. Gold and silver walls, along with a marble floor that glistens in the lights, make the richness of the venue complete. Various candles perch in a chandelier that hangs low enough for people to admire every small detail of it, as it was custom-made in France. Dark round oak tables are filled with exquisite dishes cooked by the best chefs, while some famous band plays on the stage, creating a luxurious yet calm atmosphere.

People have gone out of their way to purchase the most expensive and fashionable dresses to impress everyone and showcase their status and rank amongst everyone else.

And I won't say they are mean people who don't appreciate what they have in their life, but lately this whole charade of acting while in public has brought me nothing but a headache. "Right," I finally reply, because she clearly expects an answer, and a forced smile spreads on my lips. "Mom chose right." But even saying it seems wrong, because although I love Victor, it has nothing to do with his money.

A soft hand touches my shoulder and I glance back to see my mom joining us. My brows furrow at the excitement shining brightly in her green eyes. She practically jumps in place as she moves her head in the direction of the men. "Victor asked for you."

"Why?" The request is unusual, to say the least; he is usually so busy during these events. I never bother him. Besides, I'm always at my parents' on Sunday afternoon, so it's not as if they miss me or anything.

"Just come." She pats Becky on the cheek. "Forgive me for stealing my girl."

She shrugs and winks at my mom, while murmuring into my ear, "Good luck." Mom is already dragging me to Victor while I ponder my friend's behavior.

If Becky is as excited about it as my mom, it has to mean something.

"What's going on?" I ask, but she just waves it off and sends a huge grin to Max, who stops midsentence and then sweeps his gaze over me, appreciation evident by how his eyes sparkle and the soft smile that graces his lips.

"Valencia," he murmurs, leaning toward me and giving me a gentle kiss on the cheek that instantly sends revulsion through me.

Lately, I can't even stand his touch.

I should have known a relationship with him was a dead end, but I kept going, hoping to feel something. But no matter how much I try, the situation seems hopeless.

I need to break up with him tonight, because, by the looks of it, he thinks he's in love with me.

"Hi," I say, avoiding his weird gaze as if he expects something from me, and focus my attention on my stepfather, who opens his arms widely. At once, I'm hugging him close, calmed a bit by his familiar scent that always reminds me of protection and power.

Mom met Victor six years ago through her job, and they have been inseparable ever since. He's a famous oil magnate and his net worth is around one billion dollars. Not to mention his larger-than-life family. His son Braiden is three years older than me, and the minute they became serious, she introduced us to each other.

He might be a stepdad for me, but in everything that matters, he is a real dad. "Hi, darling." He kisses the top of my head and then steps back. "You should know that I approve. I think you are the perfect match."

Confused as hell, I have a second to ponder his words when he picks up the fork and champagne glass from the nearby tray and clicks one against the other.

Perfect match?

The music quiets down as everyone spins around to face us, curiosity written all over their features, but they don't have to wait long.

Max clears his throat from behind me, and I turn around only to gasp as he slowly drops onto one knee, a navy blue velvet box in his hand. And with a swift exhale, he opens it up to display a magnificent five-carat yellow princess-cut diamond ring with several smaller white diamonds surrounding the center stone.

Most girls would go crazy for such a ring. But me? I want nothing but the floor to swallow me whole so I can disappear from this place right now.

"Valencia," he says, but I barely hear him over my pulse ringing loudly in my ears as panic builds inside me. "You are the love of my life. Will you do me the honor of becoming my wife?" He raises the box higher to me as I hear women oh and ah at this, while a slight hiccup from behind indicates that Mom is moved by all this too.

It's what she and Victor want for me, the perfect prince to complete my good-girl image that will last me a lifetime and suffocate me to death.

Licking my dry lips, I open my mouth and close it, trying to find the words to say but failing, because, frankly, how can I escape this situation?

"It's okay," he murmurs, catching my gaze, and he reaches to grab my hand, but I step back. I notice the hint of anger slipping into his eyes, but it's so quickly gone I think I imagined it.

"Valencia?" My mom's worried voice snaps me out of my stupor, and I finally find the strength to do what's right.

I've made a lot of sacrifices in my life, but not this time.

And to hell with consequences.

"No." My answer is so low it's barely audible.

A woman whispers loudly among the crowd, "What did she say?"

Max stays on his knee, and says, "Didn't get that." Excitement is radiating from him in spades, which indicates to me he thought this would quickly be a done deal.

Why? Doesn't he see how wrong we are for each other?

Clearing my throat, I gather all my courage and proclaim to everyone so there is no doubt about my answer. "No, I won't marry you." The silence that follows is almost deafening, and one of the waiters even drops a tray on the floor. "I'm so sorry," I add, because it's not his fault I'm incapable of feeling deeper emotions for or attaching myself to anyone; he is a great guy.

Who I wish wouldn't have proposed to me in front of a roomful of people.

"Valencia." I close my eyes for a moment as Victor's steely voice reminds me once again of the fear that runs deep in my veins for the rejection I have inflicted right now.

Glancing at him and Mom as they stand next to me, shock and displeasure evident in their expressions and stances, I address them. "I'm sorry, but I can't do it."

Max finally rises as the people murmur loudly, no doubt discussing my refusal, which will be the main topic of gossip in high society for days to come.

Anger simmers within me, but I quickly push it back, because I shouldn't show those emotions.

Showing emotion usually has a catastrophic ending for me.

Victor clicks his fingers and the music starts playing again. Then he motions with his head to Jeckie, his assistant, and at once, he runs to the waiters who swiftly place drinks in people's hands, doing their best to distract them from this fiasco.

"It's the attention, isn't it?" Max says, hiking his thumbs into the pockets of his pants. "I shouldn't have proposed here," he muses, while I shake my head in disbelief.

Does he really think that's the only reason for my refusal?

"I'm sure she is just overwhelmed—" Mom starts, but I interrupt her.

"I don't want to marry you. There is no other reason than that."

My words bring hollow laughter from him. "So this three-year relationship meant nothing to you?"

For a second, guilt slips in as all our moments together flash though my mind, reminding me that this man stood beside me in so many life-changing events, first as a friend and then as a boyfriend.

When I was accepted into Juilliard. When I had an accident and couldn't dance for the whole year. He was always there and offered his silent support. I've loved him dearly and have been so grateful for everything he has done for me.

But gratitude isn't a good enough reason for me to walk down the aisle with the man and promise in front of God to love and cherish him forever, when my heart is not in it.

"I'm sorry."

I don't have anything else to say, but he just snarls and addresses my parents. "I'd like to go now if you don't mind." He doesn't wait for their reply and heads in the direction of the gate. His anger must be written on his face if a scared-looking waiter who jumps back is anything to go by.

My parents silently run their disappointed gaze over me, their lips thin, probably wanting to say something but failing.

And suddenly, it all becomes too much. Their scrutiny, Max's anger, my guilt that tells me to fix this for everyone and be the perfect girl who makes everyone feel good, even if she screams inside at the chains imprisoning her in *their* perfect image.

So I do the only appropriate thing in this situation.

I pick up the hem of my dress and run to the balcony, ignoring my mom calling after me. Once there, I hurry down the few stairs to the garden, my heels clicking noisily on the concrete.

I don't care about the frigid air or the way goose bumps pop up on my skin from the cold. I don't feel it, because my body is functioning on an adrenaline high.

The moonlight shines brightly, highlighting the stars above, as the garden is lullabied by the sounds of the fountains as water pours from them. The groundskeepers must keep the water hot for it to function so well, considering the time of the year. The garden design focuses more on various trees and flowers interspersed with benches and pathways that spread in different directions for people to stroll along and admire the beauty of nature.

However, I have only one place in mind, and that's the greenhouse located in the bushes, which is only a few feet away. I found it the first time Victor hosted a party like this one, and oddly enough, the door is always open, so I've had a reprieve from all these social events.

While enjoying the smell of roses all around me.

A puff of air leaves me as I exhale in relief while turning the knob on the door and stepping inside, closing it quickly and leaning on the door. Warmth instantly greets me and I close my eyes, drinking in the peacefulness of this place.

Heaven.

"Well, isn't this a surprise?" a deep, husky voice echoes in the room, and my heart stills, because if there is one person who can disturb my peace...

It's *him*.

CHAPTER FOUR

Houston, Texas
Christmas 2000

Valencia, 7 years old

The minute Daddy stops the car on the side of the road, he shouts, "Valencia," behind me as I get out and run toward the wooden bench, my eyes drinking in the beauty of the ranch spread out in front of me.

And although we are surrounded by green grass and many acres of woods and fields, all my focus is on the moonlight-colored mare that stands in the middle of the horse ring. A cowboy, his hat low over his eyes, murmurs something to her and she nickers in approval.

"Oh my God!" I scream, and the man turns to me, his eyebrows rising as I hop on the fence, grabbing it tightly in my hands as I point at her. "She is magnificent!" The mare just stares at me for a moment and then nickers again, shifting a little while the man pats her on the muzzle and then winks at me.

"We have a guest, I see." He waves me over. "Come here, darlin'. Want to

touch her?" I gasp in delight and hop down, rushing to him while the sand scatters, slipping into my ballerina flats and probably smearing dirt on my white socks, but it doesn't stop me.

Finally, I reach my destination and my eyes widen as I stop next to her and lean my neck back to see her properly; she is so tall! The top of my head barely reaches her middle. She vibrates as she looks down at me and huffs with her nose. I giggle as her breath fans my cheeks.

"Hi, horsey!" She doesn't seem impressed with my greeting, just goes back to the cowboy's hand, and that's when I notice he keeps slipping little carrots to her. "Can I do that too?"

The man nods and leans forward to pick me up when Dad's stern voice comes from behind. "Valencia!" The cowboy freezes and the horse immediately makes a displeased noise and shifts slightly, so I step back, not wanting to annoy it even more.

"Shhhh," the man soothes the horse, then shouts over to my dad. "She is safe here." I catch Daddy's eyes and he shakes his head, sweeping his gaze over me, and then says, "Stay close to Levi. I'll be back shortly." With that, he moves in the direction of a very small house. I notice a few holes in the doors and empty stalls in the far corner.

Daddy said we needed to travel to Texas for him to help innocent people find strength through God in their difficult times. They send him letters and he can't refuse.

"Okay, come here, little lady." Levi picks me up, settles me on his hip, and then places the carrot in my open palm. "Feed it to her gently and have patience. She is an old mare, but she's friendly."

Holding my breath, I extend my open palm to her and she sniffs it, still watching me closely but then quickly nicks the carrot from me. I can't help the laughter that spills from me from the ticklish sensation as she touches me. "She is so sweet!" I say, and Levi just chuckles.

Then he offers, "Want to ride her?"

I want to reply yes, but my dad comes back from the house, calling, "Valencia, we need to go." I sigh heavily and wiggle in Levi's arms to get down and, with a wave, run back to my father.

He picks me up, just as a woman with tears streaming down her cheeks exits the house, holding some kind of brochure in her hand. "Thank you so much,

Pastor, for this chance." Behind her, two small boys around my age rush outside and give me a curious stare.

Dad's eyes linger on them for a second, and I roll my eyes. Mama always said he wanted a son but that God didn't give them such opportunity and they only had me. That's why Dad spoils any boys rotten, in the church or his classes.

At least, that's what I've been told.

New York, New York
January 2018

Valencia

He emerges from the shadows of the greenhouse, his dominating presence shrinking the space into a tiny place that barely allows me to breathe.

The only source of light is the moonlight, and it cascades down on him, emphasizing each rigid muscle and his handsomeness that would rival anyone present in the grand room.

His silky, sun-blond hair falls down, barely touching his shoulders, creating a contrast with his ocean-blue eyes that hold me prisoner whenever he drills them into me.

He does it a lot, stares at me, and on most days, I hate him for it. Because it disturbs my peace in more ways than one.

The three-piece suit he wears hugs his body, tightly emphasizing the muscles that speak of dominance and power, while his strong, clean-shaven jaw indicates a stubborn yet playful character. Tattoos are splattered all over his hands and neck, disappearing under his collar, and I try not to wonder if he has more ink under his clothes.

More than the last time I saw him naked.

He steps closer, his familiar scent of cigarettes and expensive cologne tingling my senses as he smirks, showing a dimple on his right cheek. "Darling," he says, and I retreat a step, my back pressing against the door, but it doesn't stop him from coming nearer. He rests his arm above my head, leaning closer as his breath fans my cheeks, and I hate the thrill that instantly rushes through me. For a second, I find it hard to breathe, as unfamiliar images play in my mind with him and me naked on the bed and— "What is New York's good girl doing here?" And just like that, he snaps me back from my haze and I shake my head.

This is insanity and the main reason I always stay away from him. How can my body react to someone, if I feel nothing but resentment for the guy? Or that's what I try to tell myself.

Licking my dry lips, I don't miss how his gaze shifts to them for a moment, and reply, "Don't call me darling." And then I ask before I can stop myself, "What are you doing here?" He chuckles, and my cheeks heat up as it dawns on me that it's a secluded place and perfect for a secret rendezvous. Without thinking, I quickly scan the place for a female or clothes as she might be hiding somewhere here. Who knows with whom he has an affair? I've heard a lot of stuff about him, and somehow I believe he lives up to his reputation. He laughs, and I snap, "Is there someone else here?" I won't stay and humiliate some woman, or that's the excuse I give myself.

Because dwelling on the fact that jealously fills me and I want to scream in his face is irrational and insane and... there are just no words to explain how wrong that will sound.

"A woman I fucked here?"

I wince at his crude words, and the amusement that coats his voice annoys the hell out of me. "You are disgusting, you know that?" I spin around and open the door to get out, but his hand shuts it again, leaving me trapped between his rigid chest and the door.

Instant heat surrounds me, and I feel him move behind me, as he leans to my ear and murmurs, "So the princess is not as cold as everyone claims." His voice creates some kind of trance as he shifts closer, and my eyes close and my breath hitches as I expect him to do something.

But instead, he steps back, leaving me alone, and says, "Don't worry, darling. There is no one here but me." A beat, and then he adds, "For now anyway." He taunts me and we both know that.

Arrogant jerk who thinks the sun and moon rise with him.

My brows furrow at that last comment, and I turn around to face him again. "What are you doing in my greenhouse?"

"Your greenhouse?" He chuckles again, and I really start to hate that. "The entire place belongs to me. As does this. But be my guest and call it *your* greenhouse. I don't mind."

What? He's the owner? No wonder though. The words luxury and power define him, so it's only fitting he built this freakishly expensive place.

Kaden Scott is a king who rules his kingdom with an iron fist, or at least that's how I see him amongst his company and the people who like to be attached to him.

A powerful businessman who owns companies worldwide. Notorious bad boy who loves extreme sports and makes the press talk about him for days.

And let's not forget about the women. I heard he has those in spades too, everyone so willing to grace his bed as long as he lavishes them with attention. But that information is based only on rumors. I've never seen him with one.

Come to think of it, no one knows much about him period, other than all those exaggerated stories.

His brow lifts at my stupor, and I wish I could go back, leave him alone, just so he won't have the satisfaction of being right or ending up in my company. But just the idea of facing the mess I've left behind gives me a headache. "You can help me put orchids in the soil and prepare everything for spring. I think they should bloom by then." I blink a few times at such an unexpected change of subject, and then I cast my gaze on the table full of terra-cotta pots. "Or is princess afraid to get her hands dirty?"

"I'm not." I'm quick to defend myself, and I groan inwardly, because this is so childish, and by the amusement flashing in his face, he thinks so too.

"The gloves are there. Join me in the back." He scans me from head to toe. "Good thing you don't have a phone with you. I wouldn't check it if I were you." He waits a beat. "The fiancé might send a not-so-flattering message."

"You know," I whisper while he half smiles, although it doesn't reach his eyes.

"I know everything that has to do with you."

Ignoring his statement, I say, "He's not like that." Max doesn't have a mean bone in his body, and although he is hurt now... he'll never go and post his heartache. One of the reasons I kept coming back to our relationship was because Max was a hundred percent safe.

"Right. I forgot our Max is a saint." The way he says it makes it seem as if he has never heard a dirtier word than that. "Yet you still don't want to marry him."

"Marriage shouldn't be about convenience." Where the hell do these words come from?

"Yet convenience is exactly what played a factor in you leaving me and going back to him," he says casually, putting on gloves as he grabs a pot and bag of soil.

"We had to be *something* in order for me to leave you."

I can't believe we are having this conversation, as we've ignored our connection during any meetings for the last six months. And he's never even given me an indication he remembered we spent an entire week in Italy, exploring the city and making love every single day.

Until the reprieve from the real world ended and I came back to New York to my life where everything was organized. And doesn't make me question myself, and my entire existence, like I experience around Lachlan.

That's his middle name, but he always prefers me to use it.

"Kaden," I moan, pulling at the ropes as he skims his lips down my stomach and settles between my thighs while his fingers slide down my hips.

"Lachlan, darling. When you are in my arms about to be fucked hard, you call me no other name but Lachlan."

"That's true," he agrees, and then crooks his fingers at me. "Come help me out. Gardening clears the mind."

I join him as he hands me a pair of gloves. As I put them on, he dispenses the soil into both pots, settling it inside. "Why orchids?" I wonder, quite surprised by this. I had no clue he was interested in gardening.

The only thing we did in Italy was make love, eat ice cream, and visit all the historical and artistically fashionable places. I'd bought the ticket to Florence on a whim after a breakup with Max and fights with my teacher, wanting to let go for a while and have a proper vacation.

I got more than I bargained for when a blue-eyed stranger bought a coffee for me and mesmerized me with his charm and attention.

"Beautiful flowers that can last for a long time."

I watch him carefully and repeat his actions, but the soil spills on the table and I curse. But then I feel his heat behind me as he places his hands on mine, pressing them into the pot. "Before you pour more, dig it with your fingers, firmly planting it inside," he instructs, and immediately electricity zaps between us. He leans over my shoulder, pointing at the orchids. "Plant them now and check them out in spring. Or whenever else you feel like hiding here," he jokes, leaving me as I gulp for breath.

Lachlan always does this.

Envelops me with his presence as if punishing me for the past.

He grabs his jacket and throws it over my shoulders as I look into his eyes, our lips a breath apart. "Don't get cold on the way back, princess. There is a narrow path in the garden in the east. You can use it and not face everyone else."

"Thank you." That's the most we've spoken in all this time. "Lachlan—"

"When you get tired of this good-girl image, come to me," he whispers and brings us flush against each other. His hand slides down my bare back as goose bumps break out on my skin. He dips it slightly above my ass, and then before I can even react, he nips my mouth and licks my lips as I open them with a gasp, soaking in the feeling of protection yet danger that always surrounds him.

Lacing his fingers through my hair, he firmly holds me as his mouth devours mine, planting ownership on it without meaning to. With each touch and lick of his tongue, press of his lips, and his burning hands that send fire through me, he reminds me of what we could have been and that I refused it because I was too scared.

He lets go. I sigh and then fist his tie, craning my neck, rising on my tiptoes and seeking him again as our mouths meet greedily. He drinks from me, fueling fire and life into me.

With him, in this moment, nothing else exists, just two people who cannot resist the needs that drive them insane.

But too soon, the moment is gone and he pushes me away as I still search for him. "Valencia," he rasps, his thumb rubbing my swollen lips. "You should have never gone back to New York without me."

And then with me still burning from our encounter, he leaves me there alone as he steps out and allows the cold air to enter the space, bringing me back to the present and to all the reasons why it's wrong.

*L*achlan

Pressing the remote, I watch the wide metal gate open for me. My sports car's engine roars to life as I drive toward the house, enjoying the wind blowing across my skin as music blasts from the radio.

My phone vibrates in my pocket, so I take it out, pressing the Answer button. "Is it done?" I ask.

The voice on the other end of the line immediately replies, "Yes. It's already all over the internet with photos and shit, and we sold the story—anonymously, of course—to several newspapers. By eight this morning, everyone will know about the rejected proposal."

I hang up, not interested in the rest as a smile pulls at my lips.

People complain all the time that nothing in their life goes according to plan and blame it on whoever and whatever, everyone but themselves.

The secret to a success is really simple though.

Plan everything.

Pulling the car up to the main door, I get out and throw the keys to Levi, who catches them quickly, and then I enter the grand hall, moving toward the secluded area that no one has permission to enter but me.

The glorious space has a stage-like feel with a rounded ceiling that, instead of being solid, has see-through colored glass that distorts the light and cascades it down on the person below, creating an aura of mystery and stilled art. Assorted statues are placed around the chair in the middle, making it almost like a throne room where one king can gaze at his subjects who do their best to impress him with their art.

Although they aren't visible, ten speakers surround the place, making sure that whenever music plays, it can be heard from any corner clearly without interruption.

I've planned and sketched this place for months, making sure every detail is exactly the way I want it. The designer has created one of the most beautiful interiors in the world, but at the same time, the feeling of doom and desperation coats the place.

I light up a cigarette and drop onto the throne, while snapping my fingers, and instantly music echoes through the space. I rest my head against the chair back and allow the sensations to rush through me, bringing clarity to my mind that for a second disappeared with her.

While teaching my protégés, I always inform them of one, single golden rule that guarantees the victory in most cases.

Study your prey.

Without research, without thoughtful preparation, you can get caught. A lion doesn't just get up in the morning hoping to get his prey; no, he knows exactly where to hunt for it, what speed to use, and how to make sure no one knows he's there.

There are certain things humans should learn from wild creatures, that's for sure.

Valencia Moore.

I exhale the smoke and drink in the smells while the idea of making her mine sends electricity through my entire system.

Yeah, I do want to own her.

But that's not the reason why her wings will be broken.

There are secrets only she is able to crack, secrets that haunt me to this day and won't let me rest.

The brown-eyed angel has to become mine.

But for that, an angel needs to soak in darkness and own it like her second skin, and who better to introduce her to this world than me?

CHAPTER FIVE

New York, New York
October 2003

Valencia, 10 years old

"*Mommy!*" *I call out, rushing inside the house and dropping my
ballet bag on the floor while wincing in pain as my legs throb
from the exhausting rehearsal.*

*My brows furrow when there is no reply. I step in the direction of the
kitchen when a loud sound of shattering glass coming from the living room
reverberates through the wall and stops me in my tracks.*

*I quickly run to the room and gasp in shock as I see Mom sitting on the
couch, sobbing into her hands while her body trembles. Different objects, or
what's left of them anyway, lie scattered all over the floor next to her feet.*

*Our usually tidy living room looks as if a tornado went through it: pictures
ripped into pieces, vases broken, Dad's expensive wine creating a wet, red pool
on the floor.*

Even our white-as-snow expensive silk curtains that reflect the sun are shredded into pieces, and I see the scissors on the table while Mom continues to cry.

What happened here?

"Mom?" I ask, and as I come closer, she jumps in her seat, turning to me and bursting into tears again. "Mommy, what happened?" Instead of answering, she hugs me tightly to her chest, rocking me from side to side, as she rests her cheek on the top of my head.

"I will save us from this. I will, honey." Her whispers make no sense to me, and fear spreads through me rapidly. "We will leave as soon as possible." My stomach flips at her words, and I lean back to search her face, but she has a completely blank expression, looking above my shoulders as if in a trance.

"Mommy, I'm scared."

She blinks back and then finally focuses her attention on me. She palms my face, and only then do I notice how cold her hands are and how she has blood smeared on them, probably from digging her long nails into her palms.

"I will protect us. I will—" Whatever else she has to say is lost as the main door shuts, the sound startling us, and a second later, Dad enters the room, his assessing eyes not missing anything.

I expect him to question Mom just like I did, but he doesn't. I haven't seen him for a few days, because he's been out of town traveling.

Instead, he tells me, "Valencia, go to your room. Mommy and I need to have a few words."

Her arms tighten around me as she shakes her head, murmuring, "No." At this point, I return the embrace, my heart beating rapidly in my chest from fear of the unknown.

Mommy's never loses herself like this; she's always smiley and happy about everything. And there hasn't been a day where she wouldn't give all her love to Daddy.

But now she acts as if he is a bad person who can hurt us. "I want a divorce," she proclaims, and I whine, shocked to my core that she even voiced it.

Daddy and she were married in a church. How can she even think about this?

I glance at Dad and my eyes widen as his lips thin and an expression crosses his face, but I don't know how to name it. In a beat, it passes as he shifts his attention to me, giving me the soft look I'm familiar with. "Valencia go to your room."

"No," I reply, scooting closer to Mom, who exhales in relief. I don't know what's going on, but I can't leave her alone in this state, especially since she doesn't let go of me.

"Marina, you don't want Valencia to get upset, do you?" This question freezes Mom and she stops breathing, and for the first time, I notice fear in her eyes and her hold on me loosens.

She wipes away the tears and then smiles, although it does little to reassure me. "Honey, Dad is right. Go upstairs. I will come to you shortly."

"But—"

She kisses me on the cheek, patting me gently on the back, and then ushers me to the door. "Go." I listen to the command, still not quite convinced, but the tension in the air is thick, and I don't want to prolong the inevitable.

On the way, Daddy softly runs his hand over my head and winks at me. "Don't worry, munchkin. Everything is going to be okay."

With that, I go to my room and drop onto the bed, wondering what could possibly shock Mommy so much that she asked for a divorce?

*N*ew York, New York
        January 2018

*V*alencia

The high note at the end of Tchaikovsky's *Swan Lake* fades, and I fall down as the swan dies because of the bad dark lord. Originally, she does it with her lover, but Duke had an emergency at home, so he couldn't practice with us.

Silence falls over the studio as I breathe heavily, still looking down at the floor and smiling, because I've finally managed the entire dance without screwing up the final steps that for some reason couldn't register in my mind properly before now.

I glance up to Mistress Olga, who stands by the mirror while resting her elbow on the barre, tapping her chin with her finger, her face wincing on one side.

I clear my throat. "You didn't like it?"

She exhales heavily, motioning for me to get up, and I do while nervously biting my lip.

She is the best ballet mistress in the States. If she doesn't like something, it means it truly sucks. I should have rehearsed more last night instead of going to that stupid dinner, which in a way ruined my life.

I wince at the thought of my phone constantly blowing up with messages from everyone and their mother about various magazines and Twitter and IG posts that showcase me looking cold-hearted and Max looking like a loser who got his soul crushed. I read a few of them but gave up by the tenth, since the comments were all the same.

Spoiled bitch.

Poor guy.

He'll find someone else.

What's with today's society so quickly jumping to judge one person without actually wondering what could have happened? You are crucified without the facts.

Mistress Olga finally speaks up, and my stomach flips at her stern voice. "Your technique is perfect." I grit my teeth in anticipation of what she will say next, although it's not hard to guess. "But your emotions... you are like a beautiful statue, Valencia. The dance evokes so many emotions, and you have none." She clicks with her fingers. "And just like that, the beauty of dance vanishes, leaving us with, well, you." She'll never sugarcoat anything for you, aiming straight at the heart, that's for sure.

Emotions.

What are those anyway? It's not as if I've had much opportunity in life to display them. "She is held hostage. What is she supposed to do?" I grab the bottle of water and gulp it greedily. I'm not thirsty, but I'm afraid I'll say something I'll regret.

Arguing with Mistress Olga doesn't end well for most students.

Her jaw drops, almost hitting the floor. "Exactly! There is a palate of emotions. Her lover played into an evil spirit's trap, she has no hope left, and she is alone with her captor." With each reason, she flips her fingers up and then points one at me. "Yet all she can do is be beautiful."

"She shouldn't show him her weakness." Why does no one understand my point? Quite frankly, I don't even know how to portray a woman who is in such a situation, but I imagine she would prefer to keep her dignity intact and not show him how much he hurt her with what he's done.

Not to mention her lover, who apparently didn't even bother to recognize her. While I love everything about the *Swan Lake* dance and story, I never understood what's so epic about their love story itself. To me, it ended when he didn't understand the dark lord provided a decoy.

Mistress Olga huffs in exasperation, hitting the wall with her notepad. "I can't reason with you!" She exhales a heavy breath and places her hands on her hips, annoyance crossing her face. "Look, Valencia, you are the star of the show. I'll be honest; I wasn't sure you were talented enough for this... but you are. The show is in two months, but I can't have my prima ballerina displaying this." She waves her hand at me and then sighs. "You need to understand her." My brows furrow as I move strands of my hair behind my ear.

Since she doesn't say anything, I probe. "Understand what?"

"Understand why she made certain choices." She takes my hand in hers and smiles softly, although on her wrinkled face it looks more like a grimace. "You don't know what love is, so you can never see why she did what she did. Until you feel her, truly feel her... you won't ever be able to be her. And on stage, you have to." She pats me on the cheek, grabs her bag, and moves in the direction of the door, her heels clicking loudly on the wooden floor, and with each step, fear rises higher and higher in me.

What does she mean by that? Mistress Olga is never straightforward with her students; she always speaks in metaphors or between the lines. "So if I don't do that, you won't let me perform?"

She pauses at the door and then looks over her shoulder at me, indifference reflected on her face. "Not at all." Relief washes over me, but it's quickly gone, as she says, "You can still be part of the show. But you won't be a prima." With those last words, she leaves, while I stand there numbly as desperation slowly fills me.

Ballet is my everything. Being a prima is my dream, our dream.

Failing it will mean failing my father, and I can never do that. I've already failed a lot of opportunities on purpose just to keep everyone happy around me. Dancing in my hometown though is everything.

But how do I do that if they require emotions from me, emotions that can lead to my destruction.

I sit down on the floor, resting my forehead against my knees, holding back tears, because life is nothing but a mess.

This is not what I envisioned for myself, not what I've planned.

I wonder, Valencia, have you ever done what you want instead of what is right?

Lachlan's voice washes over me and I can't help but answer that, even if it's inwardly.

No, I've never done what I want except dance. But even at this, I've failed.

"Knock, knock, knock." Bella's voice snaps me out of my stupor, and I raise my head to meet my friend's worried gaze as she rests her shoulder against the doorjamb. She clucks with her tongue. "I was gone for a year and this is what I find?" She waves a bottle of wine in the air and holds up a box of lemon macaroons. "Good thing I brought these from France, huh?" she asks, and laughter slips past my lips as I get up. With a loud squeal, I practically jump on her, rocking her from side to side, while she hugs me with all her might.

"I can't believe you're here!" I say and lean back, drinking in her features and noticing a new beauty shining within her. My six-foot tall, long-legged, blonde, blue-eyed friend was always a thing of beauty, but now she has an added glow. I hug her again, while murmuring into her ear. "I'm so glad you came!" I exhale heavily as tears threaten to spill, but I hold them back.

She doesn't need to see me like this.

Bella pats my back, while murmuring, "How could I not?" She finally lets go and palms my face, pressing the cold bottle against my cheek. "I booked the flight the minute the news reached Paris." She crosses her arms, tipping her head to the side. "What do you want to do?"

Of course.

I should have expected that once my best friend knew about my trouble, she'd be by my side. No matter what happens, she is the only person in the whole wide world who will always be on my side.

"Well—" I start, but she interrupts me.

"And while you are at it, answer this too. If you don't want to marry Max, then why did you refuse to take the part in the show and they picked me instead? You could have had Paris and all the fame." My stomach drops, because it's the last question I expect, and I shift uncomfortably, not really knowing how to proceed.

We stay silent for a long while, and she finally exhales heavily, and orders, "Go change and we can go to your place and talk. But this time, I want the truth. Okay?"

I nod, even though I'm not sure.

Truth might cost me *her*, and I don't think in my current situation I can survive without Bella.

God, how did my life turn into such a mess?

*L*achlan

Locking my hands behind my head, I rest on the chair while watching the live transmission from Valencia's studio streaming to my huge TV in the media room, while other small screens show me her performances in different stages of rehearsal.

She gracefully maneuvers through the studio, completing pirouettes and techniques that rival those of legends. She is completely lost in the music, desperation filling her every expression as her body shakes in pain that feels so real I can practically touch it through the screen.

My angel is almost ghostlike in her black attire that emphasizes her delicate figure with a graceful neck, legs that go on for miles, and her fit body that can withstand hours and hours of training.

And she would have been one of the best if it weren't for the stubbornness crossing her expression any time she performs act three, showing with her entire being disapproval for the action of the female she portrays.

Ah, what a magnificent subject to break.

I pick up the phone from the table and dial a number. She answers on the second ring. "Mister—"

I'm not much interested in what she has to say, so I don't even bother to listen. "Is everything ready?"

A pause and then "Yes."

Hanging up, I allow the sinister smile to spread across my mouth while I turn on the classical music that always soothes my soul.

This charade has lasted long enough; the time has come for action.

I just left her without another pawn.

My angel is losing a game she has no idea we're playing.

Time for her to catch up.

CHAPTER SIX

New York, New York
September 2007

*V*alencia, 14 years old

*W*ith one last swirl, the music ends on the high, violoncello note
and I freeze in the pointe pose as the audience gets up and cheers
loudly, most of them clapping while I bow to them, thanking them for watching
my performance.

My feet ache, my throat is sore as I desperately need a drink, and I can
barely catch a breath, because I still have to keep my smile intact, but I've never
been happier in my life.

My first solo performance as the prima ballerina of my ballet school!
Although Mistress Megan didn't say it out loud, she did mention a few sponsors
attending today's performance and they might take notes for the future. Any
recommendations will be a great addition to my resume.

I have only one goal in mind, and that's the Juilliard School. To be able to study there... it's nothing but a dream. I've seen videos from the school and their ballet masters and mistresses. It would be an honor to study under them. But I know my family won't be able to afford it, so I have to get a scholarship.

And for that, I need to be the best, even if sometimes I want to cry from how much pain my feet are in.

Or how on most days it costs me friendships with my friends who have interests outside of ballet and don't understand my devotion to its "religion" that forbids most of the fun they like to have.

The curtain falls as all the dancers still keep their positions, and finally, once we're out of the curious gazes, we all relax as Bella laughs, jabbing me with her elbow. "Congrats, girl! It was awesome!"

I grin at her and hug her close. "You were great too! Can you believe this? Our first show where we got to do a solo!" I say excitedly, jumping in place and immediately regretting it as pain travels from my calf to my knee and I wince.

Bella's watchful eyes don't miss it, and she murmurs, "You need to sit before someone else notices it." I nod and we go toward the changing room when a voice from behind stops us.

"Valencia."

I freeze, my heartbeat speeding up as I slowly turn around and face my father. A shocked gasp slips past my lips. "Dad?" He grins widely, opening his arms, and I run to him with a squeal, ignoring everything and everyone.

I can soak my feet in a hot tub later, but missing an opportunity to greet my dad properly?

Never!

He catches me easily, locking his arms around me tightly. "Hey, munchkin! You were amazing out there!"

I lean back as he palms my face. "What are you doing here, Dad? I thought we'd meet this weekend."

His gaze softens, as he replies, "How could I miss your performance, Valencia? Even your Mom couldn't have stopped me."

I sigh at his words, my chest heaving.

The relationship between my parents is tolerable at best, if Mom's hostile attitude toward him can even be called that. After their big fight three years ago, she decided to divorce him anyway and never explained her decision to me. We moved out of our house the next week and she rented a small apartment in Brooklyn for us. I had to take the train to get to my school, because I couldn't *leave my dance program. Mom went back to work and refused to take any money from Dad; she even shouted at me whenever I accepted his gifts. Although I stressed over this, I kept declining Dad's clothes or expensive things, because Mom got too upset and would cry for days, looking at it as if it was a gift from Satan. So on most days, we barely made end's meet, and I had new ballet clothes thanks to Nora's mom, who bought them for me too. Mom didn't argue with her, but silently she cried in her room as she came home exhausted from yet another shift at the restaurant.*

Oddly enough, Dad didn't fight for custody or even argue with her much. He came once a week to pick me up for the weekend and usually took me to a show or galleries. On Sundays, we always attended church, where during the morning service he read to those who listened.

Although their divorce was hard on me, I never asked what happened. I loved both my parents, and if they thought splitting up was the best option, I couldn't argue with that.

"I'm happy you're here," I say, but then add, "but Mom is here and we are supposed to have a celebratory dinner tonight." I hate how sorrow crosses his face, but he quickly covers it up with a smile. I don't want to hurt my dad, but I won't hurt Mom either.

I refuse to choose sides on this.

"It's all right. We can do it on Friday." He leans forward and kisses my forehead, lingering there for a second, and my brows furrow.

It's not like my dad to act so odd and impulsive, breaking the rules that Mom placed on us. "Are you all right, Dad?" Instead of answering, he squeezes me in his arms, holds me there for what seems like forever, and then finally lets me go.

"I love you, munchkin. Always remember that, okay?" Fear rushes through me, but before I can comment, he winks at me, and says, "I better go before your Mom finds out."

He goes to the doors behind the stage where Mistress Megan let him in, and I call out to him, "I love you too, Dad."

He looks over his shoulder, nods, and disappears while I'm left standing there alone and confused.

New York, New York
January 2018

Valencia
Entering my apartment, I inhale the fresh smell of peonies and turn on the light. Immediately, my cozy one-bedroom condo comes into view and Bella whistles. "Nice place. Last time I checked, you lived in Brooklyn with three roommates where sweat permanently coated the walls." She points at my living room and strolls inside, slipping off her sneakers on the way then dropping onto the couch with a loud plop. "If I'd known this, I wouldn't have checked into a hotel," she jokes while I just shrug.

I glance critically at my condo as if seeing it for the first time and try to understand her awe, because everything looks relatively modest to me.

The living room is connected with the kitchen through an arch. The counter serves as a table, and that gives me more room and a place to cook, which I love to do while watching famous opera shows on the TV hanging from the opposite wall. A white, spacious L-shaped couch with lots of colored pillows faces a small, oak coffee table. I also bought a matching set of easy chairs in case my family visited and I needed more places to sit. The white walls have different quotes from classic books painted on them in addition to several black and white framed photos of legendary dancers, reminding me every day that those women never gave up and always moved forward.

The bedroom is located in the far corner and doesn't have anything but a mattress and a closet. I don't have time to shop for suitable furniture for it, and everything seems so boring—so not me. It has an adjacent bathroom that's become my favorite place, because I can soak my bruised feet for hours and relax without prying eyes.

All in all, my little place seems like a sanctuary for me and a break from the luxurious life my mom lives, but for my friend... yeah, it's a different story.

I place the bottle on the counter and fish for the opener, as Bella asks, "I thought you refused using Victor's money?" She kicks her feet up on the table, groaning in pleasure as she adjusts her back more comfortably.

Oh yeah, that thing didn't cost three thousand for nothing.

"I still do." Her brows furrow as she shakes her head, clearly expecting an explanation. "When I turned twenty-five, Dad's lawyer showed up. He told me that in his will he left me this place, but hadn't wanted me to know." I pause, my raspy breath filling the space, because remembering him always brings nothing but pain.

Valencia.

Leave, Dad.

Snapping out of the memory, I clear my throat while continuing to work on the bottle. I need to focus on something. "He had some old furniture here that cost a fortune."

"How much?" Disbelief laces her words, because Dad was always so freaking modest. While he didn't mind bringing me gifts on a daily basis, he didn't even own a car, because he considered it a liability in the city. He rented them if we needed to go somewhere, but that's about it.

"I sold it for like twenty-five thousand. Something about rare animal and reptile skins or whatever."

Her eyes widen as her jaw drops. "Get out of here."

I shrug. "Dad was loaded. I always knew that. But he left everything for charity. Anyway, I clearly didn't need all his stuff, so I used half the money to buy new stuff and gave the rest to the Dancing Wings." She nods, because it's the only thing we both have always agreed on.

The Dancing Wings studio was founded by our very first dance teacher, Miss Patricia, who believed that everyone had talent, but not everyone had the chance to explore it. She created a school that operated solely on donations, and she taught young kids all kinds of dances there. Most of them were from poverty-stricken families, and many of them had to wear used clothes. She had several college students who volunteered to help her, and still the school barely survived.

Bella and I stayed dedicated to it and continued to help her until we turned eighteen and went to Julliard. Patricia didn't tell us things got bad, so we had no idea the studio was about to be shut down due to failure to pay the rent.

But surprisingly, some wealthy guy paid the debt and allowed her to stay, and even gave her a salary. She is extremely happy now, and we help out whenever we can. I just knew in my gut it had to be Victor, because he knew how much it meant to me. Whenever I thanked him for it, he just raised his brows and shared a weird look with my mom as if I'd gone insane. I chose to ignore it, thinking he didn't like when people expressed gratitude to them.

There is nothing like teaching young minions the beauty of ballet, to discover the dance within them for the very first time, to see happiness instead of constant competition and the worry of not making it.

Come to think of it, Wings is my sanctuary.

Not my studio.

"How long are you staying? I'm teaching KG beginners tomorrow. You can come with me, give your wisdom to the little munchkins," I tease her and she chuckles, clapping excitedly as I place macaroons on the plate, grab two glasses and the bottle, and join her on the couch.

She helps me pour the drinks, and I finally rest against the cushions, moaning while stretching my toes on the table. "Your favorite ballet mistress is a dragon," I inform her, and she rolls her eyes as she munches on the macaroon.

"Please. You were always her favorite. I just played by her rules more." Yeah, right. The woman always criticized everything about me, so I shouldn't have been surprised with today. I just hoped that if she gave me the part, it meant she trusted me to handle it.

Instead, she fed me the stupid crap about love.

Taking a large sip, I say, "She threatened to remove me from the production."

Bella's glass pauses midway to her mouth as she chokes on her food. "What?" She coughs and quickly drinks, washing it away.

"Yep. Told me I suck at showing emotions, and if I don't get myself together, then bye-bye Odette."

Bella blinks a few times, then opens her mouth and closes it, and my heart sinks.

No freaking way! "You think so too?"

She pulls her legs onto the couch and tucks them under her while exhaling heavily. "Well sometimes... when we are on the stage... it's just that you are judging."

"What?" Of all the things I expected her to tell me, these words are not it.

"Whenever you don't agree with the story, you show it for the world to see. I mean... you dance perfectly, babe. But you don't become one with whoever you portray."

Slapping my forehead, I breathe through my nose, contemplating her words. There is no such thing as criticism without merit in our profession, and as much as I hate both feedbacks, I have to pay attention to them. I'm just not sure what I can do about it besides work harder.

Bella shakes my hand and I blink at her, willing myself to listen to her again. I completely zoned out for a second there. "Max?" she probes, and I freeze, because in all this, I didn't even think about him.

Sliding lower on the couch, I close my eyes and sip the wine, enjoying the bitter taste and wondering if my phone is still blowing up with messages. I've ignored it since this morning. "Valencia, stop stalling and answer me." Stubbornness and authority coat her voice, so there is no way I can escape this conversation any longer. "He proposed in the middle of the gala. I refused."

She gasps, her mouth hanging open before she covers it with her hand. "He did what?" Her face at once transforms into annoyance as she lightly pushes my arm, and I chuckle. "I already know that, you dork. Tell me everything else. Mainly why you said no when he is the love of your life."

I wince at this description, even though she's quoting the words I said to her in a desperate attempt to convince her to go to Paris. "He's been with me through everything." She searches for my free hand and squeezes it tightly, knowing what brings me the most pain. "But besides my gratitude, there is nothing else that holds us together. We have common interests, yes, but that's about it. We are like day and night, and we..." My breath hitches as I lick my dry lips, forcefully pushing the words out. "We are not compatible. Anywhere," I finish lamely, and understanding lights her eyes.

"Sex is not good?"

I stifle a laugh that threatens to break free at her question. "More like nonexistent." She opens her mouth, probably to elaborate on the subject, but I quickly add, "We are just not right for each other. I thought he knew that, but he went and... well, you know the rest."

She stays silent, rubbing her forehead while I await her next words. I know they will come, and I think about how to give her an answer that will make her feel better, instead of the truth.

Although lying is a sin, I've discovered that sometimes a lie can bring peace where truth can cause chaos. And isn't it important to care for the well-being of the people around you?

"Last year," she starts, playing with the lid of her wine glass, "when you passed on the opportunity to dance in Paris and proposed me... you told me that you couldn't bear the thought of being away from Max. That your relationship wouldn't withstand separation." She raises her eyes to me, giving me her whole attention. "Did you know you guys were not right for each other?"

I place the glass on the table and rest my cheek on the tops of my knees as I look at her. "Yes." Pain crosses her face, but she quickly masks it with indifference, taking a large sip, and guilt fills me at the prospect of it. "I couldn't go to Paris, and everyone insisted and—" God, why is it so hard to search for a believable lie? "My mom is here—"

Suddenly, she stands up, spilling her wine on my fluffy, white carpet, which immediately is stained red. She ignores it, trembling with fury, and gives me her back while taking deep breaths. Finally, she spins around, and my heart sinks as I notice disappointment reflecting in her features. "Oh my God. For once, be honest, Valencia." I wince at her loud voice; she is really pissed off. "You refused because you knew how much I wanted it. Because I kept telling you it's my life-long dream to live and work in Paris!" Her hollow laughter breaks goose bumps out on my skin, and not the good kind. "That's what you do. Sacrifice what you want so that people around you will be happy. You are missing the fact that life is not about pleasing everyone else. I bet you even think that maybe you should have said yes to Max."

I don't say anything, just listen silently as she continues to give verbal blows. She doesn't understand what kind of nightmare I've lived in.

What I did, she only knows half-truths, but those half-truths have changed my entire life.

All fight leaves her as she exhales heavily and our stares meet. "Babe, you have to stop. What happened sucks, but you can't punish yourself forever for this. And maybe the time has come to think of what Valencia wants." She leans forward to give me a quick kiss on the cheek. "I'm afraid I will say something we will both regret, so it's better for me to leave now. I'll be at Wings tomorrow." She takes one last sip and goes to the door, but not before saying over her shoulder, "Don't even think about going back to Max. Love you."

The door shuts behind her, as I whisper back, "Love you too."

I reach for my purse lying on the couch a few feet away. I shuffle for my phone then turn it on. At once, around thirty missed calls and twenty messages arrive, all from my mom and friends demanding I call them back and explain.

<Braden> I'm on your side, baby sis, but you can't avoid them forever.

Hiding my face between my knees, I'm wondering if it's possible to screw up my life more than it already is, when the doorbell snaps my attention.

Furrowing my brows, I get up and scan the place quickly but don't find anything that Bella might have forgotten. Unlocking the door, I grin. "Did you come back for maca—" I blink in surprise at finding a bouquet of white peonies in a white basket shaped like a swan.

A single note is attached to the top in a white envelope with a black stamp reminding me of the Victorian Era.

My body freezes, and then my heart gallops wildly against my ribcage as memories from my last performance come rushing back to me.

After those stupid flowers were delivered every single time... I reported them to security and it stopped, but now it's two months later, and they are here again.

How does he know my address?

I look around and don't find anyone; the hallway is almost deafeningly silent. With a shaking hand, I pick up the note and quickly take it out, hoping to find anything but cryptic language.

But my hope dies as I read it, and fear sweeps through me.

What does that even mean, and more importantly, why is this person targeting me for his or her sick games?

An angel lived in her bubble truly believing that life is about her art and faith.
She brought nothing but happiness to those who surrounded her.
Until the monster decided otherwise

*L*achlan

Wiggling my fingers, I imagine a piano in front of me as my fingers play in time with the music blaring from the speakers. The man behind me groans, disturbing my nirvana. "You know, this behavior will only prolong it. I would really advise you not to piss me off," I say, and although he shuts up, I hear the chair scraping against the floor as he mumbles something through the tape.

Sighing in exasperation, I spin around to face a man around my age who is pinned to the metal chair situated in the middle of torture room number five.

One of the places I'm proudest of, considering the care and money I've invested in the devices here. The room consists of a single chair and several glass walls with expensive insects, spiders, and snakes living behind them. They watch their prey with fascination, especially if they weren't fed before my little play.

And per my request, they never are.

A single bulb lights the area, placing all the attention on the victim while keeping everything else hidden. He can only see me looming above him with my favorite cane, made of the finest steel.

Leaning closer, I see him shift as he mumbles something through the tape covering his mouth. Sweat soaks his white shirt and tears slide down his cheeks.

I've been nothing but gentle with him so far. Moving closer to him, I remove part of the tape from his lips, and say, "You know what my question is, Matt. Answer it, and it'll be over."

He gulps a breath, and croaks through his dry throat, "You will let me go?"

My laughter echoes through the space, mingling with the classical music.

Truly, some people are too stupid to live. "No, Matt. You are dead either way." His eyes widen as he shakes his head, wanting to say something, but I press my gloved finger against his lips to shut him up. "It's just that with the right answer, it'll be less painful. I can afford to be generous, for the right price of course." I rest the cane behind my neck, hanging my arms over it. "I wouldn't advise testing me," I add, although I can see he is weighing his options: the chaos crossing his face and his feet drumming on the floor as he looks around, especially at my torture table. He probably wonders what I will use to bring him harm.

Ah, building it in here sure provides a great decoy. "I don't know anything," he finally replies, and I nod and then hit him in the face with all my might. His nose cracks under the pressure of the metal handle and a scream of pain fills the space as blood runs down his chin, neck, and onto the floor. "Let's try again, shall we?" I exhale heavily, finding all this boring and time consuming for nothing.

Some victims are interesting to interrogate; there is a certain high in breaking them or watching them suffer. Then there are those who are interesting to catch, as they provide good entertainment even if during torture there is no fun.

And then there are victims like Matt.

Boring as fuck and completely useless, so much so that any minute spent with him is a minute wasted on not killing someone else. "Matt, tell me the location and I will kill you with let's say... five knife wounds. You'll just suffer for around thirty minutes. How does that sound, hmm?"

A tremor rushes through him as he shakes his head and mumbles while wincing in pain, trying to get free from his knots. "No, please, no. I really don't know. And if I did, my father and faith taught me—"

At the mention of his father, my hand squeezes the cane tighter as, for a second, memories take me back to the past, when the explanation for everything that happened in my life was only one thing.

Because faith said so.

I pull my hand back and deliver a blow to his stomach, hitting the gallbladder, the impact of which will provide a chain reaction of sending gastric juices into his mouth and burn his insides. He cries out, bending forward and barely breathing, as his skinny ass has never experienced anything but a fucking pat on the head from everyone else.

The golden boy.

Who would ever trust secrets to someone this weak or dumb? He doesn't have the information I need—or rather, he thinks he doesn't. So spending my time with him serves no purpose while I have a victim waiting for me in room number two. "Too bad you didn't cooperate," I say, walking to the table and wiping my cane clean. Then I throw the tissue in the bin, pour myself a whiskey, and grab my jacket. I press the first button that will open the blinds and turn on the speakers for my students who before watched only from cameras.

In case Matt had the answer, the information would have been only for me, but now they can enjoy the show.

I notice them lounging on the chairs like in a movie theater, while some of them snack on food and take some pics on the special cameras they leave in this place, which are kept for study purposes.

Sipping my drink, I whistle loudly as I move in the direction of a door, when a ragged voice asks, "Where are you going?" I ignore it, because I won't waste a minute longer on a useless subject. Instead, I snap my fingers twice and immediately the room lights up, blinding Matt as he stammers and squints his eyes, adjusting to the glare, and then fear penetrates him, as he stammers, "No. No. No!" But his words don't change the reality.

He is surrounded by lizards who can't wait to feast on his flesh. And I just pressed a button to let them out and have free rein. "Pray, Matt," I tell him as I step outside, and a chuckle slips past my lips. "Pray and maybe someone will listen." With that, I close the door while his terrified screams continue to echo in room number five.

CHAPTER SEVEN

New York, New York
November 2009

*V*alencia, 16 years old

*T*urning on the old CD, I grab the soda, and scream, "Hell yeah!"
while the rest of the people join me the minute Nirvana's "Smells
like a Teen Spirit" starts to play.

Everyone immediately gets on the dance floor while I just stand in place and
move to the beat with my arms and head, almost forgetting about everything in
the high of the moment. Strong arms wrap around me from behind as I'm pulled
back into the muscled chest and I grin, although my eyes are still closed.

Jason places his mouth on the spot between my neck and shoulder,
peppering my skin with kisses as his hands slide over the front of my body, and
all I can do is give in to the feeling, pressing myself against him. "Someone is on
fire," he murmurs and turns me around, spilling soda on us a little, and I giggle
while circling his neck with my arms and rising on my toes so our mouths can

meet in a hard kiss. He roams his tongue inside me and slides his palms down to my ass.

He hikes me up, and I wrap my legs around him, and then he takes us upstairs to his room with catcalls from his friends following us, but I don't care.

All I want is to be alone with Jason and have all the wild sex in the world.

Jason and I met during my first year at this school, and we've been inseparable ever since. Although most people told me to stay away from the bad boy from the wrong side of the tracks, I didn't listen, because none of them really knew him.

How sweet he was. How he wrote songs and played with his band in club gigs. Or how he helped his mom raise his sister.

Dad gave me speeches about being a good girl, and that relationships and sex would make me a bad one. He didn't know about Jason, and I had Mom's full support anyway. It was the first time I decided not to follow Dad's faith and rules because they seemed too ridiculous to me.

A few months ago, we finally did it. It was the most magical thing in the world and I will never regret it. He was gentle and sweet. How anyone can call it a sin is beyond me.

Currently, we are celebrating their very first solo gig in one of the school concerts, and our mutual friends are all here at Jason's house while his family is away in Florida for a visit.

Jason pushes me against the door, his finger slipping under my T-shirt, and I moan into his mouth just as a loud crash from downstairs snags our attention.

Jason drags his mouth from mine as we breathe heavily. His forehead rests against mine. "If Duke broke my guitar after I told him not to touch it, I'm going to kill him."

We share a laugh and are about to resume kissing, when my dad's raging roar freezes me and my heartbeat speeds up, and not in a good way. "What is going on here?" A beat, and then an even louder roar. "Valencia!" I rush downstairs, my bare feet slapping against the wood, and step into the living room. My dad's eyes widen as they land on me and then fill with something unfamiliar when he looks over my shoulder, probably noticing Jason. "What are you doing here?" he shouts, but then steps closer to me and grabs my hand. "Doesn't matter, we are leaving." With that, he drags me out.

We are outside when I tug on my hand harshly, and he has no choice but to let go when I stumble back. "Dad, what are you doing?"

"What am I doing? Look at you!" he shouts, his hand waving up and down over me, "Drunk, half naked, and in a house with that boy who is barely eighteen years old. You should thank God I didn't call the police."

He reaches for my arm again, when Jason steps in front of me, blocking him. "Don't touch her. You are upsetting Valencia."

That's the wrong thing to say, because my dad laughs, although it's shallow and lacks any humor. "Get back to the house, kid, before I do something I will regret."

"Oh yeah? Bring it on, old man." Jason pushes his chest up, and Dad just shakes his head in disbelief.

"That's the boy you're dating? He has not an ounce of respect."

"Dad, you need to calm down." Then I address Jason who still keeps his eyes on Dad. "Jason, back off."

"No one shouts at you." Which is sweet really, him protecting me, but I don't need protection from my dad. He might be pissed as hell, but he'll never hurt me.

"Jason, please," I plead, looking straight at him, and his emerald green eyes finally focus on me. Although I see his internal struggle, he cups my cheek and nods. "I'll be waiting by the door." He gives me a peck, and whispers, "Don't apologize."

Once he is a few feet away, I face my dad, who pinches the bridge of his nose and exhales heavily. "Valencia, let's leave."

"I don't want to, Dad. And I'm not drunk!"

"If we leave now, I will never speak about it. You made a mistake and you are sorry. That's enough. You will pray in church on Sunday, and it will all—"

My jaw drops at his words, while I wonder when I ever gave him any indication I would follow his path blindly. "I'm not sorry, and loving Jason and having fun is not a sin." He freezes, his eyes narrowing, and for the first time in my life, fear caused by my father washes over me.

Up until this moment, I didn't realize how much he worshiped what he did and that he had certain plans for my life. "Get in the car, Valencia. This boy has clearly filled your head with nonsense. A bright future awaits you, and he is nothing but trash."

"Accordingly to the Bible, all people are equal."

"That's true. But this boy doesn't look religious to me. And my daughter will not date an atheist." Clearly fed up with all this, he steps toward me, but I move back, disappointment settling through every bone.

How didn't I see it? Dad is some kind of fanatic who divides people by good and bad solely on religion. Even tough religion is not about that.

It's about love and freedom and faith. When did it stop being that for him? Is this why Mom left him? Come to think of it, he has been acting weird all this time. Always having strict hours and even choosing my friends for me. It was just a matter of time before we ran into an argument.

Jason is just someone who forced us to face it.

"I love Jason, Dad. And I'm not going anywhere with you. What's the matter with you? It's my life."

He snarls, placing his hands on his hips. "You are sixteen. You have no life or right to make decisions. Get in the fucking car, Valencia, before I call the cops." Loud thunder erupts around us, and only then do I look up to see the sky has turned dark blue and it'll be raining any minute. "You are drunk apparently. That's why you feel like you have the right to speak to me in this tone. Where is my princess?" he mutters to himself, but I just shake my head.

"I'm not a princess, Dad! I am just a girl and I'm not going anywhere. Call the cops, I don't care." I know he won't do it, because no way will he allow his perfect child to be tainted with a record, and we both know that.

His lips thin, and that's when rain starts pouring on us in heavy, big drops that instantly wet our clothes. "Leave, Dad. Just leave." I'm afraid we will say even more stuff to each other that both of us will regret, so it's better to part now so we can talk in the morning.

No way will I ever change my mind.

"Valencia—" he starts, but I shout, "Leave, Dad!"

"We will talk in the morning. I will fix this problem," he mutters and then goes to his car, sits inside, and a second later pulls from the driveway as I watch him drive away.

Tomorrow.

We will fix this tomorrow. I'm sure he acted this way only because my relationship was unexpected to him.

We still have tomorrow.

I spend the night with Jason, finding solace in his arms as he sets my fears to rest. In the morning, he takes me home, where my mom and the police greet me to announce that my dad has died in a car accident.

All because he was driving in the rain and smashed into a tree.

*N*ew York, New York
            January 2018

*V*alencia
            "Now let's get back into first position," I say, straightening up, placing my feet at thirty degrees from each other while my hands face each other, my thumbs inside my palms. "And gracefully bow to the audience," I finish, while leaning down as the kids follow my lead, but a few of them stumble and giggle loudly, and I wink at them in the mirror.

Most ballet teachers are strict from the very beginning, but it's the time for them to fall in love with dance, so I believe it should be about fun first.

Then it's going to be about technique, sweat, pain, and unconditional love and devotion.

The music cuts off and moves to soft jazz as I clap my hands, regaining their attention. They all relax, jumping up and down, and some of them sway as I lean to the side and stretch my back. They follow me, and then I do the same with the other side.

I also stretch my legs and hands all while they watch me carefully and repeat. They must do it so their tiny feet won't hurt in the morning. I remember my first classes; Mistress Patricia treated us like army recruits who owed her a debt. She claimed it would help us in the future, but it wasn't much of a consolation for bloodied feet every night.

The image in front of me is almost comical considering they all wear pink tutus along with high ponytails and lots of toothless smiles, as it's my kindergarten beginners' class. So many five-year-olds who have no clue what they are even doing here.

My favorite kind of class. "Girls, practice the first position at home while listening to this music." I shake the box full of USB drives and they squeal excitingly.

Shaking my head in amusement, I usher them to get in line as each one picks out theirs. Thankfully, I bought them all in purple, so no one will fight over one, and they each give me a long hug. "Valencia, will you come next time too?" Marcia asks, batting her eyelashes at me, and I chuckle. This little blonde angel with doll eyes will break a lot of hearts in the future.

"For sure, every Monday and Friday, as I promised."

She raises her arms up, and screams, "Yay!" and then runs off to the others as they change their shoes. I slide the window open, allowing in fresh air, as I can barely breathe through the sweat coating the air.

"Are we going to watch a video next week?" Tina crocks her head to the side, her ponytail swaying along with her. "Mistress Patricia said it was your first play."

I cringe inwardly; that freaking play should never have been taped. My first-ever performance ended up being a disaster with the piano teacher falling off the stage as I swirled on the wrong side and then couldn't stand on my toes, so I ended up in her arms and she slipped down. Everyone laughed, while I stood on the stage crying my heart out.

Since then, Patricia shows it to all prebeginners classes, claiming that mistakes happen, but you should push past them. Which is a cool lesson and all, I just wish I didn't have to see one of the most embarrassing moments in my life every single semester.

"You sure will," I reply, ruffling her hair, and she gives me a smile before walking to the door, limping slightly. I catch her hoodie collar. "Honey, are you all right?" She shouldn't be this tired after one class with me, but I noticed during training she wasn't placing her foot correctly, and whenever I told her to do so, she'd wince.

"Yes," she says quickly, too quickly, so I keep my hold on her and wave to everyone else as they emerge from class one by one, and then I drag her to the side. "Tell me the truth, Tina." I kneel in front of her, so we are on the same eye level and she won't be intimidated by me.

She sighs heavily, her hair blowing up. "The shoes are a bit too small and dig into my toes. It hurts during dancing and when I remove them, especially on this foot." She raises her left leg and slips off the sock. I gasp, because her foot is purple and has blisters all over it. It's a wonder she has been able to dance at all!

"You have to put ice on it. I need to tell your mom." The minute the words spill from my lips, her eyes fill with tears, and she begs, "Please don't do that. I told her they'd fit till December. She needed to buy a hat."

"A hat?" Confusion laces my voice and she nods. What the hell does a hat have to do with it?

"She always gets cold, but never buys herself anything. It was either a hat or new shoes for me. I can take it, but Mommy needs the hat so she won't get sick."

"Come here," I murmur, hugging her close as she sobs on my shoulder, and my heart breaks a little with each tear she sheds.

No child should experience this kind of burden, but what do they do if there is simply no other choice? We had nothing to eat for long periods after Mom left Dad, so I'm familiar with single moms and their struggles. Tina's mom does everything she can for her daughter.

Leaning back, I wipe away her tears. "Next time you come here, there will be new shoes."

Her eyes widen, as she whispers, "Really?"

"Yes, but you can't tell anyone. Also don't wear these shoes anymore, and put some Band-Aids on your blisters." I reach for first aid kit on the side and take out the adhesive bandages, placing some on her foot as she groans in pain. "They will come from a fairy. I will tell her about your struggle, and I'm sure she will help."

She glances around before lowering her voice even more. "The ballet fairy who gives Patricia notes on who behaves well?"

"Uh-huh."

She nods and then presses her finger against her lips, sliding it in a zipping motion. "Won't say a word."

"Good, now go. Your mom is probably waiting for you." She runs away while I go to the board to make a few notes regarding their progress, when Patricia's voice breaks the silence.

"You can't help them all."

I sigh heavily, as it's an ongoing argument and I'd hoped she'd be too busy with finances today to hear Tina and me. "I can help Tina."

She shakes her head, sipping her coffee. "Valencia, this school was created for kids who have less chance to attend a private establishment. But it doesn't mean you have to give it all to them. There should be work on the parents' part too."

"Tina's mom works two jobs, I think she does her best," I state while she barely lifts a brow, more amused with my anger than bothered by it.

But then Patricia is weird like that. Sometimes I think my old teacher lives in her head by her makeshift reality. She doesn't have a family besides this school, so she's naïve about a lot of things.

"Ballet is work but not only for the kids. For the parents too. They have to involve their soul." She sips her coffee again while I put my hair in a bun, hating the humidity in the room. This window AC is not working fast enough for me. "You constantly buy new stuff for them. You need to stop."

"I'm not your student anymore. I can do whatever I want," I singsong while she frowns, wiggling her nose in disgust, but she grabs my arm when I pass by her going to the administration desk.

"You are working here. You give a lot to this school. You can't help and save everyone. Stop it."

Gently pulling my arm free, I wink at her while she huffs in displeasure, and I resume my walk to Adriana, who is on the phone with someone and gives me a folder.

I read through it and just roll my eyes, because all it contains is some talk about a new progressive ballet technique they found. You just teach kids with your heart, and that's about it. How can they learn something progressive if they didn't get the basics?

"Valencia," Patricia calls, and I sigh heavily, so not in the mood for her lectures.

"Look, I won't change my mind, and I have tons of things to do, so how about—" I pause midsentence, blinking rapidly, but the image doesn't go away.

Kaden Lachlan Scott stands in the doorway of the ballet school, shrinking the spacious hall into a tiny place filled with his dominance and power.

As freaking always!

His black coat has traces of snow that he dusts off with his leather-gloved hand, and for a moment, I imagine what it would be like to have the leather touch my skin, and I bite the inside of my cheek.

What the hell are those thoughts? I act like a horny teenager whenever he's around.

As always, his blue suit hugs him perfectly, and although it's annoying, he is nothing but perfect.

The perfect jerk who kissed me in the greenhouse.

"What are you doing here?" I ask in a hostile tone, crossing my arms while he grins. But before he can answer, Patricia gasps and quickly goes to his side.

I don't think I've seen my teacher do anything this fast for another human being!

"Forgive her, please. We just had a dispute. That's why she is rude." Adriana's jaw drops too, and I lift my chin, silently asking if she knows anything, but she just shrugs. "Mr. Scott, I'm glad you came."

"Well, I couldn't resist your invitation. I'm sorry I'm late." He kisses the back of her hand, bowing slightly, showing off as the gentlemen he is *not*.

Why does no one but me see him for the arrogant jerk he is?

Her cheeks legitimately freaking blush as she waves her hand in the air. "Oh, no. I understand you are a busy man." She circles the place with her palm. "Would you like a tour? So you know you've made a great investment."

Investment?

At these words, I straighten up, panic swirling through me as I try to find meaning for this.

Victor promised Patricia that no one will ever be able to destroy it and the kids have a safe haven. He did mention lately though that the place brought nothing but costs, and since Patricia refused charities, the school couldn't even benefit from those.

He didn't sell it, right?

Maybe I should have answered one of their calls; they are probably pissed off as hell for my silent treatment.

But then something else strikes me. He never said out loud he bought this place. He just told me his opinions on the matter as a businessman whenever I brought up the subject.

And Patricia never mentioned his name either.

Oh my God. Could I have been wrong all these years and Victor wasn't the one who saved this place?

"No, I've seen it before. Although I wouldn't mind knowing about the dance routine to see how progressive you are for the neighborhood and what kind of supplies you might need."

Patricia covers her mouth with her palm as she sighs. "You are a gift from heaven, Mr. Scott." The minute she says it, something weird happens.

The aura around him changes as he tenses, fisting his hands, but still keeping his smile intact, and if people weren't watching him closely, they would probably miss it. But since I'm that idiot who always has my eyes on him, I catch it.

Deep rage settling in his blue orbs as if she said something insulting.

Such a strong reaction to one simple word?

"That's a stretch, Patricia." He shifts his attention to me, "Shall we? I don't have all the time in the world."

Yeah, and I'm what? His employee? He can take it all and shove it down his throat for all I care. People like him are sharks, and I sincerely doubt he cares much about the center. Patricia has no head for business and will even believe in unicorns if someone gives her a believable-enough story.

I'll have to call Victor tonight to figure out what is going on.

"Of course. Valencia will show it to you."

"I'm not—" She sends me a warning glance and I huff. That's as much as I can act out; she can make my life here impossible with her restrictions. It's not as if I can be rude to the elderly, and this job is the highlight of my week.

Dropping the folder back on the desk, I see how Adriana gives me a thumbs-up. I go back to the studio, opening the door widely, and call over my shoulder, "Mr. Scott, welcome to the Dancing Wings Ballet Studio." Nothing but sarcasm laces my voice, and it's followed by a chuckle.

God, give me strength to survive this meeting before I commit a sin and kill him!

*L*achlan

Valencia still sends daggers my way, but she manages to keep a forced smile on her face as she points to the studio for me. With a light bow and wink to the receptionist, whose cheeks heat up, I follow her lead and enter the spacious studio, only to frown at the smell. "Sorry, we didn't expect royal guests," she informs me, closing the door behind her with a loud thud.

I shrug, fascinated by the anger flashing in her eyes. What does it take to break an angel out of her angelic shell? "That's okay. You'll do better next time."

She opens and closes her mouth and then exhales heavily, placing her hands on her hips while waiting a beat. Finally, she raises her chocolate, confused yet furious eyes to me, as she asks, "What are you doing here?"

She makes it too easy to taunt her. "I own it." And then it finally happens, and I barely contain my laughter.

She darts toward me, poking her finger in my chest while fury coats her words. "Do you own every single thing that I like? What are you? A fucking king?" She gasps and covers her mouth with her hand as my brow lifts.

"Princess, don't curse, darling." I press my finger to her lips before she can add another insult. "And yes, I am." She has no idea just how right she is.

Although, I prefer the word *mentor,* but she is yet to discover that.

"It's your fault. What are you doing here?"

Resting against the ballet barre, I motion at the studio. "Checking out investments my company has made."

Her brows furrow as she crosses her arms. "Really? You are telling me that all this time you are the one who has kept this place running?" Disbelief and a little dread lace her voice, so I smirk and she fists her hands.

Ah, my little prey gets very passionate around me. Can't say I don't like it. "Correction. I don't want to tell you anything, but if you are throwing facts, then yeah. My company keeps this place running, as you put it."

"Uggh!" she groans, pulling at her hair as she paces the studio while I watch her, studying her fairy-like body.

She is gorgeous, like a statue that cannot be touched; otherwise, her magic will be gone.

I intend to carve a real woman out of this fucking stone, who will live and her heart will beat for her passion and desire until she will crash and burn in her devastation and pain.

"Is it because of Italy?" she suddenly asks, focusing her accusing stare on me. "Is it because I refused a relationship with you?"

"Refused?" I repeat, rubbing my chin. "I don't remember asking for it in the first place." She grits her teeth, while I say, "We spent a week in Italy, doing all sorts of things. Among them was hot sex. That's about it."

"You are—" She searches for words while gulping breaths. "You are so arrogant, so—"

"Honest?" I supply, then unbutton my jacket, and her eyes land on my six-pack visible through the white shirt.

Yeah, baby, admire it. It belongs to you anyway.

At least while we are both alive.

"Valencia, you never wanted more, but now it seems you are mad I didn't either."

"We met in Italy, and then when I came home, Victor told me that you were doing business. You mean to tell me those two things are not connected?"

Laughter slips past me, as I'm finding it fucking hilarious that she thinks her stepfather had anything to do with Italy. "What's so funny?" She practically foams at the mouth, and I've had enough of this bullshit.

She clearly needs a visual of what I'm after.

Or what she needs to think I'm after.

Catching her hand, I pull her to me while spinning her around so we are both facing the mirror. Her ass firmly plants against my hard-on that digs into her as her breath hitches, and our eyes meet in the mirror. "Do you see this woman?" I ask, sliding one hand down her breast and stomach that dips under my touch, while my other fists her hair, propping her more comfortably on my shoulder as I run my nose over her neck. Tugging on her hair, I demand, "Answer me."

She exhales heavily, but replies raspily, "Yes."

Nipping on her sensitive skin, I still her in my arms. Her back arches under my touch when I kick her legs apart a little and slide my hand lower to her pussy. "Do you see how gorgeous she is? Flushed, against me, with her body begging me to touch her and pleasure her. Why would I need any reason but that to want her?" Sucking on her earlobe, I quickly bite it before skimming my lips over her ear, and whisper, "What would you want me to do, Valencia? All this sassy attitude needs punishment, doesn't it?" She moans, pressing harder against me. "Do you need my fingers?" I probe her a little, just enough to give her clit a little friction through her leggings. "My tongue? I remember you could get off on it for hours."

She groans, moving her head and seeking my mouth, but I pull her hair again as she cries out softly, and I know it only intensifies her pleasure. She is close just from the talk alone. That's what happens when a woman like her is left unsatisfied for a long time.

She is a very passionate creature.

My passionate creature, because if any other men had access to that, they'd be dead.

No one has the right to touch Valencia but me.

For the time being.

"No, I—" she croaks, and I bite her neck, sucking on the skin and leaving pale marks. "No? You want my cock, then? How was it last time? 'Deeper, harder, Lachlan.'" She practically burns in my arms, her eyes closed, her skin flushed as her chest rises and falls, and then she surprises me.

She turns around, wraps her arms around my neck, and smashes our mouths together, and our tongues meet without hesitation, already attuned to each other. Hiking her up, I push her against the wall and she tightens her legs around me while I dry hump her through our clothes, needing her as much as she does me.

Six months without her is too fucking long.

"Lachlan," she moans, pressing even deeper while her hands scratch my back and hair as she tries to push off my jacket. "I need—"

"I know." I'm about to rip her fucking clothes off and grant her access to me, when I hear footsteps outside along with greetings.

And then I come back to reality... in the kids' studio... where I almost just fucked Valencia against the wall.

Before she can even blink, I place her down and step back, breathing heavily while cursing myself inwardly.

Who do I become when I'm around her? Not once has a woman evoked such emotions from me.

And that makes Valencia very dangerous.

*V*alencia

He steps back from me and my eyelids flutter open. We are both breathing heavily as I touch my burning lips that are tender from all the kissing. I have a moment to see an unfamiliar emotion cross his face, but it's almost immediately replaced with indifference. Within a second, nothing is left of the man who passionately ravished me in the ballet studio, and he is once again the ruthless, arrogant businessman I've known all this time.

A knock sounds on the door, and then it opens with Bella entering, holding two coffees. "Next time, you're going to stand in that fucking qu—" She halts and blinks in surprise, her head moving from me to Lachlan and back again.

I groan inwardly, because anyone finding us together like this is not what I need right now.

She quickly pushes back her shock and nods in greeting. "Bella Alvarez."

He lifts his chin as he replies, "Kaden Scott. A pleasure to meet a ballerina who makes us proud on the worldwide stages." Her cheeks heat up while a fury unlike anything settles in me, a red haze covering my eyes at the idea of him touching her.

Jealousy is not an emotion I'm familiar with, but right now, I'm ready to scratch my friend's eyes out for running her appreciative gaze over him. But more importantly, I want to sucker punch Lachlan for showing her attention.

What is going on with me? He can do whatever he wants.

We share nothing but physical attraction, because if we are not kissing, we are arguing or he's making fun of me.

"Valencia." Bella's voice snaps me out of my haze and it takes me a second to realize she already called my name. Clearing my throat, I reply, "Yes?"

"I was telling Kaden here that it was your idea to change the name of the school to attract more parents."

I can feel Kaden's stare on me but purposely ignore it, shrugging. "Good thing Patricia agreed." Before she can add anything, I go to my bag and address Lachlan without looking at him. "We need to practice for my show, so if you don't mind leaving us alone."

From the corner of my eye, I see Bella mouthing to me, *What the hell are you doing?* But she nods in agreement anyway, probably not wanting to bust me.

My back is still to him when his deep voice speaks, leaving prickles of awareness on my skin as my heart still beats rapidly in my chest from the earlier kiss. "Have a nice day, Valencia. We will speak again." He doesn't ask but orders, almost warning me. But I don't react, and he finally leaves, shutting the door loudly as Bella fans herself with a dreamy look on her face.

"Oh my God, woman, are you shacking up with *the* Kaden Scott? That explains a lot," she muses, tapping on her chin with her finger as my bag falls to the floor.

"I'm not shacking up with anyone, and what the hell is that supposed to explain?"

Bella can be a little insane when something excites her, and with her bouncing in place as she gives me my coffee and sips hers in long swallows, clearly tells me the idea of me and Kaden excites her beyond measure. "Your rebellion stage. Finally, you decided to say fuck everyone else and live your life."

Rubbing my forehead as a slight throbbing ache starts to appear, I think of how freaking noticeable my sadness must be that almost everyone feels they have the right to tell me I need to live a little. What happened to compassion? Why do we selfishly need to put only our desires ahead of others? Shouldn't we worry about everyone else?

"Okay, okay!" Her voice laces with panic as she waves her hand in front of my face. "Forget I said anything. Are we still on for tonight?" My brows furrow at her question, and then I remember I promised her a night out before she has to go back to Paris tomorrow.

After yesterday's argument, we'd met at the school and she hugged me as if nothing happened. That was how it usually was between Bella and me; we might argue but she has my back no matter what. Patricia had sent her to the more advanced class to show off her new skills and inspire them to strive hard for success so they could travel to Europe too. She finished earlier than me and rushed to grab a coffee for both us since I still had things to do.

"Of course. We just need to stop by our places to get ready."

She squeals, giving me a light peck on the cheek. "Yeah, baby! Where are we going?" I open my mouth to reply, but she presses her index finger to my lips, and I roll my eyes as she continues. "Don't tell me. Let it be a surprise! I just want to know what I should wear. Something sexy or sporty?"

A smile tugs at my lips as I envision her in sporty attire for the place I've decided to take us, and how she'll kill me if she doesn't look her best. "Sexy."

She bounces in excitement and chats about all the renovations the school is going to get while I pack my stuff and think back on Lachlan and how, with one simple touch, he gave me something I've never experienced before... with such intensity.

Pleasure.

Shaking my head, I focus on Bella and the night of fun we are going to have tonight. And then everything will go back to normal, because that's my life.

Perfect, organized, and right.

It has no room for chaos.

*L*achlan
Mine.

And I'm fucking done walking around with a constant hard-on that needs to sink balls deep into her so she'll remember forever not to avoid me.

Or use another man to place distance between us.

CHAPTER EIGHT

New York, New York
October 2009

V alencia, 16 years old

S itting numbly on the chair, I watch as my father is put in the ground while the pastor says a prayer and tears stream down my cheeks.

My mom's hold on my hand tightens as if giving me her strength, but I slip it out from under hers. "Honey—" That's the moment the pastor finishes his prayer and we all stand to say our finally goodbye. The thorns on the roses I bought for Dad dig into my palms, drawing blood that slowly drips on my white dress.

Dad hated the color black, so there was no way I'd wear it today. A barely audible sob escapes me as I cover my mouth with my fist, not wanting to show anyone my pain, because they won't have the words.

It shall pass.

There was nothing we could do.

Just one of those things.

The car crashed.

"Goodbye, Dad," I whisper, throwing the rose on the casket, and that's when Jason wraps his arm around my shoulders.

He has been with me since I got the news, waiting by the door and constantly sending messages begging me to talk to him, but I ignored him. The only people who were allowed in my house were the girls, and if any of them tried to give me something from Jason, I told them to get out.

I immediately step back, ignoring the guilt at his pained gasp and focus on the guilt that eats me alive every single day. "It's my fault," I say, and he shakes his head, grabbing my chin and lifting it so our eyes can meet.

"Circumstances. Life happened. It's not us, baby." He tries to comfort me and circles my waist, but I push his hands back.

"With you, it's always just life, isn't it, Jason? You never take responsibility for anything!" I shout at him, and disbelief crosses his face as he takes a deep breath.

"You are grieving, I understand. But don't give up on us. Valencia, I love you and you love me."

A tear slides down my cheek because he's right. We love each other, but it means and changes nothing.

"We are done, Jason. Our relationship died with my father."

"Baby—"

"Please, stop calling me that. Just... stop, Jason, okay? We are done. Accept it. Don't bother my friends, forget about me, and build your life away from here. Chase your dreams. But without me." It's a wonder I can say all those things, as each one of them is like stabbing a knife into my heart, but I have no choice.

I will live with this burden my whole life, but Jason doesn't have to.

If only I hadn't said all those mean words to him... if only he didn't drive up to rescue me from the party... if only I could hear his voice one last time.

I'm not okay. And I'm afraid I never will be.

Jason waits a moment, but then with a quite curse, he leaves, and I know he won't come back. He is proud and my rejection stung him; he already tried to talk to me three times.

Some part of me wants to run after him, to beg for forgiveness and find solace in his arms as always, but how can I?

The solace in his arms is why my dad is dead in the first place. Allowing my relationship with Jason to continue would mean betraying my dad once again.

It might be irrational, but then people in pain do all sorts of things to numb it. And besides, a relationship with constant guilt won't bring anything good anyway.

Mom comes closer to me, offering me her silent support, but I don't need it. "I want to be left alone."

"Valencia—" Even her voice grates on my nerves, not to mention her presence.

"Mom, please. You didn't like his company when he was alive. I don't quite understand why you are here anyway." She steps back from my verbal blow, her eyes widening at my cruelty, and I want to take it back, to run into her arms and cry on her chest, to let her comfort me in this moment when the world is crashing around me.

But I can't.

For the first time in my life, I can't.

I expect her to insist some more, but she just nods, quickly wiping away the tear at the corner of her eyes, and spins around to walk to the car where she'll most likely wait for me till I've had enough of being here.

I sit on the ground, ignoring the dirt around me, and cover my face with my hands, finally letting myself weep.

My dad is dead.

Because I allowed myself to be reckless, and for once I went after what I wanted, not paying attention to rules.

My dad is gone.

And the only thing I have left of him is his faith.

*N*ew York, New York
January 2018

*V*alencia
Bella jumps out as the cabbie gives me a side eye, clearly exasperated with my friend at this point. I grin subtly, fishing for a twenty in my clutch while shaking my head at Bella who takes a selfie with the club in the background.

She has been acting like a freaking tourist, pressing her nose to the window and squealing anytime we pass monuments or buildings, to the point of the cabbie turning the music up louder, hinting at us to shut up.

Not that it helped or I cared one way or the other. Someone has to have fun in this world.

Plus, I really understand Bella; New York is our hometown. Why shouldn't she be happy to spend the evening out before going back to Paris?

"Is she always this hyper?" he asks, and I shrug as I get out.

"Most of the time." I shut the door in his face and have a second to tug on my freakishly short dress before my friend is all up in my face.

She grabs my hands and shakes me while I just grin at her childlike excitement. "We are freaking here!" Yeah, we came to the Dungeon.

Or that's what this place is called anyway.

People stand in line just to get to peek inside, but they'll have no luck, as it's by invitation only, the one that currently hides in my purse.

A bright yellow sign says "The Dungeon of Burlesque" while two huge-as-hell bouncers stand by the gate, scanning everyone with their hawk-like eyes, and they send most of the people away who cry or fight their decision.

"Come on! Let's get inside! I can't believe you snagged those invitations!" Bella murmurs into my ear, and I just wink while we move in the direction of the men who focus their attention on us, sweeping their gazes over our attire.

The invitations came by mail the other day, claiming that one of the investors who had something to do with Victor's company was inviting everyone for the weekly show, which would have all the stars performing to old hits, and it would be a performance we would never forget. I had no idea such a place even existed in New York, and the dancer in me longed to check it out.

However, I knew asking anyone from my group of friends was impossible, as some dancers frowned upon it, claiming it was about sex and not art. My hands always prickled to push their bigheaded egos into the TV so they could see the beauty of it without their judgmental outlook. Max forbade me to even think about it, but thankfully, he is gone too.

God, it feels good for once to do something for myself. Once Bella travels back to Paris, I can go back to my routine life where everyone's desire means more than mine.

But for a moment in time, I want to be selfish and reckless.

I extend the plastic invitation to the bouncer, and he takes it, but before he can say anything, something makes him stand up straight as he presses his finger to his ear. A second later, he removes the red rope that blocks the entrance and motions with his hand for us to go through. "Welcome to the Dungeon," he greets, and I give him a thumbs-up while Bella drags me inside, our heels clicking loudly on the marble floor.

We pass through a narrow gate, and then a waitress beams at us with a bright smile, holding menus in her hands. "Welcome to the Dungeon," she repeats the line. Does the owner make them do that or what?

"Thank you. We'd like a table for two please."

She nods and turns around as we follow her. My eyes drink in all the beauty as I hold back a gasp.

Whoever built this place sure as hell didn't count his money.

The space is wide and huge with old music blasting through the speakers, giving a type of vibe as if taking you back in time, when the burlesque dance was born. The black marble floor shines brightly under the golden chandeliers filled with expensive crystals that display the place in a magical light that the gold walls emphasize. Portraits of burlesque legends are scattered on the walls, with little quotes about the dance written on several tablecloths. Small round tables fill most of the place, with candles and a bottle of wine on each, ready for the taking.

It doesn't surprise me that almost all the seats are taken as people engage in conversations while giving sideways glances to the stages.

A spacious bar is located at one end where most of the waiters are, and a central stage is on the other. The curtain is down, so it means we came just in time for the show. Near it is a smaller stage, where musicians wearing the same uniform are getting ready, placing their instruments in position.

The guys wear black vests with a bow tie along with black jeans, while girls have knee-length stockings, shorts, tight T-shirts with the logo on it, and navigate gracefully in high pumps. All in all, the place reeks of luxury and high maintenance, but at the same time keeps the sexy vibe of burlesque, almost taking you back in time and drowning you in the energy of the past.

"This is the best place ever," Bella says as we drop onto our chairs and the waitress gives us menus.

"Do you want to start with some drinks first?" I shake my head since there is wine at the table and she nods. "Just press this button once you are ready to order." Then she leaves, winking at us while I watch several men trailing their gazes after her behind.

"I will never know how they do that on those shoes," I mutter.

Bella laughs, sipping from her glass. "And that comes from a ballerina who has to stand on her toes."

"That's probably why you almost broke your neck two years ago while trying to run in them." She throws a nut at me, but I dip so it doesn't hit me.

"Did you invite Nora and Becky?" Isn't that a million-dollar question? She reads my face as she chuckles, but it lacks any amusement. "They refused to meet with me? Or let me paraphrase it. Becky refused, as she still holds a grudge over Paris, and Nora supported her since Becky married her brother." She takes a large sip.

Well, there is nothing to add since she covered everything. Becky was one of the best when it came to dancing, and we all got into Juilliard except Nora, who went into marketing and management. She studied ballet till she turned eighteen and then flipped off anyone who insisted she stay. Becky would have won the part for Paris if it weren't for the injury she got during the last audition that ultimately destroyed her career forever.

After that came the drinking and several bad choices in men. Nora's brother was pretty decent. I know most people judge them for being together, but I saw genuine love between them, and in a way, I'm glad she has him and doesn't drown in self-destruction.

"Bella, it's none of your business." She wants to say something but I shake my head. "And Becky shouldn't hold a grudge. But it's a beautiful evening, so let's enjoy it instead of arguing, okay?" Nothing will mend our group of friends, and oddly, I'm okay with that.

We grew up and everyone found their own path. Sometimes, though, paths don't cross anymore, and that's all right.

Musicians slowly start to play an old tune I don't recognize and everyone quiets down, the lights going dim as the stage brightens up. The red curtain rises up, up, up, and then a red-haired woman in a red dress stands on the stage, frozen in position with one hand on her hip.

"Jessica Rabbit is here, I think," Bella mutters, resting her chin on her palm, and I chuckle. But indeed, with her curvy body and sex appeal, she can easily be that without blinking.

Swaying to the beat of the music, she slowly walks across the stage and plays with her dress, fingering her zipper while turning around to give us a view of her behind. "Well, she is hot," I comment, popping a nut in my mouth and wondering if it's possible to look this hot with my thin body that has almost no curves. I can go braless and no one notices.

"Yeah, I'm going to join the catcalls soon, just saying." She takes a sip of her drink, but the minute the light hits the dancer's face, she spits the drink back in her glass. "Holy moly! Is that Mia?"

Our glasses-wearing, cute dancer who barely says a word to anyone?

"Are you dru—" I join her shock though, as indeed the sexy goddess on stage is none other than Mia Parker, one of our classmates who currently performs with me.

Mia is one of the best dancers in the group, and she would go places if it weren't for her younger sister she has to support. For some reason, the teachers never give her a chance, and as much as I've tried to get her into a higher position, she always refuses. She is always sort of there by my side with no explanations. The girl is the sweetest.

But what the hell is she doing here? "Olga will have a fit once she knows."

"Bella, we can't mention it," I warn, because I don't care about her reasons. She will not be kicked out of ballet for this. My stomach growls and I decide to occupy my mouth with something before we can speak with Mia, who notices us too. Her eyes widen as she freezes, but I send her a reassuring smile, and she continues to dance, though her focus is still on us.

I open the menu thinking about ordering something light, when paper falls out of it and onto the napkin in my lap. My heart stills and then beats with power again.

No.

Not here too.

Bella's brows furrow, as she says, "Valencia? Are you all right? You've gone pale all of a sudden." A beat, and then, "Don't worry, I won't tell anyone about Mia." As much as I love Mia, she doesn't occupy my thoughts right now and isn't the reason for my shock.

With almost shaking hands, I read the paper that has the exact same cryptic language on it, and the words make me question my sanity.

An angel stepped down from her pedestal, joining mortals.
Not expecting the secrets that she might uncover.
The monster chuckled at her shock, anticipating the bigger blow.
What happens when an angel comes into a monster's dungeon?

"Oh my God," I whisper, and stand up while Bella's concerned gaze is still on me. "Everything is fine. I just need to go to the bathroom," I say, and she nods, although it doesn't seem she believes me.

I quickly run toward the secluded area and step inside, closing the door firmly behind me, and place my hand on my chest that rises and falls rapidly.

These notes are not funny anymore. Someone is doing it on purpose, trying to keep me off balance, but who? Should I tell someone about them? What kind of person can the man possibly be if he refers to himself as a monster?

I turn on the water, wet a towel, and press it to my neck in hopes of the cold calming me down. My reflection in the mirror resembles a deer caught in headlights. My eyes are exceptionally big in a pale face, especially with my hair pulled back in a high bun. "Just someone's prank," I chant, turning off the tap and taking a deep breath. "A prank that most likely is supposed to scare me."

But how can a prank follow my every move? I need to speak to someone about it.

I might endanger other people close to me if it's some kind of stalker or something. Instantly, my mind goes to Frankie, as she has a brother who is an FBI agent. While this case doesn't require the feds, he might know someone who could help.

Police can't really pursue a case without any real evidence, and since the words are printed, they won't even have a reason to believe it's addressed specifically to me.

With those thoughts swirling in my head and calming me down, I emerge from the bathroom and dart to my table. I almost bump into a waiter, who sways a little with his tray full of drinks. "Sorry!" I mumble, but he just flashes me a grin.

"No worries, doll." My brows lift at this rather familiar word, but he just winks, so it's hard not to join his amusement. He picks up a red drink and gives it to me. "Have this. Should add some color to your cheeks. It's a crime to look this bad in a place this hot."

A laugh slips past my lips, because it's just impossible not to like this guy. "I will graciously accept it." My hands wrap around the cold substance, and I suck on the straw and moan loudly. "This is heaven."

"I told you so, doll. Going to go now though before anyone else gets thirsty." Then he leans closer, and whispers into my ear, "Stay till the end. The guy will give you quite a show on the stage." With one last wink, he goes to another table while I laugh again.

Some people are awesome by simply being themselves. I can already see myself coming here again in the near future.

The music ends, and I see Mia finishing with one leg in front while she blows a kiss to the audience, leaning forward slightly in lacy panties and heels with her nipples covered with something. She waves and then leaves the stage while the audience whistles and shouts her praises.

Bella is clapping the loudest it seems, giving her a standing ovation. "The girl is on fucking fire! Who knew she could move like that?"

"Certainly not us." I fist the offensive paper and drop it in the ashtray, sipping more of my drink. This stuff should relax me for sure.

Sitting more comfortably on the chair, I place the napkin in my lap and press on the button to finally order food; otherwise, the drink will go to my head.

"I mean, she should leave ballet really, considering how they treat her, and just make money here. I imagine they pay well." She shifts her attention to me, sliding closer. "Which reminds me. What do you think of Paris?" She has the most random thoughts ever.

"Em... it's a beautiful city?" And loud.

She rolls her eyes. "I meant what do you think of going there with me?" She digs in her small purse and then slides open her phone. She searches for something and then practically shoves it in my face. "I bought you a plane ticket with an open date."

"Bella, this is—"

She wiggles her index finger at me. "Don't answer now, but think about it. Nothing keeps you here anymore, and in Paris, you'll have lots of possibilities. They invited you the first time, after all. It will be a good start for you, away from everything else."

"The situation with Max doesn't change anything else though." But as betraying as it sounds deep down, I think about what my life would be like if I listen to her and follow my heart, without thinking about everyone else.

Without feeling like I owe it to my mom to stay her little princess so nothing bad will happen. To remember that girl who could sing her heart out with Jason in his car while Queen blasted from the radio.

To be a girl who can make love under the stars because she feels like it, unafraid of consequences.

Simply to be a girl who doesn't live under the weight of an ax that always hangs above her head.

"Maybe it's a push to start anew?" She pats my palm, and I open my mouth to reply when a shadow looms over us. The hair on the back of my neck prickles, sending now familiar awareness through my entire system, and my breath hitches.

My eyes close as a deep voice speaks softly yet firmly, almost caressing my skin. "Valencia."

Lachlan.

*L*achlan

If a woman's beauty could have been described in symphony numbers, then Valencia would be *Symphony No. 9* by Beethoven. As beautiful and as rapidly changing pace.

A white dress hugs her slender body. The open back provides a perfect view of her flawless skin, inviting me to leave an imprint on it, imaging how it will dip under my touch. Her chocolate hair shouldn't be enclosed in the stupid bun, but cascading down her back freely so I can tug on it whenever the fuck I want. Her locks are shiny and silky, and look gorgeous around my fist.

I never wanted her for myself, but with each passing day, the obsession to make her mine and own that angelic body of hers drives me insane, to the point of threatening to lose my control. I should worry more about it than I do, but at the end of the day, she is mine either way.

Tortured or fucked.

And it's about time she knew it too. The information needs to seal forever into her brain so she won't display what belongs to me for every willing man to see.

If a hunter trains his prey well, she seeks him without realizing it. She is already following the path I have so carefully placed to trap her.

But I want more.

She is mine.

It's time to train her to remember that too.

CHAPTER NINE

New York, New York
January 2018

Valencia

It should be a crime for a man to be this handsome.

Lachlan places his palms on the table, his mouth lifting in a half smile as he greets us. "Welcome to the club, ladies." Then he focuses his drilling blue eyes on me. "Glad you came."

Bella's cheeks flush and I can't really blame her. He is the epitome of masculine sexuality, especially with his sleeves rolled up, showcasing every rigid muscle. And the five o'clock shadow only adds to his charm.

"You own this place?" Bella asks excitedly, and Lachlan chuckles while I huff in annoyance, because I can already predict the answer is yes.

"Afraid so."

"It seems you acquire every place that has me in it." I'm mortified by my words, which earns me another grin, and that makes me want to kiss him and punch him at the same time.

"I'm yet to buy Olga's studio and your condo. But the time will come for that too." He lingers his eyes on my lips before adding, "Among other things."

Bella blinks in surprise, but I only shoot her daggers. No need to encourage his behavior!

Out of nowhere, Mia, wearing a silky dress over her voluptuous figure, joins our table. "You guys are here. I can explain," she says, but then her face beams as she wraps her hands around Lachlan's middle while he pats her on the back. "I'm so happy to see you." He gives her a peck on her hair, and I squeeze the napkin on my lap.

She wrapped herself around him like an octopus around its prey!

An awkward silence follows, because I can't stop staring at her freaking hand. A red haze makes it almost impossible to breathe, because I want to snatch her hand from him.

I'm officially losing my mind. First, Bella, and now Mia. Why am I acting this way? He is not mine, and I should stay away from him.

Not experience jealously when he shows an interest in another woman, or rather when one shows an interest in him.

"Well, no worries. It is sexy." Bella kicks me under the table, nudging me for a reassuring reaction, and I muster a smile on my face, hoping it looks convincing enough.

"You were amazing on stage. And don't worry, we won't tell."

Her grin widens as she finally lets Lachlan go and claps her hands. "You are the best, Valencia. I can't wait for you to perform the swan. You'll rock!"

"She will," Lachlan agrees with her, his gaze still on me, and our stares clash as electricity rushes through me, reminding me how he gave me the same look right before he kissed me in the studio.

I wish he would stop it; he studies me as if I'm his to do with whatever he pleases.

But more importantly, I wish my body could stop reacting to it and thinking it's hot.

I left him in Italy for a reason; nothing can ever work between him and me, because the man is dangerous to my sanity.

Or sainthood, depending on how one might look at it.

"This club is awesome, by the way," Bella says and raises her glass to him. "And if the rest of the show is like that, no wonder everyone wants an invite to this."

He nods. "I have only the best."

She chuckles into her wine, winking. "Your modesty is truly astonishing." Before my move can even register, I kick her under the table with my shoe and she almost spills her drink on the table, giving me a confused look.

Oh my God.

Then she understands it, smirks, and wiggles her brows. "Feeling a little possessive, are we?" she whispers from the corner of her mouth, and then speaks louder. "So, since this is your establishment and all that jazz, does this mean everything we order is on the house?"

"Bella!" I snap, but she hears none of it. She waits for Lachlan to react on her assumption and it follows quickly.

"Of course. Be my guests." He calls for someone with a whistle and at once the waitress from earlier shows up at our table as he points at us. "Make sure they get everything they want. No bill." Then he addresses Bella, ignoring me. "Have a nice evening, Bella. I hope you will get everything you want from this place." With these last words, he moves to the crowd, disappearing down a hall that leads to I don't know where.

Mia gives Bella and me a peck on the cheek before waving us off. "Need to get home quickly, and then study a bit more for my exams." Right, I forgot she is working on her master's degree alongside her dancing.

"Be careful, it's dark."

She rolls her eyes at my warning. "Valencia, always the caring mother," she says, and bounces back behind the stage while Bella exclaims, "So?"

I munch on the straw and ask around it, "So?"

"Are you going to explain to me what the hell is going on between you and Kaden, or why I got a bruise on my leg for nothing?"

My cheeks flush as I quickly apologize. "I'm sorry. I didn't mean to. I—"

"Whatever." She huffs in exasperation. "No biggie. But I do want to know all the dirt on this guy. So spill, my friend."

Maybe I should talk to someone about this, to get a better perspective on the matter. Plus, she will understand and not judge me, right?

I open my mouth to share my secret with her, when her phone beeps and her brows furrow. Whatever she reads in her message must have really shocked her, as she quickly gets up while dialing her phone. She picks up her purse and runs to the door, and I only have time to blink before snapping out of my stupor and darting after her.

"How is this possible?" she shouts into her phone, and then nudges a bouncer. "Could you please catch a cab for me?" He nods and goes outside while she paces back and forth with her phone, worry written all over her, and my stomach flips.

She rarely worries about anything; what could have happened? "Okay, I will be back in Paris on the first flight. I love you too. Bye." She hangs up and I shake my head, expecting an explanation. She exhales heavily. "That's Pierre." Her latest boyfriend, but they seem pretty serious according to her. "His grandmother is ill, and she is amazing. They give her just a few days to live, and he just can't handle it—" She stops midsentence, and I hug her close while she hiccups into my shoulder. "She is really a nice lady."

"I'm sorry, sweetie." She tightens her hold on me, but then the bouncer calls, "Your cab is here."

She leans back and graces me with a teary smile. "As always, our get-together didn't end as planned. I'm going to the hotel to pack and then jump on the next flight."

"Let me grab my purse and I'll go with you." She'll need all the support right now.

She shakes her head, blowing me a kiss. "Nope. I need to be on my own right now." I nod, because I understand it too. It's devastating when a loved one suffers and you can't do anything about it. "Think about my words regarding Paris." With a final wave, she hops in the cab while I'm left standing as the breeze hits me in the face.

A low growl sends shivers down my spine. "Get inside." Lachlan turns me by my shoulders in the direction of the club and practically drags me back inside.

The warmth of the place quickly brings back my common sense. "Let go of me, you brute." I pull at my hand and stumble back when he doesn't retain his hold on me. "I'm leaving anyway. Thanks for the invitation. No need to send it again." I spin around and go to my table, quickly grabbing my purse and jacket while gritting my teeth at the disappointment filling me. He doesn't follow me or even try to change my mind.

Does he care or not? His behavior is giving me mental whiplash.

The waiter from earlier shows up and points at my mouth. "What's with the face? My magic drink was supposed to lift up your mood, not make it even worse."

I give him a soft smile. "Something came up."

"Well, you know—" He shuts up, saluting me. "Have a nice night, umm, lady."

Lady? What happened to doll?

I don't have to wonder for long as I notice Lachlan scowling at us and roll my eyes. If he can't have it, apparently no one else can either.

I walk past him, but he grabs my arm, stilling my movement as our eyes clash. Mine annoyed and his stormy, reminding me of the sea. "I'm fucking tired of this cat and mouse game, Valencia."

"Don't play it then." All of a sudden all this is my fault? "You show up in my world, doing business with my stepfather. Our fling was supposed to stay in Italy. Yet you come here and confuse me, and...." I can't believe I spill all this right in the middle of the freaking burlesque club!

He brings me closer, his breath fanning my cheeks, and I raise my chin, not wanting to back down under his harsh stare. "I never said I wanted a relationship. But I do want what you denied me." My brows furrow as I wait for him to elaborate and he does, and his words send heat through my entire system, reminding me of the man hiding beneath the cold exterior. "One last night. We promised ourselves seven days and nights. And you only gave me six."

"This is—" He wants me because of some unfulfilled promise? Is he insane? "I won't sleep with you just to be done with our seven days."

He trails his knuckles over my cheek and presses us flush against each other, so it's impossible to miss the heat coming from him. "Live a little for yourself, perfect angel."

Licking my lips, I reply, "What's that supposed to mean?"

"Tell me you don't want my cock sinking deep into your tight pussy, to feed the need that drives you insane." I gasp at his crude words, but he only leans closer, splaying his open palm on my back as he continues to murmur into my ear. "Tell me that you didn't let that limp dick touch you. Because how could you after what you experienced with me?" He bites on my earlobe, right before saying, "Tell me that no self-satisfaction brought you relief."

I stay silent, my eyes closed as I drink in his smell and words that hold so much truth I can't deny them. "This is wrong."

"I'm not looking for anything right. Just one night, Valencia. Let's feed each other's need so this insanity can finally let us be and move on." He pulls tightly on my bun as I breathe heavily and can only see his handsome face in front of me.

He is right, so right. The past six months have been nothing but torture, and maybe to get over Lachlan I need to sleep with him one last time.

Sort of like a goodbye to the rebellious person I tried to be, and failed.

Close the loose end before moving on to something different.

And even though it's probably the stupidest decision I've ever made, I speak the words nevertheless. "One last night."

God help us both.

*L*achlan

My little prey will always find a way to her hunter. A bond that's unbreakable. Sort of like the victim and victimizer, a never-ending circle unless the victim rebels and shows strength.

That's what I should focus on instead of the insane need to erase every touch of another man from her skin and make her pay for every day she belonged to him and not me.

Wanting her shouldn't be a driving force in any of this. Indifference and cold calculation, that's what any hunt should be about.

Anyhow, this doesn't follow any plan, but it'll make the game even more interesting.

Valencia will be introduced to her captor's castle sooner rather than later.

Valencia

Lachlan presses the remote, and the iron gates slide open as two security guards nod in our direction. He roars the engine to life, driving inside, and I hold back a surprised gasp.

The mansion is freaking huge and reminds me of a castle in the cartoons I watched when I was a kid. Just how many properties does he have?

The huge horizontal brick building spreads across the land. The magnificent architecture includes several statues in arches that create a mysterious allure, but also a little fear, and it seems there is no escape from it.

It has two levels with a lot of windows with balconies attached, and most of them are made from stained glass, reminding me of cathedrals.

It appears to be surrounded by a beautiful garden by the short snippets I manage to see before Lachlan stops the car by the massive wooden door with three sets of stairs leading to it, all made out of marble.

Freaking marble! I knew he was rich, but this is just too much. Why would someone need this kind of house? The only thing missing is the storm and lightning, and this place would be straight out of a horror movie.

"All you need now is a butler waiting for us." I speak for the first time since the club, hoping to break the tension that filled the car the closer and closer we got to here.

He laughs and my brows furrow, but he doesn't elaborate.

He doesn't have a butler, right?

Lachlan turns the car off, gets out, and walks around it to open the door for me as he points at the house. "Welcome to my mansion, Valencia." The way he says it casually, yet so possessively, fills me with dread and wonder at the same time, and my heart starts beating rapidly as I take a deep breath, confused with myself.

Stepping inside this castle-like place creates weird sensations all over me, as even the walls beam with something, something so unfamiliar yet scary, as if holding secrets that should never be uncovered. "Did you change your mind?" he asks, drilling his blue orbs into me, and I shake my head.

If anything, I will give myself tonight and think about consequences tomorrow, even maybe curse myself for it. But tonight, nothing exists but this brief moment in time where everything besides him and me goes still.

When we enter his house, my heels echo off the walls and my eyes widen as I cover my mouth with my hand.

Everything is lit up with candles spread all over the hall, on the floor and banisters, and even dangling from the ceiling. Like we are living in the eighteenth century and Thomas Edison hadn't invented the electric bulb yet.

The door shuts behind me and then I feel his heat against me, as he murmurs, "Like it?" And he pulls me against him.

A raspy breath escapes me. "This is surreal. Why would—"

He spins me around and crushes his mouth to mine, changing my question into a moan as he slides his hands down my ass and hikes me up, leaving me no choice but to wrap my legs around him while my arms circle his neck.

His kiss is demanding, passionate yet punishing in a way that brings me pain along with pleasure. As if he wants me to forever remember the imprint of it but at the same time hates that he is doing it.

Hates that he needs me.

His tongue glides against mine as he takes me upstairs, fisting my hair and not allowing me to move my mouth from him, even an inch. He doesn't even give me a chance to study the rest of the house.

This goes on as his feet thump on the floor, and when he enters the room, my head spins as he puts me on the floor and steadies me as I sway a little.

I look around the room that doesn't have much except a table and wide bed with a lacy black canopy that leaves the ceiling above it open. "Is that a mirror up there?" Why would anyone need this? Does he lie with his women and...?

Instead of answering me, he throws his jacket on the floor, unbut-

tons his vest, and tosses it so it lands in the same place. Then he
snatches his tie from his neck and steps close to me while I instinc-
tively take a step back, but he grabs me and spins me around, wrapping
the material around my eyes, and instantly everything is blacked out.

I try to wiggle free of his hold, but he manages to squeeze my
wrists behind my back, and even though he murmurs softly, his voice
holds danger. "Did you really think that you returning to him after *me*
would go unpunished?" He splays his palm over my stomach, sliding it
lower until he molds my core through the material, cupping it with his
whole hand, and I gasp, my thighs clamping around it. But he chuckles, removing his touch. "No fucking way." I hear the creak and swish
of leather through belt loops before he pushes my hands in front of me
and binds them together, so I can't use them.

His fingers skim over my nape as he pulls me back, my heart
beating wildly in my chest, and then shifts my face to the side, craning
my neck so our mouths can meet in a hard, long kiss that sends electricity to the tip of my toes. His mouth relentlessly takes mine, tongue
playing inside as if warning me of what will come next. My lungs burn
from his power to steal my breath, and liquid heat spreads through me,
reminding me of a volcano about to erupt.

He gives me one long swipe and then tugs on my lower lip, before
moving his attention to my neck as he runs his nose over it, tickling
my skin. Then he bites it, and I cry out, not expecting the pain that
follows.

"All those evenings and gatherings with you on his arm, smiling
brightly for everyone to see. Ignoring me," he rasps harshly, digging his
fingers into my hip while sucking hard on my neck again, and I wince,
trying to evade it, but it's useless. "I couldn't even talk to you without
you running in a different direction." He pushes me forward, his
fingers tugging on my zipper, sliding it down, and then unties the
strings at the back of my neck, releasing the halter-top. Immediately,
cold hits me, pebbling my skin as the dress slowly drops, leaving me
standing in my nude lacy panties. "You both live only because he never
touched you. Your body is only mine, isn't it, Valencia?" My brows
furrow at his growl, alarms blaring in the back of my hazy mind, but I
push them away, promising myself to dwell on it later.

He moves to the other shoulder, repeating his action, but this time
he pulls on my panties, tearing a moan from me as they rub against my
clit, bringing discomfort and short relief, which disappears quickly and
leaves an ache in its wake. "Tell me."

Sexual, it's only sexual and means nothing. "Yes." For tonight
at least.

Cold instantly slips into my bones when he steps away from me,
but then he is guiding me somewhere, only to stop abruptly as his
shoes bump the back of mine. "Look at you, all flushed and ready for
the taking. I could fuck you against the wall now and you'd scratch my
back, welcoming every thrust. Right, Valencia?" he prompts, bending
me forward, and then I feel my breasts press against the bed, the
movement arching my ass up to him, and his hand palms it, molding
and then squeezing, earning himself a moan. "But that's not how I will
give it to you tonight. You deserve to be denied a little for all the
fucking hell you put me through." And that's when he spanks me, his
palm bouncing off my ass cheek, and I still.

He freaking did what! "You—"

He doesn't let me finish, smacking me again, and this time it sends
a jolt of awareness through me, somehow intensifying the ache
brewing inside my heat, which only makes me greedier for him.

He bites my ass and then sucks on the skin, probably leaving
marks, but I don't care.

I don't care about anything as long as he continues to do what
he does.

His lips skim up my spine to my back, leaving butterfly kisses along
with light nips that awaken every nerve in my body and makes it even
more attuned to his actions, anticipating them with each breath.
"Lachlan—" Pleading coats my voice. I want him to end this and just
give me what we both need.

We can have foreplay later, once this fire inside me is sated, once I
can think about anything but the ringing in my ears, which illuminates
everything that leaves me greedy for more of him.

For all that is him.

"Your beautiful pale skin is magnificent with my handprint on it."
He slaps me again with one hand while the other moves my panties to

the side and two fingers enter me. He twists them as I bite my lip, holding back a groan that threatens to erupt from the back of my throat. "All wet and ready for the taking. Too bad no one is providing it for now." With each slap, his fingers continue to press inside me, and I rock on them, finding the friction that slowly soars me higher and higher. But then he takes it all away, flipping me on my back so that my entire body lies flat.

I hear him shuffle with his clothes, and then his heat is back. He probably places his hands on either side of my head, as the bed moves and his hard-on rocks against my core, making me arch my back, but he clacks with his tongue. "Not yet, Valencia."

He is truly driving me insane tonight.

His light beard rubs against my collarbone as he travels lower and nibbles on my nipples before sucking one at the same time as his fingers roll the other, reminding me how sensitive they are. He grazes it with his teeth, but soothes it with licks, highlighting my every reaction.

He shifts to the other one, providing the same attention to it, and I long to touch him, skim my fingers over his rigid muscles that flex with every movement, but all I can do is lace my fingers together and get drunk on all the sensations he provokes. "Lachlan, please." My body burns for him, demands his cock to soothe all the aches that play through me.

No one but Lachlan will do, but he is not listening to me. He only chuckles, skimming his hands over my waist as he trails lower, kissing the underside of my breasts and most likely leaving a mark if the sting is anything to go by.

Then he shifts lower, rubbing his face against my tight stomach that dips under his touch, and then I feel him nudge my thighs wider, practically flattening them on the bed. I groan in protest, but he just orders, "Come on, darling. We both know how flexible you are."

Pushing my tied hands against the headboard, I pant heavily, antici-pating his next move. As his hands hold my hips wide open, his breath fanning my heat, I try to close my legs around him to urge him on so he finally can provide me what I so desperately seek... but I can't.

He runs his lips over the inside of my thigh as he inhales my scent, repeating the action with my other side, but this time he pulls on the skin, nipping on it lightly. I'm about to protest and order him to continue when his mouth lands on my pussy, swiping his tongue from bottom to the clit, and my ass shoots from the bed. My senses go into chaos, feeding on the fire rushing in my veins.

He holds me still, thrusting his tongue in and out, as his thumb presses against my clit, adding to my need.

Loud moans and groans echo in the room followed by Lachlan taking his fill, not stopping even when he allows me to circle my legs around him, my heels digging into his back. "No one tastes like you, Valencia." He laps me again, but this time pushing his finger inside, grazing my walls.

"I don't want foreplay anymore." This pleasure that borders on madness only frustrates me, because I can't touch him, pull him to me, or make any demands. He rules in this bed, but can't he give me what I want just once? "Please take me."

"Why should I?" he asks right before nipping my clit. I hiss, biting my lip so a loud moan won't escape.

"Please." I don't have any specific reason, so I might as well beg. All I want is for him to finally give me what I crave.

Just when I think he will comply with my request, he shakes his head against my stomach then continues to slide his tongue inside, playing with my core as if it is his personal instrument that he controls.

Tongue, mouth, teeth, on repeat. Just when I'm about to come, he slows down, then builds the pressure again.

When I'm about to lose my freaking mind, he rises up, unbinds my wrists, and I hear the foil packet being ripped open. Then I feel him nudge against me, sliding his cock up and down over my heat, spreading the wetness all over me. He murmurs, "Fucking finally," and enters me, stretching me wide, not even giving me time to adjust to his cock as he drags it out and slides back in, matching my gasp with his as we both groan.

He is right.

Fucking finally.

His mouth finds my breasts and laves them as he continues to rock inside me. My ragged breath fills the space between us as I put my hands around his neck, pulling him closer, scratching the back of his head with my nails, needing him to be as on edge as I am.

Instantly, he removes the tie from my eyes and I blink, trying to get my vision back, but then he is all there is, gazing at me with desire and possessiveness that clearly knows no measure. "Who is fucking you, Valencia?" he asks, sucking on my lower lip while thrusting hard, moving us on the bed.

"You." I try to hike my leg over his hip, but instead he lifts it up and places it on his shoulder.

"And my name is?"

Barely thinking or breathing from the new angle that allows him to dwell even deeper, I rasp, "Lachlan." Who else? No one in my life has made me experience what he does, complete devotion and passion that has nothing to do with love.

Sweat coats our skin. As he glides up and down, I arch my back, feeling the sensation. That's when he speeds up, giving me longer strokes, earning himself a hiss and moan at the same time, and then he retreats, leaving me empty. I whimper, hating it, but then he comes right back in, and I'm back there with him.

I cry out and sink back on the bed. He continues to move, while he drills me with his stare and digs into the pillow, my core clamping tightly around him.

A few more thrusts and he roars above me, biting on my neck and sending prickles through me.

We both breathe heavily, wrapped in each other, and I don't allow my common sense to come back to me.

It has no place in this tight cocoon we've just created.

He finds my mouth and we lock in a kiss that means more to me than it has ever been.

*L*achlan

I turn on the water then step inside the shower stall.

Immediately, cool water cascades down on me, but I don't so much as flinch, letting the cold slip into every pore while hoping to squash the raging fire spreading inside me.

I burn for Valencia.

Her moans and sighs still echo in my ears; my hands still long to touch her perfect, soft skin as she forgets herself in pleasure that only I can provide for her.

Being good in bed is not new to me. I've mastered the craft through the years, as it's a perfect weapon to use whenever I feel like it. And sure as fuck, it helps to know how to get a woman off with minimal preparation, to find the blackness that illuminates everything and everyone.

But feeling anything in that bed aside from forgetfulness from the nightmares? Yeah, that's new, and I hate it.

For the first time, I didn't think about anything but the woman under me and how she felt. For the first time, my whole focus belonged to her and only her.

For the first time, sex didn't give me peacefulness or ironclad control. Instead, it allowed chaos to infiltrate me and demanded more.

Punching the tiled wall, I fist my hands to the point of almost breaking my own fingers as I will all the memories to come back so I can remember the mission, the reason she is here.

Valencia is nothing but a means to an end.

I will tamp down any emotion she inspires that has nothing to do with me punishing her. I don't understand them, because there is nothing spectacular about her. She represents everything I despise in women, yet whenever I see her, my mind chants one thing only.

Mine.

Yet the idea of hurting her, of surrounding her in my darkness, only fuels these desires longing to wipe her clean of the color white and forever bury her in the color black.

It doesn't matter though.

Her end will still be the same.

Sinners and saints don't mix.

Oh, we will see about that.

CHAPTER TEN

New York, New York
January 2018

$\mathcal{V}$ **alencia**
  Shifting slightly to the side, I dig my nose into the pillow while inhaling heavily, almost moaning in pleasure from the softness of the material that smells like the most expensive whiskey combined with cigarettes.

The sheet pulled over me barely grazes my skin and cools me, which provides much-needed relief in the heated room. My body aches in all the right places, making it so I can barely move. My brows furrow as I search my mind for what happened.

Wasn't I out last night with Bella? And why does this mattress feel like I'm floating on a cloud and it can swallow me whole? I'll willingly let it as it gives the softest of touches.

I roll onto my back, throwing off the sheet and huffing loudly, and my eyes open only to widen as I gaze at myself in the mirror plastered to the ceiling that shows me in all my naked glory.

And then last night comes rushing back at me, and with a gasp I sit up, looking around.

I'm at Lachlan's house!

He is nowhere in sight. I hastily get up, picking up all the clothes scattered on the floor, and ignore the pain between my thighs and the marks of ownership he left all over my body. I rush to the bathroom, locking the door, although it's really a laughable attempt.

What the hell are you doing?

I'm acting as if this guy kidnapped me and I'm finally awake to defend myself. Clearly he didn't even bother to wake me up, so he doesn't care what I do.

I catch my reflection in the mirror and wince at my hair all over the place along with smeared mascara and red lipstick, and then I see hickeys and bruises marring my skin after our night of sex.

If sin had a name, I'd probably be called it in this moment.

Dropping onto the toilet seat, I palm my head, groaning while images from last night dance in my mind like a vivid erotic movie that has no end.

His skillful hands on me, his kisses, his everything.

I've never in my life thought I'd allow anyone to tie me up, but it's ended up being the best freaking experience of my life.

My pleasure, my moans, they probably heard me in other rooms.

With this thought comes an overwhelming fear. I gulp, closing my eyes and trying my best to block away the woman who acted on her desire, who was uninhibited in her needs and was so selfish.

Who slept with the wrong man.

Before Lachlan, I never allowed anyone to touch me since Jason, even Max. Whenever he brought up the subject, he received only no. Plus he only asked—barely in passing—not trying any strong persuasions. Granted, I never had the desire to explore anything physical with him either, but that's beside the point.

Yet Lachlan broke my defenses in Italy and last night. I can't resist this man no matter how much I fight it.

How could I have done it? He is Victor's business partner; he is Max's partner for God's sake. They don't like him.

Everyone is still upset with me over the engagement, and I go out and do this?

How will I look anyone in the eyes? Face the consequences of my decision?

None of the decisions I make on a whim have good endings.

Getting up, I wash my face, hoping the soap will remove at least some traces of last night, and then I put on my dress, hating the heels that press on my soles, reminding me that I've overdone it with dancing and walking.

But he so feverishly loved them last night, paying attention to every detail.

I've made a mistake, but no one knows about it anyway. Lachlan isn't the type of man who will go around and tell everyone about his sex life. His absence this morning also indicates he doesn't care what I do one way or the other, so he sated his interest in me and moved on.

As should I.

I emerge from the bathroom and notice the balcony door open with the black, lacy curtains blowing in different directions as if someone is out there. I tiptoe to it but find it empty. My eyes catch a table with a chessboard, and it looks like two people are playing since the black and white pawns have been moved.

Although white seems to be losing, because the black board player has white's knights. Will be a tough job for white to win.

Who does he play with here?

Shrugging, I lean on the banister and my eyes widen.

The garden is magnificent, but it's a freaking labyrinth. How will I ever escape it? And who has a garden that looks like a dystopian quest that no one can probably win.

Finally, I find the gate where several security guards stand, but there is no other soul in sight. How will I get a cab?

God, if only I had more experience with one-night stands, I wouldn't have been in this situation!

Going back into the room, I find my purse on the table and dig through it for my phone, which still has some charge, and press the Uber button. It shows no car in the vicinity, but I can call it once I'm outside this scary castle.

I still remember the way from last night, so it shouldn't be a problem. Before I go on my grand escape, I look, for the last time, at the bed that is still rumpled from our night of lovemaking, and part of me hates myself in this moment.

Because all I long to do is get under the covers and bury myself in the smells of us. For the first time in years, I've found peace and complete surrender in Lachlan's arms.

Life though is not about pleasure and happiness, as I've found out.

It's about pain, punishment, and sorrow that never leaves, no matter how much you try to wash it away.

"The fairytale has ended," I whisper and close the door, forever imprinting passionate Lachlan Scott in my memory.

I'm sure we'll never meet in such circumstances again.

*L*achlan

"She left," Levi says next to me, while extending his hand to where the morning newspaper lies.

Shrugging, I run my fingers through my hair and send a message to Shon with the latest details. "Good."

I pick up the paper and drop onto the couch, while the coffee steams on the table. I have a perfect view from the terrace of the snow-covered garden.

Chance jumps from place to place out there, huffing and then lying on his back with his tongue hanging out. I don't really have much love for animals—bad introduction to them in childhood—but Chance somehow managed to find his way into my mansion and didn't want to leave.

The black Newfoundland decided this was his home, and in time, I got used to him.

In a way.

It's always fascinated me how little dogs need to find happiness. A little attention and freedom here and there, and the human has the most loyal creature on earth.

But people? They are consumed by greed and desire for power that kills their humanity with each passing day, and resisting those desires when they are right in front of you is almost impossible.

Maybe that's why there is so much evil out there.

"Lachlan, she knows the place now." Panic and confusion coat his voice, and I finally raise my eyes to him only to find him shifting from side to side, several wrinkles marring his face, especially the deep line between his eyebrows as he frowns at me. "Don't you think—" The old man just doesn't know when to give up. With his constant nagging, the only reason his ass is not out of here yet is because I grew up with him and he's stayed by my side through a lot of shit. It also helps I don't want to kill him, which in my case speaks about the deepest affection for a human life there can be.

The click of my fingers and a dismissive wave cuts him off. He purses his lips but stays silent. He shakes his head, and then with one last accusing glance my way, he exits the common room and probably goes to the kitchen where he can curse me all the fucking way.

Levi doesn't approve of my plan, not that he knows much about it anyway. But come to think about it, he never approves of any violence, but it doesn't stop him from working as my butler.

Leaning forward, I touch my iPad and immediately cameras scattered all over my place come into view in small windows, trailing her every move. She is outside now, walking to the gate while nervously looking around and taking deep breaths, most likely for the courage to face the guards who stand by the gate in their suits like watchful dogs.

A thrill runs through me at the idea of her fear that I can almost taste, but with that also comes anger that, combined with last night's lust, makes me one dangerous man to face.

My fingers prickle to play with her skin with my most favorite devices, watching the color and bruises appear on it, and how it will affect her head. But the idea of anyone else so much as scaring her?

No, that's not a possibility, because willingly or not, Valencia is mine.

And until she dies, she doesn't have to be afraid of anyone but me.

Pressing the number on my phone, I wait for the person to pick up, and then bark, "If anyone so much as touches her, they are dead. Find a cab for her." More like tell one of the men to drive up in a cabbie's car.

No one has access to my property, but I know she needs to escape after sex.

I know my prey very well; after all, she has been my work in progress for years and the most anticipated prize.

Raging desire mixes with euphoria at finally being close to my goal, of finally destroying her wings and cutting them off her so she can painfully fall and fall until she reaches the underground.

Where she will fight and fight a losing battle and then finally adapt to its rules, burning her soul in the process.

But on this path, she will find the freedom she so desperately needs, even if she doesn't think so.

And what a magnificent sight this will be.

Run, Valencia, run.

I'll give her one more peaceful day in the fairytale she lives in, where she hides behind her façade of a perfect life and believes that this world is about faith, love, and fucking unicorns.

But when tomorrow comes, the demons will come to play, to finally introduce and welcome her to the dark side.

Valencia

The pastor finishes his Sunday service, and everyone gets up quickly, increasing the noise that snaps me out of a trance. I follow, hating the pink, floral dress that almost reaches my ankles and scratches against my skin.

As a ballerina, I prefer to have my legs free for movement, but my parents taught me to always show respect and wear appropriate attire, as they called it. And although I'm no longer obligated to come here, I do it for me.

Because I made a promise a long time ago, and in my faith, I find peace. And I desperately need it after last night.

A night I try my best to forget, because it can destroy everything I've built through all the years.

"Valencia!" Pastor Aidan calls, and I plaster a smile on my face, walking toward him even though I have no desire for small talk. He is a great guy, but after my turmoil, I'm not sure I'm ready to meet people who always insist that I should be perfect.

"Hi, Pastor. How are you?" I give him a basket with freshly baked muffins, and he takes it eagerly, winking at me.

"I'm good, child. Thank you as always. The kids love them, you know." I nod, one of the reasons I still do it. Those little munchkins have no one, so baking goodies for them brings me joy. "Want to go with me to give it to them?" he offers, placing the Bible under his armpit, but I shake my head.

"I need to go home. I have an important rehearsal later on." I finish lamely, not wanting to lie but at the same time not wanting to tell the truth either.

Pastor looks at me for a second, and then asks, "Is everything okay?"

"Perfect."

He gives me another long stare but then pats me on the back. "Okay, then. Won't bother you with it. I'm sure you'll be great at the show." He picks up his glasses from the table and is about to move in the direction of the Sunday school where the kids from foster homes come every week to play, when my question stops him.

It spills out of me before I can control it. "Pastor Aidan, if we don't follow the rules, does that make us sinners?" Clearing my throat, I add, "Does it make... less... less.... Do we get punished?" I finally let out the words that have been in my head since that fateful day with Jason. I've always played in my mind my sins, as they call them, and that's the only time in my life when I did something outside the norm.

And my dad died.

Was that divine intervention telling me what to do?

"For not following the rules?" he supplies, and I nod, crossing my arms tightly, lost under his surprised gaze.

"Yes."

He motions to the bench in the front, right under the altar, and I follow, sitting next to him as he places the basket between us.

"I'm sorry if that's a weird thing to ask." I've been coming to this church almost my whole life; he had been one of my father's close friends, so he probably wonders why I even question our faith and religion.

I should know better, but lately all those voices from the past don't make much sense to me.

"When I was your age, I toured through Europe. Sex, drugs, and rock and roll. The whole package." My jaw almost drops from this information, because imagining Pastor doing any of those things is... well, unimaginable; that's what it is.

He smirks at my shocked expression. "Yeah, I thought life had nothing but endless possibilities, and no one should ever place any holds on me. I even dropped out of college, because I considered it too restricted." I don't say anything, just blink with each new piece of information. "It was a great experience. I've met many people, visited so many places. In about the third year, I understood I couldn't drift forever and came back home." A beat, and then, "I visited the church, and I just... found peace. I wanted to make a difference, and I felt like this job allowed me to."

Shifting my hands on my lap, I finally speak past the shock. "Did something happen that made you come back home and choose your faith?"

His brows furrow, and then he chuckles, amusement crossing his face. "No divine intervention or life threatening injuries that made me turn to God, no. Religion doesn't punish, Valencia."

"My dad said it did," I whisper, and he exhales heavily, running his finger through his hair while gazing ahead.

"Your dad was obsessed with right and wrong." My heart stills with this information, because that's the same thing I thought back when I was sixteen. "We joined the church together, but he thought everyone should follow a specific path, a path he thought was right. I didn't agree with him, which ultimately led to our dispute."

"But we always came here."

"Your mom allowed you to come here even after the divorce, but we lost touch with your dad long before he died. He was a fanatic, Valencia. If people didn't live the way he thought was right, then they lived wrongly to him. He wanted a perfect society, a society where he was always right."

I swallow past the bile in my throat at all this, and flashes of the past come crashing back at me. How Dad never listened to anyone if they weren't following religion. How he forbade me to hang out with kids if their parents didn't attend church. How he always claimed that love is pure and right only if it follows the rules.

I always thought he just followed the religion blindly, but what if he lived on the extremes of it, preaching something ugly instead of truthful?

"Faith is about love. It doesn't really matter what you believe in or what you call it. If you have that in your heart and look at everything and everyone through that prism, then life is happiness. We came into this world to learn how to be happy. And sometimes for that, we need to experience pain, heartache. There are lessons to be learned for sure. But we didn't come here to get punished. Or to follow paths that bring us only pain and sorrow." He touches my chin and lifts it so our eyes meet, his silver ones holding nothing but kindness as always. "Valencia, you didn't come here to follow the rules your dad placed on you. You live this life only once. Make the most of it."

A tear slides down my cheek as I inhale deeply, pushing through the memories that only bring pain. "Last time I tried to do that, Dad died. I fell in love with the wrong boy and—"

He shushes me. "Who said he was wrong?"

"Dad." Maybe it's irrational and maybe I should have found professional help a long time ago, but he always said that if we follow the rules, life is nothing but bliss.

The minute I stepped outside the boundaries, he died and my life was never the same. It was impossible for me not to connect the two things in my traumatized teenage brain.

"Did you love him?"

"I did, yes."

"Did he do anything?"

"No." Only if one looked through the prism at perfection, otherwise Jason was like every other teenage kid with hopes and dreams. "I left him after Dad died. He moved to another city, and the last I heard, he has a successful band. I think he even has a daughter." I don't lie in bed wondering about what ifs, because ultimately I don't think we were right for each other, but sometimes I wish I would've taken his offer and moved far away from New York. As much as I love this city, I don't think I've truly been happy here since Dad died.

Since their divorce really. No matter how much I asked though, Mom never explained what made her do it. Maybe she was fed up with Dad's teachings as well.

I should talk about this with her, to put to rest all those puzzle pieces in one picture.

"That's good. Love is what keeps us alive and what makes us choose our faith. Don't come to church to atone for sins. Come here, because it's what you want. Otherwise, it's a punishment and that is not what it's about." Pastor finishes and stands up while patting me on the head, just like he used to when I was five. "I've got kids to feed now. I hope our talk helped you."

"It did," I reply. With one last nod, he goes to his destination while I'm glued to the bench, his words playing in my mind on repeat.

What if life is not about punishment, but love?

What if life is not about fear, but freedom?

What if life is not about pain, but happiness?

I have some thinking to do before I reach a final decision, but I think I'm going to use that ticket of Bella's sooner rather than later.

*L*achlan

"Everyone out," I say in the conference room, and Alex pauses midsentence, as he was in the middle of his finance report in front of the board of directors.

My CEO wanted to implement some modern changes that will triple our income according to him, so I found time for it, but it doesn't matter now.

"Lachlan—" Alex starts, but he must read the barely contained fury on my face as he hastily picks up all the papers while addressing everyone. "How about we move it to another day? Something came up." The board of directors give me side-glances, but they listen to him, their chairs scraping loudly as they get up, slightly annoyed. As much as they don't like my behavior, they will keep their mouth shut, because they like their bank accounts too much.

The minute the door closes after them, I crush the phone in my hands after reading the information of Valencia's whereabouts.

I throw it against the wall with a roar, along with everything else nearby, a wild beast raging inside me from her going to church to cleanse herself of her sins.

A sin being me.

May this holy water wash away all the devil's thoughts from your head, Lachlan. It's the only way for you to live in Heaven.

I roar again, slapping the table with my palms as I take deep, calming breaths, blocking away the voice from the past that nags at my sanity and threatens to strip me from my carefully held control.

I never had issues with anything until Valencia showed up in my life, until she awakened unfamiliar emotions of wanting to own every part of her while dirtying her in a way she'll never be able to wash away.

I've always needed to catch her in my trap so she'll become a broken angel who can never get her wings back.

But now?

Now I want to drown her in my darkness so she will never find escape from me, keep her in my dungeon forever to punish her, not only for the sins she did not commit, but for the weakness she has become.

The game has gone on long enough.

She doesn't get a day longer.

Tonight.

It ends tonight.

*S*omewhere in the world...
     Fall 2018

*V*alencia

Digging deeper into the pillow, I cover my other ear with my free hand, hoping to eliminate the sounds of the Newton's cradle that have been going on for hours, but I can't. My body is exhausted, reminding me of the sleepless nights that always greet me in this place.

Then the sound of the lock turning snaps my attention, as it's exceptionally loud in the room, and the thud of heavy leather shoes echoes through the space and my heart stills.

Why did he come? He almost never visits me here, finding my "terrible state," as he calls it, too disgusting to look at for long.

I swiftly turn around to face him as he graces me with a tentative smile that doesn't reach his cold eyes when he scans my appearance. "Valencia," he says in a patronizing voice, and fury penetrates every bone as I sit up on the bed despite the pain, only to be pulled back to my side because the cuff is not long enough.

At one time, they used a chain that allowed me to move freely, but I tried to get free by hitting the caretaker in the head and taking his key so I could escape.

They found me on the second floor, where I stumbled on the slippery floor. That had brought more punishment, using knifes to leave permanent scars on my back.

Disobedience is the one thing he hates the most, and I was nothing but that for the last eight months.

He clicks his tongue, placing his hand on my head, and I move it to the side, doing my best to evade his touch, but it's useless as he pulls my hair, sending prickles of pain through my scalp. "If you'd just learned a little bit of discipline, we wouldn't be in this situation." His voice is filled with regret, as if he truly believes his words.

The man is insane.

"Don't touch me," I say, but instead of listening to me, he pats my head, removing the strands of hair that have fallen over my face, and lifts my chin so I can meet his stare head on. I can barely talk through my dry throat, as they give me water only every six hours, too afraid to leave it with me. God only knows why. What can I possibly do with it?

"I will never accept this," I hiss in his face, hoping determination coats my features so he'll have no doubts left about my intentions.

His fingers on my chin tighten and I wince in pain, but I hold back a groan, not wanting to give him even the slightest satisfaction. "Be grateful for your condition, Valencia. Otherwise, the consequences would have been severe." He leans forward and stops the cradle. The silence that falls on the space is almost deafening and the ringing in my head slowly stops. "Another twenty-four hours should be sufficient punishment, and for the sake of—" He doesn't finish, his voice halting as if even the idea sends a tremor of anger through him. Darkness crosses his face, a look I don't know or recognize. "Matilda will come to you tomorrow." He lets go of me and leaves while I sink back into the pillow, breathing heavily, my heart beating rapidly against my ribcage.

I don't have all the time in the world. I have to think of an escape before he destroys the thing I hold dearest to my heart.

So I do the one thing I have always done in situations where hope was an illusion with no solution in sight.

I pray with all my might. My faith and prayers are the only things that keep me sane in this never-ending nightmare that my life has become.

CHAPTER ELEVEN

New York, New York
January 2018

*V*alencia
        Breathing heavily, I finish the last position and bow to
the imaginary audience as the music ends. I raise my head to face the
mirror, and a completely devastated woman greets me, tears sliding
down her cheeks as sorrow and grief are reflected on her face,
displaying the emotions of a betrayed swan perfectly.

I just finished Act III when the prince falls into a trap, and instead
of sealing his fate with the princess swan, he chooses the dark lord.

He has won again, and my heart is broken.

I pause at that thought and straighten up, wincing slightly at the
aching muscles and shaking my leg a bit, because ever since the last
performance, it's been bothering me.

My heart.

Does it work? Do I feel her pain now as if it's my own?

Pressing my palm over my chest, I close my eyes and concentrate on my emotions, and with pain comes rage that prickles my fingers as I live through her.

Poor, poor swan. The prince she loved broke her trust and lost in the game for the dark lord. She will forever stay his prisoner now.

At least she thinks so.

Suddenly, the image of Lachlan comes to my mind, playing like a colorful movie as he introduces me to his mansion and the darkness that surrounds it. With his wicked sense of humor and ultimate power around him.

If he played a role in *Swan Lake*, he'd be an evil spirit that creates webs of lies to get what he wants. I can't imagine him as an innocent prince who can be easily fooled or believe in love.

The image doesn't suit him, but instead of scaring me, it intrigues me.

Clasping my hands, I snap mentally out of the character and bring myself back to the present, where I'm Valencia whose heart is quite all right.

Confused, but far from broken.

And the time has come to mend it.

I pick up my phone and write a quick message to Bella.

<**Me**> I'm coming to Paris.

The reply comes almost instantly.

<**Bella**> No fucking way! YES! When?

<**Me**> In a month or so. I need to finish all the stuff here and find someone for the kids. Otherwise, I'm good to go. Time for changes.

<**Bella**> If I knew sex with a guy would make you do this, I'd have pushed you to it a long time ago. :D

Rolling my eyes at her, I just send her an emoji of a tongue sticking out and place my phone back, pondering if I should finally call Mom back.

After all, she doesn't deserve this silence of mine.

I slide the phone open again and dial her number. She answers on the second ring, and I expect a scolding or shouting or anything other than her soft "Valencia." Invisible knots that held my chest together disappear as I take in a deep breath, leaning on the barre, stretching my back in the process.

"I'm sorry, Mom." There is nothing much to say except this.

There is silence on the other end of the line, and then a ragged breath. "Honey, why did you date the boy if you didn't want to marry him?" Yeah, my mom doesn't beat around the bush and gets straight to the point.

"I thought that was the right thing. A perfect guy for a perfect princess. And you liked him." Which sounds so lame and it's probably not true. I may act like a victim in all this, but truth be told, I spent all this time with Max, because he was a safe choice.

He didn't require emotions from me, nor did he want more. He was happy with a porcelain princess who finished his appearance and fit into his life and the dreams he had.

I don't think he ever truly loved me either; we just grew up together, and maybe he wanted what I represented.

However, the time has come to take responsibility for everything that has happened in my life and own up to it, dust myself off, and start anew.

"Are you upset?' I ask, feeling like a small child who desperately seeks her Mom's approval.

"I'm upset because you didn't come to me with this problem. I'm just—I'm upset, yes. But with myself."

"Mom—" This is the last thing I wanted, but she continues to speak.

"I love you, Valencia. You are my baby girl. And I want you to be happy. Whatever that means to you. Stop making decisions by weighing everyone else's desires. Choose the path that is right for *you*."

An image of Lachlan rushes through me, along with all the dreams I've had regarding Paris since I was a little girl. "What if what I desire is not right?"

A silent moment follows while my heartbeat rings in my ears, finding it vitally important for her to reassure me. "Does it hurt anyone?"

"No, not in the sense you are putting it."

"Then I don't see a problem. Follow your heart. It will lead you to—"

"The right place?" I supply, and she laughs, her colorful laughter mending one of the broken parts in me.

"To *your* place. Okay?"

"I love you, Mom." Through all the years, she's the one who has always supported me in my dreams and stood by me through everything. Even when she divorced my dad, she never once made me choose between them.

Even to Victor, she said that we were a package deal.

"Well, I'm glad." I grin at her words. "I love you too, honey. Now make your mama proud and give the best show New York has ever seen."

That's my mom.

"I thought you told me to follow my path?" I tease, and I can practically see her shrugging as she lifts her brow. "Ballet is your path. This is a truth set in stone and nothing will ever change it." Victor's voice comes from the distance. "I have to go. Your stepfather can't find his glasses. It's a wonder he can survive without me at work at all. Oh, and he says he loves you too." Warmth fills my chest at my parents' support, knowing that as long as they have my back, nothing can hurt me in this world. "I love him too. Bye bye."

She hangs up and I exhale in relief, even my shoulders feeling lighter.

All my fears seem so silly in this moment.

Packing all my stuff, I smile brightly, feeling hopeful about the future, when the phone in reception rings.

Who would call this late?

*L*achlan

Moving soundlessly through the night, I place a mask on my face, finishing the black sweater and jeans attire that makes me almost invisible.

After I turn on my phone and get inside the studio that I memorized during my last time here, I turn on the computer.

Valencia is still on the phone with her mother as I program the laptop by connecting it to my phone. I put on a playlist and send a message to Shon to follow the plan exactly.

What's a chase without a little play?

I preset the phone to dial the studio number and disappeared into the corner, using all the skills I've acquired from the master who taught me to be invisible, no matter what the situation is.

*V*alencia

"Hello?" I ask again, but the other end of the line is silent. "Hello?" Sometimes this phone has connection issues, so I lean down, sliding my fingers over the line and checking if it's attached to the phone, and it is. "I think it's useless," I mutter, hanging up and frowning, as a folder on the desk catches my attention.

Picking it up, I read through it and gasp in shock.

He wants to sell the freaking studio? I blink again, making sure I'm reading it right, but there is no mistake. Patricia signed over all the rights to Lachlan, and he is evicting everyone within a month, claiming this place can no longer act as a studio.

Freaking asshole!

I knew it! He just can't be trusted. "I won't leave it alone, Lachlan!" I hiss, rolling it up and hiding it under my armpit. But before I can dwell on it, music blasts from the studio, and I blink as I recognize Mozart's "Turkish March."

We never use it for ballet classes.

Confused, I dart to the studio room and see the stereo playing. Maybe Patricia updated the playlist? I quickly turn it off and shrug, almost laughing that for a second fear penetrated me because it's so freaky to have music suddenly begin in a silent and lonely studio.

But then the music starts again, this time from another stereo located at the end. Patricia usually has two per studio. I do the same with this one as well. Maybe there is a glitch in the system? Adriana said recently some tech guy updated all the systems and made it easier to control the music from all corners; clearly, he did his job right. "All because someone felt too lazy to adjust the music by themselves," I grouse, snagging my bag, and I'm heading outside when the music starts back up again, and this time I freeze on the spot.

The different sounds come from all over the place: music blasting from different directions while the lights in the studio go up and down, along with a crashing sound from the administrative area.

"What is going on?" With trembling hands, I fish for my phone, only to find it crushed inside my bag. How is this possible? I left it for just one second when I went to pick up that call.

A call that no one answered.

My pulse speeds up; ringing in my ears erupts as all the information I've heard through the years about kidnappers hits me.

My notes. Is it the same person?

This is not a simple prank all right.

Another crashing sound and I jump into action, running to the bigger studio at the end of the hallway where there's a back door.

Then I see a flash of a baseball bat barely lit by the moonlight as a tall man hits the walls with frames displaying Patricia's diplomas, and they fall to the floor, shattering into tiny pieces. I scream in fear, dipping while covering my face, and resume running.

The man doesn't really hurry after me though, snagging computers and papers and everything by the sound of it as he destroys the studio in a methodical, almost planned way.

I can barely see in the dark, and only my knowledge of the floor plan allows me to reach my destination and grab the knob and twist it, but it doesn't work. I twist it again, pushing at the door with my arm, but it doesn't budge.

Panic swirls through me as the crashing stops and footsteps, leather boots by the sound of it, come closer and closer to me as he taps the bat against the wall in time to the music.

I frantically do my best to open it, but it's useless. "Valencia," he says, and my brows furrow at the familiarity of his voice, but I can't concentrate on it now.

Abandoning the door lock, I dash to the side, where the opening leads to the narrow hallway to Patricia's office. She has a phone there; it should work! The police are my only option at this point.

But I don't make it two steps before he grabs my arm, tumbling me to the floor. I cry out as my knees hit against the harsh wood but manage to scoot back from him, hitting blindly at anything, but he doesn't budge under my assault.

I kick him in the shin and that slows him a little, and I have a moment to escape him. Barely glancing to his right, I see it's not a baseball bat as I originally thought.

It's a freaking metal cane!

I crawl to the office, managing to get inside and shut the door behind me as he bangs on it loudly. I close my eyes, practically feeling my heart in my throat from the fear. Limping, I get to the desk and pick up the phone, but it's silent. I press on the button a few times, but it's still silent, and the freaking cable is cut.

Oh, no.

No, no, no.

That's my only out. He called me by my name. Why would anyone need to hurt me?

I didn't do anything.

What do people usually do in situations like this? I try to focus, but it's next to impossible with him pushing against the door as it thumps and thumps and thumps.

Looking around, I don't find any weapon to defend myself from a man who is freakishly strong.

The window!

There is a window, but the minute I get to it, I see it has metal bars that are unmovable. "Oh my God, what am I going to do?" He destroyed the studio.

This is not just a spur of the moment crime. It's filled with hatred.

Then I hear it.

The snap of the lock, and then the door is kicked open and it bangs against the wall. He enters. I don't know who he is, as his face is covered in a mask, but with each step, I retreat farther and farther, while asking with a trembling voice, "What do you want from me? Who are you?" He doesn't respond, just continues his movement, breaking everything that gets in the way of his cane. "Please."

That's when the music by Mozart ends on the softer note, and he hits the only light bulb above us with his cane and everything goes black.

And then I hear only my raspy breath as he flicks something and digs into my skin as my screams fill the space.

CHAPTER TWELVE

Lachlan, 5 years old

*T*he car moves swiftly on an empty road while nothing but desert greets me as I gaze out the window. Songs are blaring through the radio as Aunt Jessica hums the tunes under her breath. She looks over her shoulder at me while still navigating the car and winks. "You will love it in Peaceful Heaven, Lachlan," she assures me while opening her window. Hot air fills the car, and the added breeze offers some relief from the heat. "Everyone is so nice there."

Resting my head on the windowsill, I mutter, "I miss Mommy and Daddy."

"Me too, honey. Me too. But they are in a better place now and it means their time has come. The only thing we can do is accept it." Tears form in my eyes, and one of them trickles down my cheek, but I quickly wipe it away so she won't see it.

Mommy and Daddy died in a car accident two months ago, because the road was slippery and it was too dark for them to get out in time. I had been at school in my kindergarten class, so I survived and they placed me in foster care till they could locate my family. Although it was hard, they finally contacted Aunt Jessica who lived with her husband and daughter in a town called Peaceful

Heaven. I couldn't find it on a map and always wondered why the social workers winced whenever it was mentioned.

I'd never seen her before, 'cause Mommy always claimed we lost her to some cult, but I never understood the words. When she came after me yesterday, she hugged me close, rocked me in her arms, and promised me that even though she couldn't bring my parents back, she would give me a real family.

I don't want a real family. I want just my family.

Why did God take them away from me?

Wiping away another tear, I glance down at my newest gift, a Holy Bible from Aunt Jessica, and flip it open, wondering if I can find the answer there.

I close my eyes, hoping that wherever that Peaceful Heaven is, it'll be kind to me.

* * *

I *startle awake as the car stops abruptly and I hear Aunt Jessica say, "Hey, Carl!" She takes out something from her shirt and shows it to the man standing on what seems like a big fence or something in front of the city, and he nods, opening the big gate. She drives inside while I sit up higher to see the town better.*

The sun is shining brightly, giving me a good view of everything. My heart falls as I understand it's not really big, and only lots of little, white houses are there, and I don't see any people. "Where is everyone?" I ask, and Aunt Jessica jerks nervously.

"At church, darling. It's Sunday. And we are late." I blink at the fear in her voice. But she quickly adds, "But it's all right. There was traffic on the road."

My attention is still on the view, and I question, "Why are all the houses like this? There is no school?" She doesn't answer and pulls the car to the side, near the square white house with short grass. Everything is fixed nice, but it's almost squished with other houses, not leaving even an inch between them.

"Let's go, honey." She gets out and then opens the door for me, and I hop down, wincing slightly at the pain traveling from my numb neck. Her small car isn't comfortable to ride in. "This is your new home now." She wraps her hands around my shoulders, squeezing me lightly, but all I feel is sad.

Because this doesn't feel like my home.

"Just follow the rules, and it will be the happiest place on earth for you."

Rules.

I will soon learn that they are the most important part of this "Peaceful Heaven."

*N*ew York, New York
January 2018

*V*alencia
Wincing, I slide my head to the side to avoid some-thing annoying poking my face, but the touch follows me. "Bella, go away," I murmur, wondering why my best friend has showed up early in the morning at my place and is annoying the hell out of me. She always has this stupid habit of waking me up while playing with my hair.

It doesn't stop though. Instead, something sprays on me, and with a loud huff, I snap my very heavy eyelids open and still in shock.

A man looming above is splashing me with water from a glass while holding a towel on his arm!

What the freaking hell?

I sit up on the bed, raising my hands to push him away, when they are pulled back.

Chained. I'm chained to the headboard attached to the... I glance to my right to see I'm way down from the guy and that I'm on the floor, occupying a white-as-snow mattress, and held in place by metal rails next to it.

I pull at my wrists, but it's useless. "Don't be scared." The man gives me a reassuring smile, but I just scoot back and kick him in the knees as he steps closer. He stops with a pained expression on his face. "Valencia—"

"Who are you?" I scrunch my eyes hard and then open them again, hoping that maybe I'm having a nightmare and just haven't woken up from it.

But the image doesn't change, and that's when the panic overtakes me. I scream my lungs out as I try to get away from the source of danger.

"For God's sake, child, you have strong lungs. Please have mercy on my ears," he begs and finally retreats, giving me time to study him.

He wears a gray suit with a slightly longer jacket and white gloves that have not a single stain on them. His gray hair is perfectly put together, and his wrinkled face mostly holds indifference, even though his voice doesn't support it. He must be around sixty or more years old.

But what surprises me is his eyes. They are green and hold so much kindness that for a moment I stop screaming, because there is no threat coming from him.

Wrapping my hand around my neck, I croak past my abused throat, "Who are you and what do you want from me?" And then I remember the studio and a man chasing after me, and fear envelops me even more. "Why did you kidnap me?"

What do victims usually do in such situations? I shouldn't analyze all this like that, should I? But then that's me. I've always been put together during stressful situations, and then I allow myself to cry once the stress is over.

However, the over part is nowhere in sight.

"He didn't."

The deep yet husky voice sends tremors down my skin, yet not from its tone but the person it belongs to, because I would recognize it anywhere. Back in Patricia's office, I couldn't concentrate properly.

Lachlan.

My head swings toward the sound, and then I see him through the glass as he steps down from the door, his shoes making thumping noises as he walks in with his cane held level in front of him.

He grins at me while sweeping his gaze over his own creation, and only then does it register where I am.

One word that can describe it is insanity.

Four glass walls surround me, creating a cage-like atmosphere while the mattress, small table, and toilet in the other corner are the only other things occupying the inside of the space. The harsh light comes from above me, bright like on a football field, and someone is trying to blind me.

Outside the cage, there are various knives and ropes displayed on the wall, along with a very long metal table and a sink that has water dripping, drop by drop. The sound echoes through the entire space, grating on the nerves.

And cameras.

Cameras that are above me in every corner, giving whoever is sitting and watching a perfect view of everything I do.

AC blasts on my skin and I shiver, then gasp as I see a long, white flannel nightgown on me that reminds me of those Victorian Era nightgowns that cared about a girl's modesty.

"Child—" the older man starts, but Lachlan interrupts him.

"Leave, Levi."

He opens his mouth to protest, but Lachlan gives him a look and points his cane behind his back. He finally goes to the door and shuts it, while I gaze at Lachlan, who presses the button and enters the glassed cage, tsking.

"Pathetic state, Valencia. It took you what... a minute to scream your lungs out? No one even touched you." He wiggles his finger. "I expected more."

I stand up but fall down on my knees, because the chains are too short to move around. He sighs dramatically, kicking the chair closer and dropping onto it while rubbing his chin with the top of his cane. "It's short for now. Maria will change it once we are done so you can... well... roam around freely I guess." I don't even bother to ask who that is, probably some other psycho who thinks all this is acceptable.

"Why are you doing this to me?" If he orchestrated this, then... "The notes?" I need to know, and he nods. I puff out air, not knowing what to make of it all.

What if it was his strategy to get me in a panic just to prove something? But as I rack my brain, nothing explains it. "You want to kill me? Is that it?" Is this the kind of thing they show on TV, where a man is obsessed with a woman, and he creates a web around her to trap her in? Because he has some unexplainable cravings and he's focused them on me?

He chuckles, inspecting his cane, and I really have a deep desire to knock him off the chair with it just to not see that smile of his. "Valencia, if I wanted that, you'd be dead. I don't do anything in half measures." He says it so casually, as if we are discussing the weather. "Your father owes me a debt. And I will collect it. From you."

"Victor?" It's about him? He wants to use me in some kind of business deal? That calms some of my fear, because it means he won't do anything to me. He knows my stepdad will need proof that I'm all right. Braden was kidnapped once, and Victor handled the situation brilliantly.

I don't have to be careful with my words, just withstand this environment that at least doesn't have rats or gross things. Granted, the toilet is open, but I can take some humiliation.

As long as I'm not dead.

Mom won't survive losing me.

"So all this... Italy... and what followed after... it was a game to lure me in?" Maybe it's not the question that is supposed to be important to me. After all, isn't the answer obvious? Yet I demand to hear the answer from him, to cement my stupidity more.

He stays silent, but I see his jaw tic. Otherwise, his face is completely indifferent. He rises on his chair and comes slowly to me, then flicks his cane open and the tip of a blade extends from it.

Lachlan presses it against my chin, urging me to get up. I have no choice but to sit up on my knees. He taps the blade on my skin while still holding my chin high. "No. Fucking you has everything to do with your charm and nothing with your father," he says seductively. Then he slides the tip lower and digs it into my collarbone as I cry out and try to move away, but he stops me. "Careful or it might touch the artery." I still as I feel blood slip down my breast, and then the metal slides lower, nudging slightly at my stomach and bruises on the skin there.

Enough to sting, but not enough to do permanent harm. "Your skin was made for torture, you know that? Pale, so pale. It will show every bruise, every drop of blood." He slides it back to my neck, and before he even does, I know what he will say. "It's a beautiful sight along with my mark for everyone to see and never wonder who you belong to."

"I'm not yours." I fume. Does he really think this kind of thing will turn me on?

"We will see about that." He flicks the blade back and taps the cane against my cheek. "Be the good girl that you always fucking are and cooperate, Valencia. It will be easier."

I snort. "You mean I will be safe?"

He turns around and walks to the door, then says over his shoulder, "No, it will be easier. The word safe doesn't exist in my vocabulary." And with that, I'm left alone to ponder his words, while nothing but the buzzing of AC and dripping water sound in my ears.

*L*achlan

Emerging from the torture room, I bark at Levi, who still stands by the door. "What the hell was that?" He doesn't reply, so I shift my attention to Maria, who immediately casts her eyes down, tugging on her long, black uniform dress. "Feed her in a few hours. Leave water there. Also change the chain for a longer one so she can move freely inside the cage. And put the screens around the toilet so she has privacy there." Levi's brows rise, but my harsh expression keeps him quiet. The last thing I need is for him to gloat that I can't dish out a proper punishment. "Also, turn off the lights inside the cage and leave one bulb on outside. No one enters besides you and Levi."

She nods, holding the card tightly. Maria sold her body on the streets for years until Levi found her half beaten to death. He brought her here and we gave her a job. Last time I checked, she married one of the security guards.

At this point, I could be considered a fucking matchmaker or something.

She trails off to the kitchen, probably for the tray of food, when Levi says to me, "Folders are on the desk. Jaxon sent them in."

"Good. No one disturbs me. Keep an eye on her." Before I go, I add, "Don't gloat."

"Wasn't going to."

As I go down the hall, all I can think about is the woman who is left in the torture room.

And how I hate leaving her there. But at the same time, I love having her completely at my mercy, not knowing my next move.

Victor.

My laughter bounces off the walls.

If she only knew.

V alencia

Pacing the cage, I knock on the glass, but it's so strong my knuckles hurt. Huffing in frustration, I go to the table as the heavy chain on my leg drags behind. I wince as it presses on my ankle exactly on the spot that always throbs after rehearsal.

The meal the woman brought earlier is lying on the floor untouched, as I only hydrated myself with water. I want to be conscious for whatever he dishes out.

Nothing here can be used to help me escape, so I drop back on the mattress, hiding my head between my knees, and wonder about my calmness. I've tried breaking the wall with the heavy chain, but all it did was bruise the pads of my fingertips.

Why am I not freaking out? This is too calm, even for me.

But deep down I know.

Maybe I consider it a punishment once again for wanting to do something for myself.

Why can't God just allow me to live my life in peace without sacrifices?

Leaning against the wall, tucked into a ball, I allow a single tear to drop on the mattress, hiding it away from the cameras.

My pain should always be only my own.

The monster got the angel.

CHAPTER THIRTEEN

Lachlan, 7 years old

The loud footsteps that make cracking sounds on the old wooden floor snap me wide-awake. My breath hitches, sending my body into alarm. I glance at the clock, which shows seven o'clock, and whine in desperation when I realize I'm alone with him tonight.

Aunt Jessica is at her evening church service.

I grab the blanket from the bed and throw it over me, hoping to escape the monster that slowly creeps into my room. I chant the prayer my aunt has taught me.

She said if I do it while in pain or fear that God will always help me out. That I won't be left alone.

I chant and chant while tears stream down my cheeks, and my whole body shakes while I squeeze into a little ball, hoping he won't find me. Even though it won't help.

Too soon, the door bursts open and a bright light shines in the space. His voice makes me shut my eyes harder, hoping it's just a nightmare that'll go away soon. "Lachlan." The word sounds funny, which means he's been drinking again while Aunt can't see.

He does a lot of things when she doesn't pay attention.

"Please, God. Please help me," I murmur, holding on to the belief that something will take me away from him, that he will stop his actions and won't harm me again.

But all my prayers don't get heard, 'cause he pulls the blanket off, leaving me lying in my pajamas while he stands over me. The light behind his back hides his face, and that scares me even more when he cracks his head to the side.

He looks at me sadly as he squeezes the cross around his neck. "Lachlan, you understand I don't want to do this, right?" he asks, as I shake my head and sit up, moving until my back hits the headboard, my body shaking to the point of my teeth clacking against each other. "You are a devil's temptation, and I'm too weak to fight it." My eyes widen as he flicks his belt open, pulling it out of his pants with a loud whoosh, and I shiver at it, knowing what that leather thing can do.

My back holds the scars that will never go away.

"Please don't." The room is so quiet, but my voice can barely be heard, and he frowns, slapping himself on the cheek while bending in two, and my tears drop down on the bedsheets. I hope that this time my begging will make him stop, that this time he won't do what the devil tells him to do.

But my hope goes away when he raises his eyes on me, and orders, "Get on your knees."

I shake my head, scooting back even though there isn't space to do that. "Lachlan, get on your knees." He hits the belt buckle on the floor and it makes me move. With my heart beating fast, I slowly get on the floor, but not before trying again. "Please."

He cups my cheek, running his thumb over my skin. I can't help but pull away at the touch, and he doesn't miss it. He squeezes my chin, making me hurt through my bones. "You are a sinner, Lachlan, for bringing these desires in me. And sinners need to be punished. I'm helping you to get to heaven. Otherwise, boys like you will go to hell. Do you want to go to hell, Lachlan?"

I just want to get away from him, and it doesn't matter to me if it's heaven or hell.

He roughly pushes me on my knees, and I hit the floor with a groan as he rests me against the bed and wraps the belt around my mouth, pressing it against my lips so I have no choice but to open my mouth and dig my teeth into it. I close *my eyes as he hikes his fingers in my pajamas bottoms and slides them down, opening me to him.*

And because it's not the first time he does it—I've lost count of his Thursday and Saturday visits to my room—in my mind, I go to the beautiful green field where I think about lying on the grass as the sun shines on me. There is nothing but endless sky, and I make myself not feel the agonizing pain that pushes and pushes into me, the groaning and heavy breathing that threatens to suffocate me, the smells that forever stay in my brain.

Instead, I breathe in the flowers blooming on the pretty green grass, the sound of a waterfall, and go to a place inside me where no one holds me prisoner and does bad stuff to me.

The pulling of the belt from my mouth and the taste of blood on my tongue brings me back as Uncle gets up, stepping back, and then I bite on my fist, 'cause I know what will come next.

And that I can't make a sound.

The hard metal buckle hits my back. My entire body is full of pain that tells me my skin didn't heal from the last time and it'll hurt for more days. He continues his blows two, three, four more times until he stops, and says, "You had to be punished for tempting me, Lachlan. It's all for you to go to heaven." I don't turn or reply, just press my forehead against the bedsheets and breathe in and out, as it holds the tears that threaten to escape me any minute.

Finally, he pulls his zipper up and leaves the room, closing the door, and I let myself cry on the sheets that still smell like him.

As soon as I can, I wash myself in the bathroom and put on my pajamas. Aunt Jessica comes back while Anna, my cousin, sleeps soundly in her bed. I climb on mine, cover myself with the blanket, and wish with all my heart to go to hell.

Because if heaven is like this place, then I don't want any part of it.

ew York, New York
January 2018

*V*alencia

The bright light blinds me as Lachlan steps inside the cage, wearing his fucking three-piece suit. Does he not have other clothes or what?

I've lost count of time in this place, as they keep me mostly in darkness where the dripping water in the sink is the only sound that keeps me company. They don't forget to feed me, but that's all sent back untouched.

He clucks with his tongue as he leans forward, his finger trailing my chin, and I move my head to the side, avoiding his touch. He grips my chin tightly and a slight moan of pain escapes me. "Valencia, I do like your stubbornness, but when it borders on stupidity, it quite annoys me." His voice is void of any emotion as he points at the food scattered all over the floor where I threw it the minute the "nurse" brought it inside.

"I'm not a pig who you'll get ready for the slaughter." I spit into his face, and he merely lifts a brow, wipes the spit away, and places the strands of my hair behind my ear with his other hand. He finally lets go, stepping back and scanning me with those assertive icy-blue eyes of his. "I will never beg my father for a ransom." If he thinks I will beg Victor for anything, he has another think coming. Victor mentioned having a new important project with Lachlan, but also that the man was dangerous. He probably refused to have anything to do with him, and that's why I've been kidnapped.

What else can explain this madness? And besides, he doesn't look like a serial killer anyway.

All this is a carefully placed tactic to create panic inside me and scare me, but ha-ha on him, because I'm not falling for it.

I push back the thought of what I did with him, avoiding those memories like a plague, because they meant nothing. He used me in his game, and like the idiot I am, I have been caught in the trap.

This has only solidified the truth I've lived by all these years. Emotional decisions lead to chaos that has the power to destroy your life and those close to you.

He takes out a cigarette from his pocket, lights it up, and says

before taking a long pull of it, "Oh really? My plan went to shit." He
mocks me, exhaling the smoke all over the place, and I wave it away
with my hand, hating everything about it.

He grabs the single chair next to him that is close to the table and
sits on it, placing his cane between his legs as he crosses his arms over
it. If anything, he reminds me of a pirate who has kidnapped a lady.

I groan inwardly, because who the hell compares this guy to a pirate
in my current situation? "So, using your logic," he says with his patronizing tone that grates on my nerves, "keeping you alive has no point,
right? Since you won't ask for ransom." He chuckles as if finding this
idea truly hilarious.

I freeze, searching for words, because I have no answer to that.
Will he kill me if I won't comply with his wishes?

Focusing my attention back on him, I notice his watchful gaze on
me as he cocks his head to the side and scans me as if trying to search
for something.

Like weak spots that he can press on in case he needs leverage. His
whole demeanor is about indifference, control, and dominance, but he
is not using it in a threatening way.

Yet.

But beneath the cold exterior, I see flashes of fury and barely
controlled emotion I can't name when he squeezes the cane harder as
his cigarette ash continues to drop on the floor, barely used. Half the
time, he doesn't actually smokes those things. Why then does he light
them up?

With his handsomeness, one could compare him to a lion, but he is
a hawk. He doesn't miss anything and always has the advantage over
his victims who never see his attack coming, and then he is free in
the air.

You are pretty much doomed in his grip.

"It doesn't matter what I say," I hoarsely reply and curse myself for
not drinking more earlier. Being dehydrated won't bring me anything
good. "You will do whatever you want."

If I don't come willingly, he will make me. That much is clear from
him. God, how could I have been so wrong and not trusted my
instincts that told me to run away from him at the very first glance?

How could I have succumbed to my desires and shared all those moments with him?

How did I allow those hands, which have cut me to touch me and bring me pleasure? A tremor rushes through me as disgust forces bile into my throat.

A man who can hurt a woman deserves nothing.

"Ah, darling. You finally registered in that head of yours I'm not a good guy." I pull on my restraints, but it's useless. The metal just digs deeper into my skin and I groan quietly. "Don't do that." Suddenly, all amusement is gone from him, as he barks, "It will only damage your skin more."

A hollow laugh erupts, and it takes me a second to understand it's me who laughs and laughs to the point of tears streaming down my cheeks and my stomach hurting from the effort. "Now you care about my well-being? How thoughtful of you," I spit.

His gaze darkens. He stands up and is by my side at once, his cane stopping my movements, but before I can say anything else, he presses it against my mouth, and I still, because I don't know what he will do next.

The metal is harsh and imbedded with a few stones. I can imagine how much it will hurt to have it hit against my skin. No way in hell will I risk it, no matter how much I want to. "I don't give a fuck about your bruised skin." His voice is so cold it could freeze a fire, and chills run through me as he continues pressing it harder. I tighten my mouth so he won't touch any teeth. "But I need you healthy for what I have planned next. Don't fuck up my plans, Valencia. Or you will live to regret it." Then he turns around, going toward the door. He is almost outside when he glances over his shoulder, and says my way, "Since you do not appreciate kindness, you won't have food for three days. We will see what you say then."

"Whatever!" I shout, but he is already gone. I wrap my hands around my knees, rocking back and forth, as I finally can let go of the brave, and maybe stupid, façade and succumb to the desperation and fear that consumes me.

What did I ever do to him to deserve this?

Three days? Is he not going to ask for a ransom?

Lachlan

Flipping the page on the recent accounting update, I read the fucking last line again, but it doesn't register in my mind. No matter how much I try to concentrate on the multimillion-dollar bill that will bring me much-needed power on the East Coast, I can't for the fuck of me understand shit and reply to the offer.

Instead, the brown-eyed beauty, who is in my dungeon built specifically for her, occupies my every thought as an unfamiliar sensation spreads in me, stripping me of my iron-willed control.

Throwing the contract on the table, I get up and go to the huge window that looks out over the fountain and its alcove in the garden as thousands of thoughts rush in my mind.

None of them make sense to me.

Resting my arm on the window, I let the memories of her crying on the floor play in front of me as the deep desire to soothe her, yet hurt her, rages inside me.

Seeing her bruised and in pain... unsettled me. On some level, it even angered me, as no one should ruin a skin so pure.

But she always reminds me with each glance and turn of her head who and what she is.

What she needs to become for me to win this chess game she has no idea we are playing.

I always thought breaking her spirit would be easy; after all, she's lived nothing but a sheltered life. What do princesses know about resisting dragons? All they do is wait for the princes to save the day and release them.

But maybe, just maybe, I'm not dealing with a princess... but a warrior who has managed to hide her armor from me all this time.

My fists clench and I hit the glass with all my power, cracking it under the assault, as realization dawns on me.

That's why I feel complicated emotions; her strength appeals to me on some level.

I laugh at and destroy weakness.

But strength? That, I respect. Not everyone has the ability to fight while in extreme circumstances; most just die accepting whatever so-called fate throws their way.

A soft knock on the door pulls my attention back, and I say, "Come in."

He takes a beat and then clears his throat, exhaling heavily. Levi is nothing but consistent in his fucking sighs.

"Tell me," I order, barely containing myself from spinning around and demanding to know all the details. I showed restraint an hour ago and decided not to look myself.

"Maria went to her and acted the part that she would feed her without your permission. But she refused, so that makes it roughly forty hours for her without food." Of course, the little angel doesn't want anyone to get in trouble on her behalf. Everyone else comes before her.

Selflessness along with stupidity will be a human's ultimate downfall, because rarely anyone will show it to another, and most only feed on those who give it. "She does drink the water though," Levi adds in reassurance, as if it's supposed to make me feel better.

At least she is smart enough to keep herself hydrated.

"Lachlan," he starts, but my splayed hand stops him and I turn to him.

"What did I tell you when we started on this journey?" He plays with his thumbs, avoiding my gaze, so I ask again. "What did I tell you, Levi?"

"Never feel sorry for the subjects."

I clap my hands together, the sound exceptionally loud in an otherwise silent space and he winces. "Look, you remember. And now with Valencia, don't forget it. If you cannot follow the rules, you know the consequences." Not the words I ever expected myself to speak to Levi of all people, but he left me no choice.

"She is so young. She is—"

"She is not *her*."

His body trembles as he places one of his hands on his chest, probably rubbing the silver cross at his neck. After a second, he raises his disbelief-filled eyes to me as he points his trembling finger at me. "You don't get to talk about her."

"I wouldn't have if you didn't bring it up. You think I don't see it? From the very beginning, you've been involved much more in this situation than you should be. Valencia is a subject like everyone else." I quickly turn on the cameras from the torture rooms and bring the tablet closer to his face as he turns away from it. Blood never pleases him much. "She is just like all those people. Remember that."

He nods as disappointment crosses his face. "You cannot run from the truth forever, Lachlan. Make sure this path doesn't burn you." Before I can reply, he is out, leaving me alone with my hectic thoughts that won't settle, no matter how much I try to rein them in.

She shouldn't matter. She means nothing. She is a means to an end that is twenty-three years in the making. There is no hope for her. At the end of this all, she'll be dead like all the other victims.

But why doesn't this thought bring me anything besides hollowness in my chest?

With a roar, I scatter everything from the table onto the floor. As it crashes in different directions, the sound reminds me that everything in life is as fragile as those things.

With the right pressure, you can break anything.

With that thought in mind, I emerge from the office and come face to face with Maria who holds a tray of food, and by the items on it, I understand it was for Valencia.

"She refused," she says softly, barely audible, and I take it from her. "I'll handle it."

My leather shoes sound in the hallways as I pass by rooms where screams and groans, and even club music, come from inside.

I gather Arson must have one of his victims in there.

After five minutes, I end up in the small opening to her place and see her splayed on the mattress with her eyes closed, her arms crossed, and curled into a ball, trembling slightly.

My brows furrow as I notice the AC running low and quickly put it higher; otherwise, she will get a fucking cold.

I grab a blanket on the way and step inside the glassed space. I place the tray on the table. Then I slowly walk to her and throw the blanket over her, drinking in her pale, soft features that, despite how much she pretends to act peaceful, give her away.

Because she is not asleep. I can recognize it by the barely heard rasped breath and how her chest contracts with my nearness. I lean down to touch her hair and almost reach it, when memories assault me and I almost roar in pain as the voice echoes in my ear.

What will you do for me, Lachlan?

My hand fists as I yank it back and dart to the table, finding the paper and envelope on it along with a pen. Since she refused to write any letters to her home, I will write one to her.

I quickly scratch the text against the paper and then place it on the tray, knowing she won't be able to resist herself and will check it out.

I know all about humans and their nature; I've studied them for years, after all. And while Valencia might be different, she is still one of them.

That is a truth carved in stone, and that's why she'll never have my mercy, even if she begs for it. Her fate was sealed a long time ago, and it doesn't really matter that she had no say in it.

Innocence is not a virtue; it's a weakness that allows demons to shred one into pieces. Some come up stronger, and some... break.

Let's see, Valencia. What will you choose?

*V*alencia

The minute the door closes after him, I open my eyes, propping myself higher on the pillow as my hands clench the fluffy blanket that brings warmth in this otherwise cold place. My skin almost turned blue from it, but I didn't ask for the blanket. I figured it was part of the torture, considering he even withheld food.

I didn't know what to expect when he showed up. Fear mixed with curiosity played tricks with me while I did my best to act and breathe evenly, but I suspect he knew I acted.

Why did he do it? Does he care about me after all, and all this is a power play just to convince me to play along so he can get what he wants from Victor? Who places a victim they want to hurt in a glass-like cage with all the necessities, even while creating an aura of doom and depression?

That's when my nose twitches and the smell of freshly baked bread with mozzarella cheese fills the space, instantly making my mouth water, and I swallow down the saliva as my stomach growls.

I place my hand on it, wincing, as the need has become unbearable in the last few hours. It would have been bad for anyone, but for me? I barely hold on.

When Maria offered me food, I refused knowing full well who organized this stage. No way does Lachlan not check if his commands are obeyed or not. And maybe this woman is brainwashed to help him out; God knows what he did to her so she'd agree to this. She doesn't deserve his punishment in case he finds out.

But he left the food himself and on the table at that, taunting me with its delicious aroma. I'm starved and long to just have a bite, but I won't.

Maybe it's stupid or maybe it's pride, but somehow deep down, I know it's a test and I'm not going to fail it. He thinks I won't survive one more day without food? We will see who can issue challenges.

There is a lingering thought that maybe, just maybe, he is doing it, because he can't bear the thought of me suffering. That maybe it's the part that attracted me to him in the first place, that kindness lives somewhere deep, buried under... well, whatever he is.

I'm about to roll on my side, when I notice an envelope next to the tray, and curiosity gets the better of me. I stand up, and in few steps, grab it and rip the seal open, wanting to read the note.

An angel resisted the orders, too proud to know any good.
Monster didn't find it amusing, nor interesting, so he wondered.
Tell me, angel.
What do monsters do to those who disobey them?
Maria, oh, Maria.

I read again, hoping I've imagined the implication between the lines, but no matter how much I replay the words, the outcome is the same.

If I don't eat the food he brought me, Maria is as good as dead.

And suddenly, the food that looked so delicious a few seconds ago brings nothing but barfing sensations inside me, and I can barely stand thinking about putting it in my mouth. But what choice did he leave me?

What did he say earlier? He needs me healthy for whatever he has planned for me.

To think that I gave him the benefit of the doubt. Nothing good lives inside that human.

And I shouldn't ever look for it again.

*L*achlan

I watch her shovel the food into her mouth while almost choking on it. Her refusal can be seen miles away, but she clenches the note tightly in her hands, probably still shocked by the words.

There was this one moment when she wondered why I brought her the blanket, if maybe there is something more than darkness. I could recognize it by the why she furrowed her brows, bit on her lips, while softness touched her face.

Well, the captor quickly stripped his captive of any illusion she might have had about it.

She has her answer now.

I rule and live in darkness, and searching for something that is not there should teach her to accept her reality.

Even if it's a nightmare of my creation.

Turning off the camera, I pick up the contract again and can finally read it without anything bothering me.

And as much as it should please me, it only angers me more and proves to me that I should speed up the process.

Time never works to anyone's advantage anyway.

CHAPTER FOURTEEN

Lachlan, 8 years old

*A*unt Jessica combs my hair, critically ticking with her tongue. *"I should have requested a bit smaller shirt for you. This one is loose."* She puts the comb on the table and then adjusts my shirt while also pulling up the tie. *"You look so handsome."* She presses her hands to my chest, wonder crossing her face.

I don't say anything, just hug her close, and she pats me on the back. I find solace in her arms, safety for one fleeting moment in time.

Besides being in this place, Aunt is the kindest person I've ever known. She cooks tasty food, lets me play with Anna in the garden, and even teaches me to play the piano.

Music is the only source of light for me. The minute my fingers touch the keyboard and the keys create magical feelings inside me, each note tugs on my heartstrings.

When I play, I can pretend I'm not in this town that has no escape, a town where no one is really your friend, and a town where almost everyone is a carbon copy of each other with similar clothes and views.

I can pretend my uncle doesn't sit on the couch and watch me tentatively while criticizing my every move.

Yes, music is truly a beautiful thing.

"We are going to be late. No need to pamper him," Uncle snarls, picking up his bible, and motions to the door with a bouncing Anna by his side. "Let's go." *Right, God forbid we be late for the Sunday service.*

Especially this one.

"Oh, I just want to make sure he is perfect before meeting the pastor." She addresses me. "Remember what I told you. Be nothing but respectful and answer his questions. Based on that, he makes a selection."

My brows furrow at those words as I follow her outside, wincing from the too-small shoes that dig into the back of my foot. "Selection?"

She nods eagerly while we trail down the small road to the church with Uncle and Anna in front of us, and she waves to some people who are doing the same. The whole town is actually going, because the pastor arrived.

Based on what I understood, he only does it once or twice a month, and everyone loves him, since he saved them and gave them hope.

Whatever that means. But Aunt said he is like a president that sets all the rules and makes all important decisions about our community, because he always knows what's best for us.

The Pastor.

"The pastor always selects several new kids for his special program. If he sees potential in you, you will study with all the other selected kids and will have a chance at college. Also, he has specific meetings with the kids so he can give you all the important stuff." She sighs heavily. "This would be a great opportunity for you, especially with your talent." She stops and kisses me on the cheek, murmuring softly, "So please do your best so he can choose you."

If it means he can get me out of this place, I will do whatever it takes.

We finally reach the church and sit in our usual row. There are voices for several minutes, but then everyone gets quiet as the man gets on the stage.

He is wearing a black robe that almost reaches the floor, the heavy cross hanging from his chest, while his assertive green eyes scan the place like a hawk watching for his prey. He seems really tall and muscled, but the glasses on his face make him almost approachable.

He looks friendlier than other pastors around him, and hope blossoms in my *chest. If he always saves everyone, maybe I can tell him about Uncle and he will tell him to stop hurting me?*

He opens the book on the stage and clears his throat. "Hello, people."

Everyone answers him, and then he proceeds to give his speech, half of which I don't understand, but people react to it. Some cheer, some cry, but almost everyone watches the stage with awe and adoration and complete happiness.

They really do love him.

He finally finishes and is met with loud, never-ending clapping, and then he sits on his chair that looks more like a throne behind the stand. No one ever sits there, so it solely belongs to him.

Aunt Jessica quickly stands up and grabs my hands, tugging me toward him. "Let's go. We need to introduce you while the line is not long." But even though she is quick, I see already about seven people lining up to him, and everyone has small kids around my age with them.

I huff, because it's too hot, and I tug on the collar of my shirt, but Aunt quietly fusses at me. "Behave." I stop my actions and just look around, noticing a boy behind me fidgeting with his hands also.

He sees me too, and then murmurs, "Hey." I smile, because in this place you don't get much interaction with anyone, since everyone is homeschooled till you are ten.

They claim it helps in the long haul, but then again, I don't understand that either, so I never question it. "My name is Logan," he says.

"Lachlan." He extends his hand to me, but it's slapped away by his mother I guess as she addresses my aunt. "Follow the rules."

Whatever they want to say fails though, as we are next in line. Several families who already went through the process seem disappointed; their kids probably didn't pass.

Finally, we stand in front of him, and Aunt Jessica takes his hand and kisses the back of it. "It's an honor, Pastor." He nods and then looks at me. As he scans me from head to toe, something crosses his face, but I can't name it.

I only know it sends tremors through me, and suddenly I pray for him not to choose me.

Please, God, please.

But as always, my prayers don't get heard.

New York, New York
January 2018

Valencia

I hear the lock being turned and get up swiftly, ignoring the pain in my knee from my previous position. Maria doesn't bring me food as I expect, but instead clears her throat and comes to me with a keychain in her hand.

"Don't do this." I stop her with my hand as she gives me a confused look. "I know you want to help me, but he will kill you if you free me."

This guy is serious, and I'm not even sure it's his plan to bring me safely to Victor anymore.

Her eyes widen at my words, and it takes her a beat to reply, as she hides her gaze from me. "Lachlan asks that you to come upstairs, take a shower, and join him at dinner."

"You're joking, right?" I ask, as laughter erupts from me so harshly that I have to hold my stomach because the hilarity of the situation is not lost on me. "He is asking me? How big of him!" I manage to say past my amusement, wondering if I ended up in some kind of other dimension.

But Maria stands still, fear evident in her eyes, and I stop, clearing my throat. "Well then you can tell him to fuck off." Why didn't I curse all this time? Nothing like expressing an emotion with one curse word.

The whole good-girl image is overrated; it's brought me nothing but sorrow.

What's his plan anyway? He's acting all weird and not delivering on the serial killer aspect of it, yet everyone is scared shitless of him.

If he didn't kidnap me for the sake of raping or ransom, then what does he want from me?

How does he intend to break me and drown me in darkness as he claims? The guy is completely mental, that's for sure. But what's the agenda?

I sit back down, resting my back by the wall while gazing straight

ahead of me, barely holding back the impulse to show my middle
finger to the cameras.

"He will be angry," Maria whispers.

I shrug. "Good. Let him." Maybe then he will finally show his true
self and stop playing whatever twisted, fucked-up game he has in mind.

"When he is angry, he does bad things," she adds, and my heart
stills as I glance at her. She fumbles with her fingers, shifting from one
leg to the other, and I notice how she glances at the ceiling from time
to time.

"Why do you do that?" The elderly guy, Levi, also has this guilty
expression whenever he comes inside and sighs heavily if he sees my
pain. Yet as much as they might be Lachlan's prisoners, they don't
seem abused or tortured.

Nor does he strike me as a man who will go around and rape his
female maids if his victims don't follow their orders. He scared me
with Maria before, but now I think it's just a ploy.

This kind of devotion they are showing him? It comes from loyalty.

I can recognize that. But how is it possible to have loyalty to such
a man?

"He saved me once. I will always stay with him."

"No matter what he does?" Shouldn't she, as a woman, feel for me?
For my state? With what does he brainwash all these people?

"He won't hurt you if you just follow the rules."

"Funny thing, I don't want to follow them." I don't know where all
this stubbornness comes from, as I've never shown it before in my life,
but it's there.

As if strength has been unleashed within me, that was kept hidden
and locked long enough and emerged to help me in this madness.

"Please," she begs, kneeling in front of me and wrapping her hands
around mine, startling me. "Just this once, do it. Don't antagonize him
right now. Not during this time."

During this time?

"What is he, a beast that's going to unleash his animal once the full
moon hits?"

She doesn't reply, and for a second, I wonder if that's what she
believes. But thankfully, she quickly shakes her head as a chuckle slips

past her lips. "No, but please. Who knows? Maybe if you do what he asks, he will let you go." There is so much hope in her voice that it's hard not to believe her.

Except I know it's not the case.

Then another thought hits me.

If they let me out, it means I will have a means to escape. I found the cab that day and have good memory of the labyrinth in the garden. If I manage to snatch the phone from Levi's back pocket, I might be able to call the police or someone to help free me.

And get lost in the garden until they arrive. Anything will be better than sitting in this cage and doing nothing.

Playing along doesn't have to mean surrender; it might be the only solution to the problem.

"Okay, then," I agree, and her face lights up as I stand up and dust my knees. "Let's go to that dinner."

And crash it.

*L*achlan

"She has agreed to dinner," Levi proclaims, holding my jacket for me as I clip the buttons on my sleeves. With Beethoven playing in the background, I study my reflection in the mirror.

"You don't say?" I motion for my jacket.

He places it on my hand, huffing. "Why did she say yes? I thought she would say no."

He blinks at my chuckle, as I put on the jacket and pour myself a glass of whiskey. "Levi, you know nothing about women, do you?"

He blushes, playing with the collar of his shirt, while mumbling, "I'll have you know my Elizabeth loved my ways." Softness crosses his features, but it's quickly replaced with sorrow. "While she was alive anyway." He wraps his hands around the cross on his neck, closes his eyes, and chants something.

I finish my glass and grab my phone while slapping him on the back. "Hide your phone. She will try to get it."

"What?"

"Why do you think she agreed so eagerly? Our angel wants to escape."

Her naivety is entertaining in some ways, because it only proves to me she has no idea about true danger and darkness in this world. She believes in fairytale stories, that it's possible to easily escape serial killers just with some "awesome" plan.

Serial killers are hunters. They don't let go of their victims or give them freedom unless they want to achieve something with it. If more people knew about psychology, maybe fewer people would live with such a useless thing as hope.

It never did anything good for me either. Hope only brought disappointment and the knowledge that no one will come and save you because simply no one gives a fuck.

She shouldn't have bothered with poor Levi anyway. I'll give her one shot at winning, and if she fails, I will resort to my grand scheme.

Either way, she'll be destroyed.

It's just up to her to choose her demise.

*V*alencia

I dip the brush into the loose powder and it spills a little on the table as I bring it up to apply to my cheeks and nose, being careful not to touch my blood-red lipstick that makes my lips fuller.

Gazing at my reflection in the mirror, I study my perfectly applied makeup that is more suitable for stage than dinner. Vivid smoky brown eyes with three layers of mascara, cheekbones standing out thanks to the bronzer, the added makeup highlighting my pale skin, and everything is finished off with my hair that Maria put into a braid that gracefully showcases my neck.

Standing up, I slide the silky white robe to the floor as I walk to the costume waiting for me on the bed. I fist my hands, doing my best to rein in my anger, but it's so hard with Lachlan's last order.

Maria brought me to this spacious room with the simple bed, carpet, and a wardrobe that rivals a princess's, plus a huge-ass bathroom. Earlier, she claimed Lachlan left instructions for me and I had to read them.

I opened the envelope on the dresser that basically said I could be either a sugar plum fairy or a swan from different Tchaikovsky plays and act out the character.

Just how fucked-up do you have to be to offer something like this?

I decided on the swan. After I washed myself, wincing and cursing as my bruises throbbed, the slightest touch bringing pain that reminded me of the reality I lived in, Maria fixed my hair.

I put on the Odette costume, the black bodice, as he chose the one from Act III when the dark lord deceived the prince and acted like a swan, the corset hugging me tightly as I zip it up. Beige tights and pointes follow, and the last attachment is a crown that gives me a much darker look than I'm used to.

It feels surreal to wear the costume I was supposed to perform in, in such vile circumstances.

A hollow laugh escapes me at the irony, though, since I know now exactly how she felt. If one day I am still able to perform it, I think Olga's argument of me not being able to perform as a swan will be invalid.

Surprisingly, instead of a tutu, there is a simple short skirt that's much easier to navigate. At least it doesn't add more ridiculousness to my attire.

Taking a deep breath, I exhale swiftly and open the door where Maria waits for me nervously, but the minute she sees me, she sighs in relief and motions to the hall. "He is waiting downstairs."

"Where is Levi?" Shouldn't they keep someone more trusted by my side? I didn't miss how close he is with Lachlan.

"He is there. He'll serve the food."

My brows raise, but excitement settles in, although I mask it under a bored shrug. If he is going to be so close to me, taking a phone should be a piece of cake.

All I need is a moment with it, and I'll find an escape.

We go through a second hall; it doesn't have much really except blank black walls and a red Persian carpet that flows to the stairs with oak banisters. We go down, and with each step, the music is clearer and clearer in my head.

Mozart.

Maria guides me to the dining room, and I hold back a gasp as an image from some kind of historical movie greets me.

The room is lit by hundreds of candles that are located all over the place, from the chandelier to dressers and tables. The red and golden curtains sway as a light breeze slips through the cracks in the balcony door, allowing fresh air inside without freezing your bones.

Although the room is spacious, it doesn't feel like it, because there are statues of different wild animals in hunting poses and expensive, by the looks of them, oil paintings that grace the walls, giving it an aura of doom.

At the center is the dining table spread with glistening china and food that smells delicious. In the far corner sits Lachlan, lounging on a chair as he watches me.

Levi stands next to me, wearing his usual clothes. His white-gloved hand points at the other end of the table with a plate that already has rice and chicken on it, and he says, "Please, sit down." He gives me a reassuring smile, and I return it as I hope my friendliness will keep him close. I scan his appearance; he doesn't have any pockets on the back of his pants, but I do notice one on his chest.

I can't be too obvious though, so I have to think how to snag it after dinner, so Lachlan will believe I'm cooperative.

Levi slides out a seat for me, and I drop onto it. "Thank you."

He nods and then tenses a little, as Lachlan's husky voice orders, "Everyone out." In seconds, we are left alone, sitting miles away but still seeing each other clearly.

At least I won't have to experience his nearness during this charade. "Well, you do really go all in, don't you?" I muse, picking up a glass of water and taking a sip, welcoming the cooling sensation in my parched throat. My stomach grumbles and I lick my lips at the food. I'll need to be strong for the chasing, so pride can wait. Digging into the chicken, I put it in my mouth and hate how tasty it is.

His cook sure as hell knows his job. But then Lachlan always wants the best, doesn't he?

"You are awfully... what's the right word?" He taps on his chin with his finger. "Ah, yes. Eager for this dinner. To what do I owe the pleasure of it?"

The bile sticks in my throat as my fist tightens on the fork. Desire to stab him with it is strong, but I push it down and shrug. "Sorry if you expected hysterics. I found them tiresome."

He rests against his seat, sipping his wine while his eyes calculate my next move, so I do my best to keep my face completely blank. "How interesting. Out of all the women I've killed or intended to kill, you are the calmest of them all." He points at me with his glass. "You have my respect for that. Cheers." He gulps it greedily when I almost choke.

My hands still on the knife and fork as they slide from the chicken and graze the plate, enveloping the buzzing sound as I gulp breath.

He kills women? He told me he doesn't rape anyone.

But there are other things a man can do to a woman that can forever damage her and kill her. Are those his targets? Does he get a high in destroying them emotionally before inflicting unbearable pain on their flesh?

What did you think? That he is some kind of a hero who kills bad guys, and deep down, nothing is like you thought? That he is a good man with a heart of gold? Snap out of it! It's not a fairytale!

"And she's back. I wondered who had replaced my angel," he purrs, and I let go of the silverware.

"This is all very amusing to you, isn't it?"

"To an extent."

"What do you want, Lachlan? Tell me already, because all of this is insane." I motion to my clothes. "And ridiculous. I'm not a swan and you are not a dark lord."

"Let me be the judge of that," he says, leaning on the table, still sipping his drink. "The lover in this case will be me or Max?"

"You are not my lover," I grit through my teeth, hating myself for ever allowing him to touch me.

"Then Max, huh? Hard to call someone who never had access to that seductive body of yours a lover."

Fed up with his cryptic language, I rise from the seat and plant my palms on the table, sending the china flying to the floor and shattering into tiny little pieces. "Stop playing games with me and tell me what your goal is. Enough!" Maybe all my screaming will bring Levi here, and then Lachlan will order me to go back to the room where I can make a call.

"Shhh, save your voice for later." I don't have time to dwell on his words as he presses a small remote in his hands and then points at the fireplace on our right. Just above it, the wall goes back and up comes a flat-screen TV.

My brows furrow in confusion as he presses on the thing again and the TV turns on, displaying some kind of black room. "That's torture room number three. The knives," he explains as if it's supposed to mean something to me. "Anything goes as long as it has a sharp edge. The floor is marble, so the blood slipping from the victims doesn't permanently damage anything. I don't like renovations much." He presses again and the view of the camera changes. My eyes widen as I see a man pinned to the wall, his hands above him together and closed with a knife stuck through the skin. His legs are a bit apart, but each one is chained to the wall, and blood pours from his wounds. His hair is soaked in it too.

"What is this? Why are you showing this to me?" Oh my God, does this place have torture rooms with more victims? Just how many desires does he have at once that he needs several rooms to sustain them?

"Ah, there is no sound. Apologies."

He clicks a few times, and I hear a female voice there. "How about a blade? Should go well with your tanned skin. It will hurt a bit." She shows a small distance between her index finger and thumb. "More pain than the kitchen knife. But I will have more fun. What do you think?" The man mumbles something through the tape holding his lips together, but because of his hair all over the place, I can't see his face clearly.

The woman sighs heavily, walks closer to him, and slowly peels it from his lips as he groans; it probably brings discomfort. "What was that?"

"Please let me go. I don't have any information for you," he rasps, and I freeze, my mouth hanging open in shock as tears well in my eyes.

I try to say something past my shock, but words don't come.

I would have recognized this voice anywhere.

Max. He has Max!

"No!" I finally scream and dart to the TV, but Lachlan is swiftly at my side, pushing me back on my seat, and I land on it hard, hitting my elbow in the process. "Let him go!" I scream to him, but all he does is chuckle, placing his hands in his pockets as he gazes at me.

"Darling, you wanted me to explain why you are here. I just fulfilled your wish." He steps closer, and I move back although there is no space, so all that's left is to dig my back deeper into the chair. "Now, if Max suffers or not depends on you."

"You are insane," I whisper with my heart almost in my throat from panic that threatens to strip me of my sanity. Max groans in the background as the woman grazes his skin with a blade. "A psychopath."

He sighs heavily. "Psychopaths have a genetic predisposition to be the way they are. Sociopaths are shaped by their environment. Get your facts right first, darling. However, I'm none of those." Another agonizing scream reverberates through the wall, and I close my eyes tight, tears falling on my hands drop by drop, as I listen to my friend suffer.

He is in this position because of me; I'm sure of it. Lachlan probably wants to teach me a lesson, and he never liked Max anyway. "I'll do whatever you want, but please let him go." I finally crack, hating everything about this surrender, but it's the only way to save an innocent man from this.

He leans forward, resting his hands on the arms of the chair with his lips inches away from mine, his smells of tobacco and alcohol enveloping me, as he murmurs, "Valencia, you don't get to call the shots here." Before I can add anything, he presses a finger to my lips, and I wince in disgust. "I'm nothing but fair, believe it or not. So I have a proposition for you." Our eyes clash as he trails my lips with his thumb. I'm sure he can see my chest rising and falling as my heart beats wildly, awaiting his response. "Dance for me. A perfect dance of act three. If you will dance for one hour straight with no stopping, Max won't suffer. That's one single rule. But if you break it, he does. How does that sound?"

One hour? How will I be able to perform in such a state and for one hour? It's almost suicide for a ballerina to hold that long on her legs, and it can lead to all sorts of injuries.

Will I be able to?

"To convince you even more, how about raising the stakes? If you win, you are free. If you lose, you are forever enchained in this castle."

He probably knew about my plan with Levi, which seems stupid and hopeless now. He is a mastermind who cannot be tricked.

But he is also a man who respects a fair fight; that much I can tell. So if I follow the rules, he will grant me my wishes.

I cannot fail myself or Max.

Our lives depend on it.

"Okay," I reply.

Satisfaction crosses his face as he steps back, and orders, "Let's go to the dance room. Show me your swan."

All the way there, I pray and pray to God to help me withstand this challenge.

*L*achlan

A French abbot and a major leader of the Benedictine monasticism Saint Bernard of Clairvaux once wrote, "*L'enfer est plein de bonnes volontés ou désirs*" which in English translates to "Hell is full of good wishes or desires."

Whatever we do in life, most of the time is the right thing or good intention. But our every action has a consequence.

Valencia so easily sacrificed herself for Max, not that I expected anything else from her, although an odd feeling of raging fury swirls through me at the idea of her having any affection for another man, even if it means nothing.

She shouldn't have any other male in her mind but me. She is mine. Belongs to me, as I earned her fair and square.

Her good wishes and desires brought her to the gates of hell, and she is about to sink into it, coming to the place that will forever change her and shape her into a person she won't recognize.

All because she put someone else above herself.

Hell is a fickle thing.

Sometimes people create it for us, and we learn to live there, holding on to the life that brings nothing but pain.

Sometimes people create it for themselves, choosing someone else's happiness above theirs. It's not always about love though, as everyone claims. Sometimes it's about selfish desire to feel good.

We rarely place the blame where it belongs.

Valencia doesn't know, but she failed my test; had she chosen differently, I might have considered granting her freedom. Had she followed with her plan to access Levi's phone and call the police, she'd have proved to me that she is not an angel.

But once again, she went to old habits and risked her legs.

More lines for my notes to her appear in my head. Too bad I no longer send her any, as this would have been fitting.

Once upon a time, there was an angel who sacrificed herself out of guilt.
Her wings clipped, her spirit broken.
She had no one but herself to blame.
As the monster gave her chances she wasn't willing to take.

Spinning her around to me as she struggles in my hold, I grab the rope from the fireplace I purposely put there in advance and wrap it tightly around her middle. It's long enough to let her dance freely to any distance, but tight enough that with my pull she will move in the direction I need.

"I'm not your puppet," she says, stubbornness crossing her face, and my laughter echoes in the otherwise silent space.

"Are you sure about that?" There is just so far you can push a person before he or she will explode, but Valencia doesn't.

She accepts it, barely giving a passing look at the beautifully designed space before standing right in the middle of it.

Let the show begin.

*V*alencia

My eyes snap open. I look straight ahead and take a deep breath, then step into a pose. I'm illuminated by the moonlight that shines brightly into the room from the glass-like ceiling above me. The silent room is filled with a mysterious atmosphere, creating an almost-perfect setting for a romantic evening.

The familiar first notes of Tchaikovsky's *Swan Lake* echo through the space, and I assume the position, rising on my toes and swaying from side to side while slowly moving to the corner and then hopping on my toes again, owning the stage as if nothing matters, blocking the outside world away.

To each dramatic note, I perform with my hands and facial expressions, giving away all the hopelessness of the swan who has been captured by the dark lord and can't be reunited with her love.

The pain and heartache fuel her desire to fight against him, so she feeds on them, even if they threaten to destroy her.

I swirl and swirl, rising up and down, up and down, and then a cry of pain slips past my lips as my feet land on the glass. I halt my movements, barely breathing from the glass digging into my skin.

I glance down to see my white pointe shoes slowly coating in blood from all the scattered glass covering the floor. If one is careful enough to avoid it, he is a master.

My feet throb agonizingly and I can barely stand on them. My rasping breaths help me concentrate on something other than the hurt.

The sound of the lighter flicking fills the space as he lights his cigarette, takes a deep breath, and exhales it in my direction while resting more comfortably on the chair right in front of me. "Ah, Valencia." He says as a sinister smile spreads across his face. "You know the rules. Never stop." His deep yet dangerous voice raises goose bumps on my skin, reminding me once again that the monster never sleeps.

He just feeds on my misery.

He tugs on the rope wrapped tightly around my waist and I stumble forward. I can't help the groan of pain when he directs me onto the big pile of glass. The air freezes in my lungs while I pray for the hurt to pass so I can continue.

But I can't.

Instead, fear unlike anything before spreads through me. Injuries like this may ruin a dancer's career forever, and if I don't have dancing, I won't have anything in this life.

But he knows that.

Somehow it's easier to pretend and think only about ballet, instead of Max's life that depends on my performance. For a second, I can block it away to get the clarity that is almost impossible as fear chokes me at the prospect of his death.

We have been friends since childhood. Our dads were friends. Each moment with him flashes before me, bringing only more desperation.

Another tug. This time I can't keep up. I land on my knees, biting my lip hard so I won't make a sound as the bare skin on my palms and knees touch the glass.

"Get up," he orders, but I don't.

He can dish any punishment he wants. God knows the cuts and throbbing skin are an indication of that, but I won't let him taint the one thing in my life that I love most.

He has already taken everything else; he doesn't get to have ballet too.

He exhales heavily at my disobedience and rises, straightening his perfectly ironed three-piece suit, and walks to me.

With each step he takes, my heartbeat speeds up faster and faster. He places the metal head of his cane under my chin and lifts it up until I meet his stare head on. I hate everything about this man.

Or at least I hope it's hate.

"So that's your choice?" he asks as his lazy gaze roams over me, but I say nothing.

I won't give him the last part of me that matters.

Even if it seals my death tonight.

I quickly come to a decision and speak. "Kill me instead of Max. It's about me anyway." I expect him to eagerly take it, but instead, rage fills him.

"Sacrifices are for fools, darling." He taps the cane against the glass. "Get up and dance, or Max is dead."

I hiss in pain but get up and try to rise on my toes but fail. I would have kissed the floor if his strong arms hadn't held me steady. "I will dance. Let go of me." If a life depends on me, I must.

I didn't want to give up ballet, but it seems it's better never to dance again than to have Max's death on my conscience.

He shakes his head. "You failed, Valencia. The terms were to never stop." He takes out his phone and presses Dial as fear spirals through me. I grab his hand, but he issues the order. "Kill him. Now." Through the phone, I hear Max's scream that lasts and lasts, and then Lachlan shifts my chin to the other TV that slides open from another wall, where I see Max stabbed in the chest, but not before the person removes his genitals all while he is conscious for the torture.

His face freezes with the scream still etched in his expression, and he is dead.

Dead.

Because Lachlan decided to play a game with me and I failed. With clarity, though, I understand that Max's destiny was decided long before now.

Lachlan is just that kind of monster.

I open my mouth wide and scream my heart out just like the wounded swan.

CHAPTER FIFTEEN

Lachlan, 8 years old

*T*ugging on my ironed shirt, I glanced over my shoulder one last time as Aunt Jessie waves at me from the car. She dropped me at Pastor's mansion, which is located almost at the far end of the city, and is surrounded by iron gates that have security men around them.

She said Pastor prefers his privacy and people usually take a lot of his time, and this way he can concentrate better on educating the boys.

"It's all for the goodness of his people," she explained.

He chose me, Logan, and three other kids and told our guardians to bring us to him the next day. All the moms along with Aunt Jessie almost jumped with happiness, and she whispered to me that now I will have a chance to do greater things for the community.

And although Pastor scared me, I understood that someone above listened to me, because the minute he selected me, Uncle changed.

He didn't snarl at me, didn't come close, and he didn't whisper in my ear on Sunday that I should wait for him. And although I shook in my bed, expecting his visits, he never showed up.

Maybe being one of the selected boys by Pastor is in fact a blessing after all.

A tall man, wearing what seems like a uniform that reminds me of those historical TV shows Mom used to watch, opens the door and smiles at me, although it doesn't reach his eyes.

"Hello, Lachlan. Come on in. Everyone else is already here." I nod and follow him while seeing huge sculptures inside the house, shiny chandeliers, and red carpets that must cost a lot. I see stairs going up, while the man points at a huge door.

I step inside and almost gasp. It's a huge dining room with several big windows, but they are covered by curtains, so the chandeliers shine brightly.

The dishes almost sparkle in the light with various food bowls scattered on the brown, wooden table, and the smells make my stomach grumble. "Lachlan," the pastor addresses me, and I come closer as he pats the table on his right. "Come sit here, beside Logan." I quickly do that, and my eyes almost bulge from their sockets from the well-done steaks, french fries, desserts, and lots of other dishes that people here can only dream of.

Mostly the houses have only rice and buckwheat with vegetables from the gardens. Meat is distributed once a month, and it counted on the number of people living in the house. I share a grin with Logan, as he shows me a thumbs-up, clearly wanting to grab the food as much as I do.

We take a moment to say grace and then Pastor stands up, sweeping his gaze over us. "Now that we are all here, let's start eating. You are a select few who have great potential. You will have an education, expensive clothes, whatever you want. And so will your families." I'm confused at this, because Aunt said the life here is about letting go of all those things in order to find God within you.

Shouldn't we follow the same rules?

"I will require only one thing in return," he adds, and everyone eagerly nods.

Everyone but me, because although I can see his expression turning blank, something hides behind his eyes.

I've seen this evil in Uncle whenever he claimed I was a sinner.

With my heart beating loudly in my ears, I dread his reply, and when it comes, I almost exhale in relief.

"You will live here for one week of the month. I will have special guests over. They will teach you things."

That's not so bad, he probably needs people from outside, because not everyone is smart enough here.

Except...

And then I ask a question before I can stop myself. "Where are the other kids that were selected before us?" If he chooses someone by the age of eight, surely they must be around?

Pastor's brow rises and something crosses his face, but it's quickly gone and he replaces it with a smile. Cold, scary smile. "Once they turn thirteen, they live among everyone else. They just have a chance to study at college outside once they are eighteen." And then he leans forward, so only I can hear him. "Do not speak without my permission anymore, Lachlan. Disobedience has consequences."

The doorbell rings and several male voices can be heard. "Our guests are here. Now each one of them will select one of you. You will go to your study room, and they will show you things." Then he goes to the hall to greet the seven men who came in, each one of them wearing a suit and a golden watch that practically screams money.

He didn't mention all this to my aunt when she got the document that stated what we would do.

I shrug it off, and we proceed to eat while the men sit opposite us. I move around on my chair as one of them, the older man with black hair, stares at me in a way that doesn't feel right.

I want to go home now and forget about this whole selection thing, when Pastor asks, "Gentlemen, have you made your pick?" Each one of them has his attention on a different kid and they nod. "Great. We shall start this, then." They get up, and the dark-haired man motions for me, and I go as he puts his hand on my shoulder. I want to push it away but don't. There is no need to be rude without any reason.

We go upstairs, as he asks, "Lachlan, right?" He pats my head. "I will show you heaven on earth."

What? What does this have to do with studies?

But I don't have to wait for long as we step inside the spacious room that has a big bed with the headboard nailed to the wall, several leather belts hanging from the wall, and a bench. Along with some tubes and packets that I don't recognize. I can see one more door, which probably leads to a bathroom. If it's a study room, shouldn't there be a desk?

Not this.

And then I raise my eyes to him and everything inside me freezes. I know that look.

No!

I dart to the door, but he grabs me hard by my neck and laughs, sending tremors through me. "Lachlan, baby. The fun hasn't even started." I try to get free, but it's useless. He tears my clothes away while sliding his hand over my chest. "Do you want to run without me showing you what I promised?"

I fight and fight, but it doesn't help. Several hours pass with him doing bad things to me, while I take it all and then cry in the shower because everything hurts. I rest my face against the hot tile.

Tears mix with water while I wonder why everyone dreams about joining heaven if it's like this?

*N*ew York, New York
January 2018

*L*achlan
         She sits still on the floor, breathing heavily as her raw
         throat murmurs something, but it comes out like a babbled mess.

Her hands are bleeding from how strongly she dug her nails into her sensitive palms while she watched Mina kill Max. With that one last stab, her eyes lost all hope and the strength she harbored during her dance. She looks into space, her mouth half open, and all I can do is watch her as displeasure hits me unexpectedly.

Outside forces have hurt her, and I don't like seeing her like this. Defeated, because another man—Max, no less—is dead.

Although it's fascinating to watch how deep compassion can go, this image starts to bore even me.

Throwing my jacket on the chair, I roll up my sleeves as I go to her, and that finally catches her attention as she focuses her gaze on me. A snarl appears on her face, as she hisses, "You are a monster."

"I am. Never hid that." She tries to scoot back from me, but I grab her by the shoulders, drag her up, and steady her as her knees weaken. "Enough of this 'great depression.' I want to show you something else." My words have created a banshee in my arms as she hits me repeatedly, although I can barely feel it. That's how weak the blows are. She screams and screams with her raspy voice. "Don't you dare touch anyone else from my family or friends. Don't you dare."

My brave one, still giving orders even though she is in no position to do so. "Believe it or not, Valencia, I'm trying to give you a cure from your... well, this." I don't really know how to properly describe her reaction, as I find it completely useless.

Dead people don't need our tears. They can't help them anyway. A simple truth that everyone should accept.

"So consider it my generosity," I inform her as the video starts to play on the TV. Her quiet sobbing stops and she blinks in shock while she watches Max pat the head of a little boy who bangs on the door, crying out for help.

"Shhh, little one. No one is going to hurt you," he says to the kid, and the boy wipes his cheeks, looking up at him.

"I want Mommy."

Max kneels in front of the boy, smiling at him softly, although his eyes don't hide the fucking gleam that is forever imprinted in my brain from fuckers like him. "Mommy is not here now. But I am. I won't hurt you. If you play with me."

The boy blinks in confusion, stepping away from him. "Play?"

Max slides his hand down the boy's shirt, unbuttoning each button as he nods.

I pause the video, asking Valencia, "Is that enough, or do you need more visuals?" I hope it's enough, because every time I see this kind of shit, I want to destroy everything in sight.

She finally snaps out of shock, whispering, "Oh my God." She swallows loudly, covering her mouth. "Is he going to... is he... the boy?"

Resting my back on the table, I say, "Going to rape him? Yeah. Repeatedly, for a few years. That boy is his favorite actually. Nick."

"Stop," she pleads, covering her ears, but I continue anyway, as I'm not that considerate.

Life isn't that kind either.

"Twice a week, Max made trips to his favorite place to enjoy the boys. Why do you think he never pushed you for sex? He didn't need to. He had six-years-olds to sustain his desires."

"Stop," she says again, turning her face away from me, but once again, I do not listen.

Why should only the victims live with this dirt and truth, while people hide from it because the information is too difficult for them to handle?

"Perfect Max, from the suburbs and all. With dark desires. And for him you cried and lost a bet with me. That's the man you've spent three years in a relationship with. How does it feel, Valencia? Who is the biggest monster now? Me or him?"

"Stop, stop, stop!" she screams. She breathes heavily, her chest rising and falling, and I expect another burst of tears, but surprisingly they don't come.

In fact, a blank expression blankets her face as she stares above my shoulder. "Can I go back to my room?"

My brow lifts. "Your room?" I wonder if she means the cage or—

"The one where I got ready for dinner. Can I sleep there tonight?" Her skin is pale, her makeup smeared all over her, but she keeps her chin high, even as her body trembles.

Control.

People learn to access it fast when unbearable pain has the power to destroy them. It's the only thing that can keep the person alive and sane.

I motion with my head for her to go, and with a nod, she does. Oddly, she remembers the way, her feet tapping against the floor as she walks to her room and finally reaches the door. I trail after her like the fucking fool I am.

"I just need time alone tonight. Tomorrow, you can do whatever you want to me." She doesn't wait for my response but goes inside, and I'm left standing there.

In normal circumstances, these things wouldn't fly with me, but I can give it to her tonight.

Valencia doesn't know that Max is nothing compared to the truth that awaits her once she is truly mine.

I have to make her psychologically vulnerable before firing the big gun, so to speak, because it will completely crush her.

And then she can become my protégée.

I head to my office, but halt midway, hitting the wall on my side as a deep unsettling in my stomach overwhelms me when I think about her catatonic state.

What will she do there alone?

The concept of caring about someone is so foreign to me I don't know what to do with it at first, but then my worry doesn't go away no matter how much I try to block it.

Instead of celebrating the death of Max and torturing someone myself, because there is always a victim lying around, all my thoughts are with Valencia and her dead, brown pools.

Wasn't that my ultimate goal? To destroy the little blind kitten living inside her and introduce her to the truth that's surrounded her life from the very beginning?

"Why now do I hate the idea of her torment?" The beast roaring in my ears demands to go back and check on her, to soothe her, even if it means angering her to gain some kind of emotion.

Anything but the blank fucking stare.

*V*alencia

As I numbly pad to the bathroom, I remove the crown from my head and drop it on the floor. Then I turn on the water in the shower stall and step inside, not bothering to undress. Immediately, the freezing water slaps my skin, not that I pay much attention to it.

I don't feel anything except the agony in my chest as images from the video play in my mind over and over again.

The little boy. How Max touched him. His voice. The implications of what would happen later.

Along with that comes all the years I've known Max. A kind man who had a wicked sense of humor, perfect grades, and always helped anyone who needed it. Sure, we didn't match as a couple, but I thought I'd forever keep in touch with him, because he deserved better than me.

He was always so understanding about my desire to hold off from sex. Even though months turned into years, he never pushed for it and just shrugged whenever I asked him if he needed it. Not that his answer would have changed anything, since I didn't want it.

Of course he didn't insist; he simply got off somewhere else.

My skin itches, so I grab the soap and rub the bare parts of my skin to the point of pain, hoping to wash away his disgusting preferences that stripped poor children of their innocence and killed so many souls.

But then another thought strikes me and the soap bar slides from my hands to my feet, hitting my already bruised toes.

Was it my fault that he touched them? Would something have been different if I provided him with sex on a daily basis? Would he have been able to control his cravings?

Is all those children's pain my fault? If I had seen his... his... I can't call it desires, just sickness. If I did that... would he have not done it?

I sob into the water, resting my forehead against the tile, my body shaking with my silent cries as tears fall, mixing with water as I let it all out.

Since I was a child, I always had one special rule. If I needed to cry, it had to be in the shower so no one would know something upset me.

That's why I asked Lachlan to give me access to this room.

"I'm sorry. I'm so sorry," I whisper to all those lost souls, and the cries don't stop. Because how can someone do that and then pretend to be a good person?

How can you hurt innocent children and sleep at night? And that man wanted to marry me?

For the first time, I'm glad he is gone.

At least this way he won't ever hurt anyone else, not that it's compensation to all those kids.

The water temperature changes and scalding heat surrounds me as strong arms spin me around and press me against the wall.

Lachlan holds me, his chest bare. He still has his pants on, along with a scowl on his face, as the spray soaks him to the skin. "Do you want to get pneumonia?" he growls, ripping my bodice and skirt and throwing them over his shoulder where they land with a splat on the floor. My undergarments follow, and then he kneels in front of me and carefully takes off the pointe shoes. I wince as my feet are finally free, and I wiggle my toes although it only brings more throbbing.

He examines one foot for a moment and then does the same with other, and finally, once I'm completely naked, he rises again so we face each other. "Do not apologize for what he did."

I could probably scream and say how inappropriate this is, that he doesn't have the right to stand here and look at me as if I'm his property. But that seems so silly after the revelation about Max, so beside the point.

Lachlan is a monster and a murderer, yes. Nothing changes that.

But at least he doesn't hide it or harm kids.

There is a code, not that it has any merit.

Killing is killing.

I tense in his arms, because he hurts women. What if he does the same to kids? I just assumed... "I don't," he murmurs, and I relax, finding some solace in that.

"Even you blame me for what he did," I finally say, coming to the realization that it's probably why he kidnapped me. "Otherwise, what was the need for all this?" I remove the pieces of hair that escaped the braid, but he wraps his hands around mine and pushes them above me.

"Trust me, Valencia, that's not it." His gruff voice only fuels my misery.

"You mean there is something worse?" Something crosses his face before he hides it from me, and I laugh, along with crying. "Oh my God, there is. Tell me now, Lachlan. Just deliver the sucker punch and end it."

The bubble that surrounded me has burst anyway; he might as well finish it.

"You are not ready for it."

I blink in confusion. "You think with time I will be?" I'm not sure any amount of time could have prepared me for Max, or Lachlan, for that matter.

"Following my rules will make it less tormenting."

"I've followed the rules my whole life. Look where I am now," I whisper, as our gazes clash, and for a second, my breath hitches at the intensity of his stare.

His sky blue eyes hold so many secrets, but underneath it all, I detect anguish that can break a weaker person.

Evil is not born either, right? His tendencies have to come from somewhere. "What made you the way you are?" My question is probably unexpected and not appropriate for the current situation, but with him and after what he put me through in the dance room, I never know how much time I have left.

I'd like to at least know the truth from him before I die.

"*Who*, Valencia. In the case of serial killers, the question is always who. We all have a creator," he informs me, and then maneuvers me right under the spray. I cry out from the pain in my feet, and he mutters something under his breath. The adjusted water quickly creates steam around us that envelops us in its warmth. He then proceeds to wash away all traces of makeup, then my hair and body. I wince as the soap touches my cuts and try to escape his touch, but he doesn't let me.

I don't protest much, completely emotionally drained. I'm not sure this shock will even pass. I should be hitting him and running away from him, yet here I stand and let him touch my most intimate places.

For how intimate this moment is, there is no connection between us. I've built walls around my heart and I won't let him in. I can't; he will so easily destroy me and not even blink.

Finally, he turns off the water, steps outside, and comes back with a towel to dry me off. He tugs a shirt onto me that reaches the middle of my thighs and then picks me up. In a few short strides, he dumps me on the bed as I focus my eyes on him. "Rest. There is always tomorrow."

"Thank you," I reply, rubbing my feet against each other, hoping to eliminate at least some of the ache. Propping on the pillow, I let the material soak up all the silent tears, as I whisper, "When I tried so hard to please everyone, I forgot to grow up." I'm so pathetic I feel disgust at my own self.

A normal person would have seen that her boyfriend and lover are evil people she should stay away from. But in my naivety, I placed one in the perfect box while the other in the seductive.

And both times, I ended up wrong.

He doesn't reply and I don't want him to. I close my eyes, as they burn from all the tears, and when I hear the door open, I think he is about to leave, but then the bed dips and something cold touches me.

My eyelids pop open only to come in direct contact with a big muzzle of a Newfoundland dog that licks my neck and then settles next to me.

He is so warm. Normally I'm afraid of dogs, but this one is so fluffy I forget everything and hug him close, needing the contact like never before.

And slowly, I drift to sleep, where I can find a small retreat from this nightmare.

*L*achlan

She is lying on the bed, breathing evenly as Chance's head settles into the crook between her shoulder and neck, sighing heavily and probably giving her all his warmth since she hugs him closer.

His watchful eyes are on me; he growls slightly and my brows lift. "That's your gratitude I gather." He shows me his teeth, so I lean down to tap his muzzle and he hides them, closing his eyes completely, content by the looks of it near Valencia.

Who wouldn't be?

Removing the strands of her wet hair from her face, I run the back of my hand over her soft skin that's still wet from her tears.

They should bring me pleasure, the suffering. But all it does is confuse me.

I want to destroy what brings her misery, but what do I do if that one thing is me?

Sliding my hand to her neck and breasts, I wonder what it would be like to keep her for myself as the only thing that has never been tainted by the dark.

Could I forget then? Not be plagued by the nightmares or voices that never leave, no matter how much I will them to?

Succumbing to these desires will mean betraying the promise I made a long time ago.

Besides, for Valencia, it's all the same. She will be my prisoner with no choice of escaping, and shouldn't it disgust me?

Try as I might though, the idea only excites me; there is no other man out there who gave her what she gets from me.

She is mine.

From the top of her brown hair to her bruised and crooked toes, every part of her belongs to me. We are connected in a way she has yet to discover.

This connection was supposed to be her downfall.

But now I think it will be mine.

Valencia

Groaning, I shift onto my side, burrowing into the pillow and hoping to evade the heat, but it follows me. My body is covered in sweat. My eyelids flutter open as I blink a few times at the ceiling that reflects the moonlight.

I blindly search for the blanket to throw it away, when instead, I find a hand thrown over my middle, and the heat next to me registers for what it is.

Or rather *who* it is.

Lachlan.

Looking at him, I see he is lying on his back, breathing evenly, one hand under his head while the other is on me, as if he just put it there to make sure I'm still in one position.

The dog is lounging on the floor, snoring loudly with not a care in the world it seems, while the light breeze comes from the open window along with the heat erupting from the ductwork.

Why the hell keep the window open, then?

But then it dawns on me that my captor is asleep while I'm awake and I can easily slip through his fingers if I want to.

Slowly, I pick up his hand and place it between us, then hold my breath as he huffs and lies fully on his back with his other hand stretched up. Once free, I get up on my knees and crawl over him, and as soon as my toes dig into the Persian carpet, I'm ready to do the hallelujah dance.

I quickly run to the window on the way, checking the curtains, and mentally thanking my dad for teaching me to escape the house from a window, even if it's high, in case of fire.

Come to think of it, Dad was obsessed with fire and was always afraid something might burn. He even hated when Mom used lighters to light the candles and at some point just forbade them in our house.

This is only the second floor and the ground is not very far below. The bed leg has a good spot to wrap the curtain around. I tug on the curtain to snatch it away and they screech over the bar. Wincing, I check over my shoulder on Lachlan, but he is in the same position, so I exhale in relief.

With another few pulls, it falls to the floor, where I pick it up and quickly proceed as planned. I secure one tight knot around the leg of the bed and check, tugging on it hard. It doesn't even budge.

Finally satisfied with my efforts, I fling the rest out the window and put on Lachlan's socks I found lying around. There is snow and I won't survive for long without them. I can find an escape through the maze, and then someone will find me.

Or that's the outcome I pray for anyway. He might have not hurt me, but he is still a man who kidnapped me and made me experience horrible things.

And I definitely shouldn't feel safe in his arms, and that's what happened back in the shower. I heard that victims develop some kind of feelings for their captors over time and grow attached to them, some syndrome I think.

But they spend years with them, and I did what? Four or five days, and most of those days I've spent alone in a cell.

I get up on the windowsill and climb over, holding the curtain tightly in my hands, and slowly go down while gritting my teeth from the burning of the cloth.

Sliding lower and lower, I hold back a cry of pain until I finally reach the ground. I drop to my feet and then instantly to my knees as a jolt of pain is sent from my foot upward.

I forgot I overdid it on the dance floor, and the carpet was much softer. How will I freaking run?

That's why I became a ballerina and not a freaking police detective. I just don't have a head for grand schemes.

I turn around and yelp as the man stands in front of me, exhaling a big puff of smoke into the air. "So what's the next stage of this grand escape?"

Lachlan.

How did he manage to get here so fast? He was just on the bed. As if reading my mind, he elaborates, taking a long pull on his cigarette. "Since you were amusing being so proud of yourself, I decided to let you run the show, but I'm really impressed." He whistles. "You are a survivor after all, darling." He tries to remove the errant strands of my hair, but I slap his hand away, stepping back.

Right. The monster never sleeps. "I hate you, Lachlan. With all my heart," I hiss into his face and expect him to snap at me, but instead, he just laughs. The sound bounces off the walls as he catches his breath, throws the cigarette on the concrete, and steps on it.

Then he says, "Get back inside the house, Valencia."

Fuck this.

Without thinking, I dart to the right, putting all the pressure on my feet, and run in the direction of the maze. The frigid air burns my lungs, but I don't care about any of it.

Everything is better than point-blank surrender.

I don't get far though, as he wraps his hand around my hair, and I cry out as he roughly pulls me back, spins me around, and then props me on his shoulder, moving back in the direction of his house.

And I want to kick him and scratch his back, do something, but when I notice the knife in his back pocket, my mind starts swirling.

If I hurt him and get to his phone... the possibilities are just enormous.

I quiet down and he slaps me on the ass. Fucking jerk! "Why so quiet all of a sudden?"

He takes us past a shocked Levi, who just gapes at us and then trails after us, the china on his tray rattling loudly with his footsteps. I expect to go back to the cage, but instead end up in his room.

He throws me on the bed and I huff, landing on my back, and have a second to see myself all flushed in my reflection before he pulls at my hand so I sit up. He snaps his fingers to Levi and he's quickly by my side, placing the cup of steaming tea by the smell of it in my palms while digging a spoon in some honey and then swirling it inside the tea. He gives it to me and I raise my brow.

What the hell is going on here?

"In case you get sick from running in the cold." He exhales heavily. "You shouldn't have done it, child." He looks like a good man, really. All grandpa-like and stuff, but his words bring little comfort.

Instead, I become defensive. "Free me from this nightmare, and I'll be all healthy."

"Child—" he starts, but Lachlan scolds him.

"Enough of this bullshit." He doesn't add anything else, but it's probably a silent command as Levi picks up his tray and, with one last pleading glance my way, shuts the door behind him.

"Don't even think about spilling it on the floor, Valencia. Fucking drink it." The barely visible anger skimming over him finally registers in my mind, and my eyes widen as I realize he is not as calm as he pretends to be.

He disappears into the bathroom while I sip the tea, welcoming the warmth that spreads through me and calms my sore throat.

Knife.

Keep your focus on the knife.

He comes back with a wet cloth and kneels in front of me, pressing it to my aching foot while growling, "Keep following your idiotic plans, and you won't ever dance again."

I shrug, acting all nonchalant. "Considering you intend to keep me here, I don't see me dancing anyway. This way at least I will keep my dignity intact." He doesn't appreciate my sarcasm apparently, as his hold on me tightens, but he says nothing.

He gets up to move something, and I use it as my chance, quickly taking a longer sip and then throwing the hot liquid on him, as he shouts, "Fuck!" I use this moment to stumble on him and snatch the knife away while he steadies me, and that's when I press it against his throat, using all my power to hold the blade near his artery.

He stills, as we both stand in the pool of tea, and then, pushing his chest toward the bed, I order, "Sit on the bed." He is more threatening when he looms over me.

His brow rises, but he follows the command easily and drops onto the bed while I still keep the knife close. "Give me your phone or I will slice your throat." The words sound unconvincing even to me, so he places his hands behind his back on the sheets and smirks at me. "Go ahead."

"I'm not joking, Lachlan. You are vile. I won't feel sorry for killing you." One big, fat lie, as I can't even imagine ever taking a life.

It destroys a soul, even if it's in self-defense. But he has to value his life, right? What do they say about serial killers? That they are narcissistic creatures. He won't want to die.

"And I say be my guest. Come on. Kill me, Valencia, and end it all," he orders, sitting up closer to me, and he takes my hand with the blade, putting the tip of the knife right below his ear while the rest of the sharp edge slightly grazes his neck. "But do it right. You start from here to slowly cut the artery that will spill blood, but the victim will still breathe and gaze at you with fear, because nothing at this point will help him. Prolong sliding the blade to create a high that you will rarely reach from any other weapon, especially not a gun."

"You are sick."

"Torture is an art form. Either do it right or don't fucking hold a weapon," he states, and then motions for me to continue. "Come on. Do it. End your misery." He mocks my state as if what he makes me go through is nothing.

As if I shouldn't even call it misery.

Tightening my hold on the handle, I still while my raspy breath fills the space between us, and I finally murmur, "If I don't do it, you will—"

"Whatever it is, the answer is yes," he replies, his voice turning low and deep. Yet I still don't move, my hands trembling as I understand with clarity that he will let me do it if I decide to go through with it.

But we know I won't be able to. Shouldn't I though? For everyone else so they won't experience this. Yes, he killed Max for a reason, but Max wouldn't have even been on his radar if it weren't for me.

And I'm not guilty of any crimes.

His hands end up on my waist, and he suddenly picks me up. Before I can even blink, I'm straddling his lap as he holds my gaze. He places a palm at the end of my spine while his other one travels up, up, up, and fists my hair, bringing my mouth closer to his, with the knife still firmly pressed against his neck. "Do what you truly want, Valencia," he murmurs, and my breath hitches when my body instantly reacts to his nearness.

Revulsion rushes through me. How can I be aroused by him? I should hate him, and that's it. Yet deep down under this hate are the feelings he has inspired in me since Italy, and I can't fight them.

Or rather, I can't kill him, because he holds a piece of me. And as weak and pathetic as that is, I can't hide from this truth.

The knife falls softly on the bed at the same moment his mouth crashes on mine, demanding entrance, and I allow it, sharing with him a kiss filled with hate, doom, and hopelessness, all at the same time. There is nothing gentle about the nip of his teeth, his aggressive pulls, and his tongue that with each meeting of mine stakes a claim that should never be there.

The kiss is coated with anger and fury, but also with overwhelming desire that sends liquid fire through my entire system, longing for the satisfaction and pleasure only he can provide. It's as if my consciousness finds solace in his touches that can for a moment in time erase our circumstances and leave us in a cocoon that nothing can break.

And I succumb to it, needing it to survive.

Wrapping my arms around his neck, I bring us even closer, not leaving an inch between us as my heat touches his hard-on. A moan slips past my lips, and he lets go of my mouth, trailing kisses down my neck while I throw my head back, groaning at his bites that will for sure leave marks for everyone to see.

I don't dwell on it much as he rolls my shirt over my head and sends it flying behind me. His tongue circles my pointed nipple and licks the tip but then bites on it hard. I cry out in pain, scratching the back of his head, but still seeking his touch as it sends prickles of electricity through my skin.

"There is beauty in the ache, angel," he rasps, immediately licking the abused flesh and driving me even wilder. "I know you like it long and hard, darling, but tonight it's going to be only hard." His hand travels down my stomach, and it dips under his touch as he skims his fingers over my skin and tangles them in my soft curls. "Otherwise, you might feel too guilty about it afterward." I gasp into his mouth as he buries his fingers inside my heated flesh, twisting them against my inner walls while thumbing my clit. "Ah, already so wet for me. Who are you burning for, Valencia?" he asks and pulls my head down so our eyes meet. "Who is making this tight pussy so wet it practically drips on me?"

I don't answer, because answering means thinking, and all I want is to concentrate on the pleasure spreading within me, a roaring inferno that burns and burns, demanding fulfillment. He pulls again, but this time my scalp hurts and a moan slips past me.

"Respond to me." He quickens his pressure on my clit, almost taking me there, but then stops all movement, leaving me with a maddening ache.

"Please," I beg, because at this point, I can forget about dignity, but he just tsks his tongue.

"Ah, no, it doesn't work like that. Who, Valencia?" Our gazes meet, his molten and mine probably confused, but the granite edges of his face speak volumes.

He needs me to surrender.

And I do, hating myself for it while my body weeps in relief. "You do."

He gifts me with his sinister smile, as he murmurs against my lips, "Good girl." I yelp as he flips me onto my back and then gasp, fisting the sheets, as he buries his face in my heated flesh, his tongue taking long licks, swiping the walls of my core as it clenches around it.

Didn't he say hard and not long? What is this torture, then?

He french kisses it for a moment before latching onto my clit, pressing and massaging it with his lips and tongue. His every flick and touch highlights the pressure building inside me, and I arch my back, but he pushes me back with his hand, stilling my movements. Digging his fingers into my ass, he raises it up, swirling the tip of his tongue through my folds, teasing, yet only arousing me more. He shifts to my thighs, sucking on the skin to the point of pain, and I moan, closing them around his head as I tangle my hand in his hair, but it doesn't deter him. He continues to torture me with light flicks as his finger slides into me, finding the perfect spot to drive me insane yet still not give me the pleasure my body seeks.

On his bite on my clit, my eyes snap open, as I rasp, "Lachlan, please." Any other words are impossible to me. My need is so strong that it borders on desperation.

I don't remember anything besides this man who awakens my entire system and makes the outside world disappear, creating a cocoon where right and wrong don't exist, and evil is just a passing thought.

I hear the belt buckle being unfastened, and then he places his palms on my knees, bringing me closer to the edge, and with one swift move, he flips me over again, and we end up on the floor, with me straddling him once more. My head goes dizzy and I can barely comprehend what's going on, as he growls in approval.

"Have to keep you off-balance so you feel nothing but this." And that's when he enters me, filling me to the hilt. My arms automatically wrap around his neck as my cry echoes in the room, followed by his low groan, our lips inches away from each other. "See this?" I follow his gaze to see us connected to each other. Then he raises me up and I instantly feel empty. His purple head glistens from my wetness, and as I watch, he sinks it back inside me. I moan as he catches a nipple with his mouth, sucking it hard before licking around it. "My darkness and your pureness will never change that. Here or anywhere else, when I take you and your beautiful body answers my call? You. Are. Mine. And no one else's." I rise again even though my knees shake, but he stills my move. "Slow and steady."

"No, I want hard," I plead, but he doesn't listen, controlling each rise, slowly dragging his cock in and out of me, making me feel every touch and harsh move, while his hands grip me harder.

He continues this for what seems like forever, the only sounds present in the room are of flesh slapping and my panting breaths as I gulp as much air as possible while clenching around him. My body barely keeps up with him, because I'm tired, so tired, yet I need for him to finish this.

To give me what he promised.

Sweat is coating my skin, and finally he fists my hair once again, kissing me deeply and cutting off my oxygen while simultaneously filling me up again. And this time it reaches that place where everything goes quiet.

And then roars back again with heat and pleasure and agony rushing through me. A moan dies inside my throat, swallowed by his kiss. I'm about to drop on him, but he doesn't let me.

Instead, he lifts me up one last time, and this time I feel him spilling into a condom, letting go of my mouth only to suck and bite on my neck as I throw my head back, giving him easier access. I don't even know when he had the time to put one on, but then he kept me in a trance through most of it.

Breathing heavily, I catch as much air as possible as slowly everything comes back and the picture becomes clear again, where the fire is finally extinguished and only hollowness is left.

And realization washes over me like an ocean wave, reminding me that this can never be right, even if it felt so just a second ago. "I hate you," I whisper. He doesn't say anything, just places me on the bed, and I scoot back, ignoring how exhausted my body feels.

He removes his pants and gets into bed, and I know our conversations are over for tonight, because he is satiated and doesn't need anything from me for now.

Rolling onto my back, I run my fingers through my sweaty hair and wince. I'm surrounded by the reminder of what we did, and he won't let me ever forget it.

But then again, I can't blame him either, because not once did he force anything on me.

"This doesn't change anything," I say, staring at myself and hating even my reflection. For how weak should a woman be to allow a monster to touch her?

He throws a blanket over us, and orders, "Sleep, Valencia." And although we don't say anything for a long time, neither of us is asleep.

This has changed something, and the connection we've experienced scares me way more than everything else.

Because if his darkness doesn't stop my desire for him, what will?

CHAPTER SIXTEEN

Lachlan, 10 years old

*P*astor Cane continues to read the Bible to us in class as he writes the important parts on the board while everyone copies it to their notebook.

For our "special" leverage, we still have to attend religion class every week with everyone else.

I press on the paper, and the pressure must be strong, because the tip of the pencil breaks. I quickly glance at the pastor, but he doesn't seem to notice, as he continues his task.

Exhaling in relief, I urgently yet quietly search for a new one on my table but don't find any. I scan our small classroom with around fifteen single tables that are occupied by boys only who wear similar white shirts and brown pants, and their hair is buzz cut, since a longer length pisses them off.

The pastor doesn't believe we should share a space with girls, because they can seduce us from our paths. Until the time comes for us to marry one of our own. But even then, he will decide the best match. We are nothing but his property after all; he reminds us each week that we get to spend with his guests.

Weeks where we are held hostage in the special room while dirty, old men *use us for their sick desires. Nothing is off limits to them, from pain to demands to companionship. They even like to cuddle sometimes, and no matter how much you want to vomit all over them, you can't.*

Because the punishment from "upsetting" them is far greater and in the long haul is not worth it. Pastor will make sure all the touches are nothing compared to what he can dish out.

I should know, considering I rebelled the most.

Anger builds in me at the thought of that man and the things he has done to me the last time he visited, but I push it back, because I have more serious matters at hand.

Like making sure Pastor Cane won't see me panicking, or else everyone will be punished for my behavior.

At the right corner, a few rows in front of me, Logan catches my eye and lifts his chin, silently asking what's going on.

Logan is my only friend, although I'm not sure what we have is friendship. We only chat leaving school and on the way here. Until you are thirteen years old, you are forbidden to interact with other kids outside your household. But there is always this deep understanding between us, shared pain and all.

Apparently they plan for a big hoopla once we turn teenagers, although I have my suspicions.

We won't be as pretty then. The "guests" are only interested in small kids; they don't want older ones. That's why after around fifteen years old they find us suitable brides.

They say those are the rules for us, that we are special and selected just for this place. That God himself gave him this opportunity, and we should be happy about it.

Why then did each one of us probably weep at night? I can't imagine anyone accepting normally what they have done to us on a monthly basis. Other kids who don't share the burden with us don't seem much happier either.

Just a never-ending circle of misery.

I show Logan the pencil and he nods, fishing for one on his side. He glances at the pastor, and satisfied he is still very much occupied with the board, Logan throws it my way and I catch it right on time.

An exhale leaves me, and I'm about to go back to writing, when all the shifting moves my book to the corner of the table. Before I can stop it, the book falls on the floor with a loud smacking noise, and all attention is on me.

Correction.

Their terrified attention is on me.

Since it's too late for any damage control, I look at Pastor Cane, who pauses midair with the chalk in his hand and his back rigid. He takes a few beats before spinning around to face us, his assertive, cold eyes scanning the environment to find the source of the disturbance.

He slowly puts the chalk back on the table, taking his time dusting his fingers off while everything inside me stills, and I mentally prepare myself for what comes next.

One of the rules is to never piss off Pastor Cane, as he has the power of a higher rank, meaning his punishment can never be undone. And he is second in command after Pastor, thus he is allowed to do whatever the hell he pleases with selected kids as long as they will heal before guests come.

And we usually always do, since, after his treatments, we have doctors tending to us. And if bruises don't fade... well, then there is always makeup to hide it.

"Lachlan," he says, his voice barely controlling the fury that comes from him, and then he clicks his fingers. "Get up and step outside. Everyone else, continue to write and open your books. If it's not done by the time I'm back here...." He doesn't need to finish his sentence.

We all know.

I get out and he grabs me harshly by the nape, bending me a little as he drags me in the direction of his office. We enter, and then he goes to the wall near his library and presses the button, and the wall sides open.

Then he takes me downstairs to his basement, where humidity greets us and I hear the distinctive hissing sounds.

Snakes.

The entire area is covered in glass walls that hold various snakes, spiders, and lizards that gaze at you like you are their favorite prey and they can't wait to dig their fangs into you.

He places me on the metal chair pinned right in the middle, straps my legs and arms so I won't be able to move, and then seethes into my face. "You will learn how to respect me, boy." I don't say anything else, although everything in me rises at the idea of what comes next. "You think I don't know how resistant you are with Pastor? And how you tried to tell on my son?" he asks, and I grit my teeth when I remember Matt.

He kept picking on Anna, but no one said anything. So I told on him to the minor security guards, and of course, they must have tattled on me.

Fuck them. I'm not even sorry for swearing in church. "Boys who point their fingers and accuse others are sinners fit for hell, Lachlan." He straps my mouth with tape, and adds, "You will spend a few hours here and then take a shower once I'm done. So your aunt won't know about this or she might get upset. You don't want that, do you?" I shake my head, even though I hate myself for it.

I hate whatever requires me to comply with their orders.

Satisfied with all this, he leaves, shuts the door, and probably presses the button as I hear the sound of the glass door opening, allowing the bigger snakes to slide out and have free rein.

Three of them slide back and forth at the far end, making loud noises that grate on my nerves, but I try to think about something else.

Like a life I will have once it's all over and I can go to college. I will take Aunt Jessica and Anna with me, and we can build our life there. That stupid asshole of an uncle brought her into this fucked-up community that lived by their religion and did unspeakable things.

But then the snakes turn and one of them slides closer and closer to me, rising to my level. My heart beats rapidly, while I do my best to keep eye contact with her.

Sometimes it helps, and I almost exhale in relief when she hisses and goes back to the floor. They were probably fed before this hoopla, as none of them pays me attention for a few hours.

But then one of them comes back, rises, and I understand that's a battle I lost. She swiftly leans to me and bites me right on the foot, and I scream although it's muffled through the tape, and then two of the others follow. However, it's not as interesting for them and they let go of me, while sweat and blood coats my body.

Those are dry bites, as the snakes were stripped of their venom.

And I have nothing else to do but wait in the dark room surrounded by lizards and wait for my freedom.

Just because I broke a pencil.

ew York, New York
January 2018

*V*alencia
This is what happens when you let emotions rule your life.

Saying this to myself doesn't help though as I wash my face in the sink. Every one of my aching muscles causes me to replay last night over and over in my mind.

Catching my reflection in the mirror, my hands fist as I see several hickeys scattered on my neck, collarbone, and even breasts. The fucker marked everything he could, as if taunting me with this.

So I'll never forget the devil seduced me easily.

But is he a devil in my mind though? He is the man who awakened dormant feelings inside me back in Italy, showing up in my life unexpectedly, yet spinning it in a way that made me feel alive. I'm not sure my subconscious can separate the two—or wants to, for that matter.

Shouldn't there be goodness in him despite all the flaws?

Tapping my foot loudly on the wooden floor, I try to glance over the guy's shoulder to see if my coffee is ready, but he is so freaking tall I don't see anything.

Huffing in annoyance, I check the time and groan. It's only five minutes till my museum tour starts, and it won't be as fun without my morning coffee.

I decide to go to the side, and due to the long line, I bump my shoulder against the stranger's and he turns his smoldering blue eyes on me.

Dangerously handsome doesn't even begin to describe him. His knuckles that drum on the counter pause midair, while he gives me the most sinister smile.
"Hi, there."

Blushing, because he totally caught me staring at him with my mouth open, I just nod and smile at the barista as he holds my cup in front of me. "Double espresso." I wiggle my fingers for it and he chuckles as he gives it to me. With one last side-eye to the man who still holds his gaze on me, I dart to the door, but to my utter horror, I slip on a wet spot and the double espresso goes flying and lands on the floor with a loud splat, while strong hands catch me from behind just before I fall any farther.

"You all right?" the deep voice asks. With nothing but his smell surrounding me and with my heart beating rapidly in my chest, I know I'm not.

Everything is freaking humiliating; that's what it is. "Yeah, I'm so sorry."

The barista guy comes to my aid, mopping the mess and shrugging. "No big deal."

So much for a perfect first morning in Florence as the "new" me.

Although creating big messes is so me. Groaning, I cover my face with my hands while the stranger speaks with amusement lacing his tone. "It's just coffee."

Just coffee?

Glaring at him, I point at it. "No, it's not just a coffee. It's my morning espresso on my vacation, right before my museum tour. I've been looking forward to it for a few days and now it's ruined." Oh my God, he probably thinks I'm a psycho who seethes like this to a stranger.

Mortification fills me, but instead of revulsion, something entirely different flashes in his eyes.

Curiosity. "Here, take mine." He places his untouched coffee in my hands and then winks. "And I think we are on the same tour, so let's hurry to make sure your vacation starts right." And surprisingly, as guarded as I am about my life, I follow him as we chat all the way to the museum and then spend the entire day together.

And soon, I think that slip was the best thing that could have happened to me on vacation.

Shaking my head and bringing myself back to the present, I understand now everything was carefully planned to lure me into his web.

Was any of it true?

Lachlan was nowhere in sight when I woke up, and it filled me with relief, because I just had no clue how to act around him when his dry sense of humor found everything I did or said amusing.

He is like two different men with me. There is this harsh killer and then the passionate and tender man who needs to own me. But none of it changes the fact that waking up with him is out of the question for me.

I rush to take a shower to wash away our mutual smells, hating the idea of him on me, even if yesterday I was a willing participant.

My body shivers from the cold, and with one last glance, I step out of the shower and dry myself off. It's when I'm quickly grabbing the shirt that still lies on the floor that something dawns on me.

Knowing Lachlan and whatever fucked-up plans he has in mind for me, shouldn't he provide me clothes too? Yes, it's his room, but he plans everything.

Even if I'm nothing but the prey he caught, the man is still very much possessive of me. I can't image him being okay with me strolling through the place wearing nothing but this.

I walk to the wardrobe and open it up, but find it empty.

So much for my freaking hope. I try the drawers and other things, but find nothing except his clothes. I huff in frustration, adjusting the towel that almost slips off.

And then my eyes land on the chair in the far corner, and my heart stills. There lay shorts, lingerie, and a hoodie along with Uggs.

My brows furrow as I snatch them up and quickly put them on, all while wondering what kind of serial killer this guy is if he provides all this for me.

What's his agenda? No matter what it is though, it scares the hell out of me, because this is nothing but madness.

It's as if he waits for me to be cooked just right in the oven, before placing me on the table and feeding on all my miseries. Truly, just what does his kidnapping imply?

A voice from behind me startles me and I spin around to see Maria holding a tray of food in her hand. Do they have orders for me to eat all the freaking time or what? Since the moment I came here, they always dangle a tray of some sort in front of me. "You're awake." She places it on the small table and smiles while passing by me. "Lachlan said to bring you breakfast and let you know that you are free to explore the mansion as you wish."

"I'm free to explore?" I repeat like a parrot with nothing but disbelief pouring from me.

Why is he giving me freedom? Is this another tricky plan? It must be; a man like him won't leave yesterday's deed unpunished.

She nods, and then asks, "Do you need anything?"

"I'm fine." At my answer, she beams and then quickly disappears while I just blink, wondering if I'm stupid or what. Maybe what happens with me is no biggie for the staff and Lachlan. I imagine they've played this game before.

They sure don't follow any scripts like I've seen in movies. I'm a prisoner who can walk freely wherever!

Ignoring the breakfast, I go into the hall with dark walls holding odd pictures that remind me of Picasso, displaying the cubism artistic style.

Considering this style focused on seeing the art from a three-dimensional view, meaning it has more than one meaning depending on who gazed at it, it doesn't surprise me Lachlan likes it.

Sort of implying everyone has their own truth.

The man even has to make statements with his own decor.

As I walk to the stairs, I count at least five rooms including "mine." Why would he need such a big house just for himself?

He doesn't host serial killer events, does he?

Shaking my head from the idiotic thoughts, I hop down a few steps and end up on the first floor, which has three directions to choose from.

One to the dining room with dancing space, one to what I assume is the kitchen and terrace if the smells of freshly baked bread are anything to go by, and finally another that leads with a narrow path to somewhere.

Taking a deep breath, I step that way, but quickly hide behind a column as I hear Levi's voice. "He wants red sheets, red. He doesn't like white. They annoy him. I always have to do everything myself," he instructs someone, and then passes by without noticing me. Once he disappears behind the kitchen wing, I look once again where he came from and dart there.

Maybe it's my chance for an escape?

I see a path leading to some massive wooden doors that remind me of an office. If I were as powerful as Lachlan, I'd probably make it one.

But then my eyes land on a wall that is moved back, with a security code pad next to it, and narrow stairs that lead down.

As in a secret passage? This place seriously used some fairytales for inspiration, but maybe that's like a safety exit? In case shit hits the fan, they can run off here.

With this hopeful thought in mind, I go into the stairwell and shiver slightly as doom falls over me, sending unpleasant sensations through me where nothing but cold and... death greet me.

It takes me around five minutes to get downstairs, and when I do, I look around only to see several metal rooms that remind me of prison cells. I see only one light bulb above that brightens the place, but it keeps flickering.

A buzzing sound disturbs my ears, and I understand this is not an exit.

More like another secret that will only cement my fear.

Right when I'm about to go back up, because oddly enough it seems safer than this place, one of the doors opens and a beautiful blonde saunters out of it, flipping her long locks back with a breezy gesture.

She is wearing tight pink shorts along with a white T-shirt, and knee-high socks with pink boots. Her huge blue eyes study me for a moment as she tips her head to the side, and then blinks rapidly. "Hey, doll! Where did you come from?" She sounds cheerful as she bounces in place, nothing but friendliness coming from her.

I want to reply, but my words still in my throat, and instead I swallow as panic swirls through my veins.

Because her hands and legs have blood smeared all over them.

*L*achlan

Twisting the pen through my fingers, I lean back in my chair while counting down the numbers in my head, hoping to evade this fucking obsession that doesn't let me do anything but watch Valencia on my screen as she occupies my room. I turned it off half an hour ago to rein in the chaos that erupts when she is concerned.

I still can't fucking believe she managed to get to the ground floor with that plan of hers, but I watched her and she did everything right, so there was no worry something would happen to her. The hope, the adrenaline, the fear... brought a glow from within her in a way that mesmerized me, and yet...

Anger filled my chest at the idea of her harming herself, so I ran downstairs to make sure she'd be all right. If it hadn't been winter, I would have allowed her to roam around the maze, searching for an escape while making my presence known so she'd use all her instincts to survive.

But I couldn't stomach the idea of her in agony.

And that's a problem.

She gave herself to me last night, but try as I might, it doesn't bring me pleasure; in fact, there is a bitter taste of revulsion.

One should never use another's body without consent, and although her body was into it, her soul wasn't.

It was the one single thing I had promised myself, and I failed.

I manage somehow to fail at all things when it comes to Valencia.

I get up and lean on the window as scenes from our meeting play in my mind. My plan escalated in a direction neither of us saw coming, and in a way, I hate I went to Italy after her.

Had I stayed, kidnapping her wouldn't involve all this. The conflict, the discomfort, the confusion.

All emotions that simply never existed in my new life.

"You are awfully eager for this trip. Fan of renaissance?"

She nods excitedly, gaping at the Michelangelo painting and sighs. "There is something magical about that particular era. Leonardo Da Vinci. Raphael. Michelangelo. They were geniuses who created such beauty... people who lived by their own rules." Her last words are said with a little sadness. She is probably comparing her timid lifestyle to the vividness of those who lived before her.

"Da Vinci is considered one of the greatest scientists of all time with his drawings of human anatomy and helicopters."

"Yes, along with Nicola Tesla," she says and frowns, rubbing her chin. Rarely anyone adds anything about Tesla; he is almost as forgotten as everyone else. What a genius though."

"Interested in physics?" I ask, and she laughs, motioning for me to follow the guide who walks farther into the museum, with tourists posing and snapping pics.

"Creation is an art form, you know? People are used to considering something artistic as a creation, but truth be told, we are all artists just in different jobs."

Gazing at her beaming face as she so passionately explains her points, unfamiliar emotions fill my chest and I do my best to squish them inside me.

Regret has no place in my perfectly laid plans, because it goes hand-in-hand with pity. And the minute those emotions settle inside someone, he cannot do anything levelheaded.

Because everything else centers on the happiness of another person. "This is our final destination; after this, we have a lunch break scheduled, and then we will go explore Florence. Ladies, get ready for amazing shopping," the tour guide says cheerfully, and it is followed with groans from the men and squeals from the ladies.

I look at Valencia, and offer, "How about lunch? Pizza and pasta sound good?" She doesn't eat on a regular basis. The reports stated as much, but she is on vacation.

I have a feeling everything will be different with her here.

She hesitates, removing some hair from her face, but then nods, her cheeks flushed. "I'd love to."

"Valencia Moore, please don't forget to get your refund for the part of the trip you missed since you joined us a day late," the tour guide shouts, and tension comes back at once.

Moore.

I should always remember her last name and what capturing her represents.

Apparently, I haven't done it enough. Women never evoked anything but a hard-on for me, and that lasted only as long as they could keep my attention on sex, which rarely lasted an hour.

Valencia though? She is on my mind twenty-four fucking seven, and this only intensifies the burning in my chest, which nothing can explain.

Pinching my nose, I think about going back to her and following my plan; the faster she is gone from here, the faster the emotions will settle and become nothing but memories in my good-for-nothing life.

I hear the clearing of a throat and my eyes snap open to see Levi standing in the doorway. "We have a problem in the underground."

I had redesigned the house specifically concentrating on the underground, since it's where all the magic happened. No one had access to it without my or Levi's permission, and only trusted ones entered. It's not as if I chased around the town hunting willing protégés, but I chose the best of the best or those who everyone pitied.

Like Shon, he was so pathetic on the New York street near my club that I figured the kid needed a little help reining in all his emotions. I generally don't believe in killing for killing.

There should be a greater mission that sends the right message to the masses.

"Then handle it." What the fuck is wrong with him? Protégés can play and learn all they want three days a week while he keeps an eye on them. I usually participate when I'm showing them something or there is an extreme situation. The rest of the training happens in the special apartment block in Brooklyn, only because Arson insisted he would handle it.

Speaking of Arson. "Arson is there to train his new student, right?" One of the reasons I can sit here and search for a fucking needle in the hay.

The answer is so close I can almost physically feel it in my heart, but it's still invisible.

Speeding up the process seems like the best course of action. I grab my phone and quickly type a message to Jaxon regarding a new finding, when Levi clears his throat again. I motion for him to continue then get the hell out so I can focus on the situation at hand. He timidly speaks up and my insides freeze.

"Valencia is there."

$\mathcal{V}$alencia

Stepping back, I glance around for an escape route, because this freaking blonde is coated in blood! But she just huffs, rolling her eyes. "Honey, don't get scared. It's not mine." She thinks that's what scares me? She leans closer, whispering through the corner of her mouth, "You should see the other guy. He is drowning in it after I cut open his artery. Perfect cut on the first try."

She puffs her chest while I just blink, faintly replying, "You don't say." I need to get the hell out of here. Who is this person? Does he have a school for the people here, or are they a gang?

"Yes. I'm talented." She pins her blonde locks higher on her head, and the gesture emphasizes the fullness of her breasts. "Torture is an art form."

This is so surreal I have no idea how to describe it, but at the same time, her words play on repeat in my head. I used to say that everything is an art form, depending who looks at it. But how can one be artistic about killing and be breezy about it? Are people just

devices for them, like for a painter his brushes, or for a dancer
the stage?

Art usually gives solace to a person in a way that he or she can bury
their pain, at least in my experience. Does torture bring serial killers
the same? Temporary escape from the demons that haunt them, even
if they became said demons?

"Doll, you're all pale. Haven't killed before?" she asks worriedly and
pats me on the back with her freaking blood-smeared hand, exhaling
heavily. "It's only hard the first time. After that, it's a safe ride," she
says to me and looks around. "Which one is your room?"

I finally find my voice. "I'm new. How many are there here?"
Playing along seems like the best bet in this situation; maybe at least I
will get some explanation.

So far, it has been nothing but a mess that each new truth confuses
me and sends me down the rabbit hole.

"Ten." She points at the nametag of the room behind her. "This
one is number two, belongs to Arson. I'm not familiar much with what
happens in the others though." She pouts, and that's when a guy
emerges from the room, and I have to do a double take, because he
is huge.

I crane my neck to study him better and to see various tattoos
gracing his skin as he stands in jeans, boots, and elastic gloves while his
blue hair is neatly put together in a tight man bun. He flips a lighter
through his fingers while scanning me and then addresses the blonde.
"Mina, get back inside."

Mina? As in the one who killed Max? A gasp escapes me, but she
just waves it off. "No worries, doll. No sex is happening here. I probably forgot to cut off his freaking—" Whatever she continues to say is
lost on me as Arson pushes her inside and then, with one last glance at
me, shuts the door behind them.

Okay then.

Clearly the guy is unfazed with my presence.

Taking a deep breath, I decide to push back all normal emotions
and reactions to the situation, because panicking or acting like an idiot
—I've done enough of that already—will bring nothing but losses.

I can lose my shit once all this is over.

I pass by different doors, and through most of them, I hear groans and moans. Somewhere there is drilling and then screams.

Filled with nothing but agony and torment.

Pressing my palms against my ears, I reach room number one and it says *Lachlan,* and there is a security code pad next to it.

With shaking fingers, I tap his date of birth into the keypad, even though it's a very far-fetched idea, but that's the only information I can work with. Isn't the password always something easy that no one expects?

Red light and enter the right password. Did I truly think he would put such an easy code?

"What do you think can destroy a powerful person?" I ask, munching on ice cream as we stroll down the road on the sunny Monday after yet another trip where they spoke about various renaissance leaders.

"Weaknesses."

"What do you mean?"

"If you possess something they hold dear to their heart... a powerful person will snap. It's just a matter of time."

Can I be, despite all odds, his weakness?

I type my date of birth, and it opens with my surprised gasp, and once I'm behind it, the door automatically closes.

And while I should be worried about it and think about repercussions, I can't.

Because the picture that greets me leaves me speechless.

One single table with pins and staples and a chair sit right in the middle of the room. Three walls surround it; each one of them acts like a bulletin board.

The one on the left from me has numerous pictures of young people either smiling into a camera or laughing while posing for the picture during some kind of camp.

Along with every happy picture, there is the same pic of them at the same age, but there is nothing but sadness. Gloomy teenagers mostly wearing black, or having pain along with anger flashing in their eyes.

And finally the third pictures have them, I assume, all grown up and with lethal expressions. It's as if they are all different people, but I can see traces of their pasts in them.

By the pain still present in them.

I read aloud the few nametags. "Shon, Sociopath, Arson, Jaxon, Isabella, Amalia." Are they his students? Does he teach something?

And then I move my gaze to the wall in the middle that has different men scattered all over it with arrows to their social circle, financial situation, family name. Their whereabouts and their weaknesses. There are around fifteen of them, and each of the pictures has a red X on it, indicating that they were dealt with. The last one is Max.

As if he eliminated everyone on his list.

I cover my mouth with my palm as I see the pictures of them all dead, torture inflicted on their body; some are burned, other have knives, and even... snakes?

What have they done to Lachlan that he shows this much cruelty to them? No one harbors this much anger for nothing, and the crimes are not done impulsively.

No, he clearly hunted them to deliver the blow they didn't expect.

On a loud exhale, I shift my attention to the right wall, which has no one but me.

My whole life spread in one horizontal line starting from my early childhood, spanning pictures of my first ballet trophy and then Jason.

Next to Jason is a photo of his daughter and girlfriend, and they seem like a happy family. I'm glad he found that with someone; his soul needed it. We never would have been a good couple, or rather, I would never have been able to give him what he sought.

But since all the arrows point at me, there is another picture, but with a question mark, right above me, connecting me to that mysterious person that has nothing but P written above it.

If I didn't know better, I'd think that having me as his prisoner was not his plan all along, but simply a way to get to the question mark.

My knees wobble and I sit down on the chair, rest my elbows on my knees, and gulp deep breaths, analyzing it all.

Successful businessman, a bad boy who chases an adrenaline high. How freaking ironic!

What a great mask to hide all that is living within him. Based on

those people and what he showed me with Max, he has here an
academy for serial killers.

He teaches them all this while in his spare time killing all the
people who did him wrong; he is too attached to them to think
otherwise.

The door buzzes, and I don't have to look up to know it's Lachlan.
At this point, I won't be surprised if he injects some kind of chip in me
to know my whereabouts. "Who are you, Lachlan?" I ask, and he walks
to the table, leaning against it as he speaks.

"A man."

"That much is clear. You've spied on me since I was a kid?"

He chuckles, apparently finding it fucking hilarious. "Our age
difference is ten years, Valencia. This is an informative board, but I
gathered the information before the hunt."

"That's what it all was then? A hunt. What a liar you are." I look at
him, and he shrugs, although I don't miss the dangerous flash of
his eyes.

"I'm the devil—that's true. I'm not a liar though. Everything I told
you is true." He leans toward me and locks my chin with his fingers.
"My desire to have you was one thing I didn't consider."

I slap his hand away, ignoring the tingling in my hand from the
contact. "Is that supposed to make me feel better?"

"Make up your mind, Valencia. You either want honest answers or
you don't."

As much as I hate to admit it, he's right. I feel like I'm so close to
discovering the truth. Even though I'm not sure how long I've been
here... it feels like forever. I need clarity on the situation.

The constant state of confusion just kills me.

"Who are these people?" I point at the left wall, wanting a clear
answer.

"My protégés."

I blink several times, clearing my throat. "Protégés?"

"I personally picked them to teach them torture. I consider them
mine if they will kill under my instructions. Because then they know
how to do it right. Except Shon. Sociopath handled him." He beams,

rubbing his chin. "Each one of them became masters of their craft. I'm proud."

"Proud that you made them serial killers?"

He tsks. "I can't say that. The circumstances of their lives have done it. I just helped them to concentrate on something specific and not kill everyone they see fit." As in focus on specific victims? "Trust me, you don't have to feel sorry for the people they kill." But then he wiggles his index finger. "Although I'm not sure about Amalia. She has her moments, but what a talent."

"It's sick." Licking my dry lips, I continue, "You had all the resources to help them, but instead you've created killing machines."

He grabs me by my elbow, dragging me to the wall, and holds my shoulders as he points at the black-haired girl called Isabella. "I found her on the streets of New York. She lived there for about a year. You know what she did during the night? Killed men. And you know why? Because her uncle dearest raped her all the fucking time at home, so she got out. But she saw him in every other man." He doesn't stop at my horrified gasp. "I gave her resources to channel it to the right people, to kill those who inflict the same damage. Not every single random guy who tries to play grab-ass."

"They are all victims. They needed psychological help."

"Yeah, well, it was too late for that."

He lets go of me and I turn to him, shaking my head. "So what? You run a hero organization killing those bad people in the name of the greater good?"

I expect him to agree, but I'm taken aback as he laughs, and oddly enough, this time amusement laces his tone. "Greater good? There is no such thing for serial killers. Everything comes from selfish desires."

"What's that supposed to mean?"

"Every time they kill their victims, they are doing it for themselves. For a brief moment defeating the demons that haunt them. Until the next time. Yes, they cover it up with these people who are assholes, but the truth is they are doing it for themselves. That's human nature. We are selfish creatures."

"So everyone gets a pass to your school?"

"No. I choose carefully who enters the mansion, usually only my students, and I rarely pick new ones. But the club in Brooklyn is fair game. I only take interesting cases, and those happen rarely. Anyhow, Arson takes care of that. I have other things to deal with."

I'm done with this conversation of his school or whatever the fuck this is! It's insane and just confuses me with each explanation.

So, willing all my courage in my fists, I ask the only question that truly matters. "What did they do to you, Lachlan, that you need me to get to X person?"

*L*achlan

Determination written all over her is a nice change from the victim-of-the-year mask she has been wearing for the last couple of hours, so a grin pulls at my lips, which she doesn't welcome. "And these men... what have they done to you?"

"You really want to know?"

"Yes! Please tell me the truth, so when I die, I'll at least know why!" she screams into my face, and I wave it off.

"No need to be dramatic, Valencia." I straddle the chair, pointing with my thumb behind me. "He is the guy I need to hurt. You are the key for that. Simple as that."

She blinks and then swallows, but before she can comment, I continue, "These men destroyed my childhood, so they deserved it. The younger ones were the sons, and for the record, not all of them committed crimes. Some just stayed silent when they should have spoken up." I watch her face as she dwells on something. I can practically see the thoughts swirling in her head.

Then she finally asks with a trembling voice, "Does this mean... does this mean... did they..." She takes a deep breath and forms a question. "Did they rape you?"

"No," I reply, and she sighs in relief, but then freezes as I say, "Only Bill raped me. I was his favorite toy. And Uncle, but he died a long time ago, so he didn't make it to the list."

She slides down the wall and sits on her calves, tears forming in her eyes as she places her hand on her mouth. "Oh my God, I'm so sorry."

I don't say anything but wait. Wait for the words that will surely come.

"That's why you are who you are and do what you do," she concludes, and the way she looks at me changes. There is still fear, but also tenderness, although one might mistake it for pity.

"I am who I am because of my choices."

Her shocked eyes travel up to me, and I go to her, kneeling in front of her while my hand laces in her hair to bring her closer. Her divine smell will be the death of me; the fucking lavender will be forever imprinted in my brain. "Don't fall down the rabbit hole, pretty girl. There is never justification for what I do. I'm a bad man who does bad stuff."

"You didn't know any better."

A hollow chuckle slips past my lips. "I'm not the first person to experience pain, Valencia. But not all people succumb to bad desires. There comes a time where you choose sides, and I choose this. But in no way does my past give me a free pass. A kill is a kill. A good man wouldn't have done it. Remember that."

She puts her hands on my chest, fisting my shirt as she trembles, probably with fury or desperation, or maybe both. "Why am I the key? Tell me, Lachlan. I'm begging you." Tears slide down her cheeks. "If you explain, maybe I will understand."

But this is the one thing I can't tell her, not yet.

And no matter how much I want her.... my plan will come first, because I cannot allow this madness to continue.

As I said, I'm not a good man.

CHAPTER SEVENTEEN

Lachlan, 12 years old

*A*nna lands on the seat next to me, excitement shining brightly from her eyes as she drums on my piano. *"Play for me?"*

"Sure." Slowly, I finger the notes, starting the theme song of Braveheart, putting my spin on it. She sighs in admiration while the music echoes between us, and I close my eyes, allowing euphoria to spread through me at the prospect of freedom.

Just two more months and I will be free of Pastor and his guests. We will finally be able to build a life and get the fuck out.

My fingers halt when I think about other kids going through the selection process, but no matter how much I agonize over it, there is nothing I can do right now.

But someday, I will; I just need to get out. I'm smart, or so some international results say, especially in science, and Pastor already told me that for my excellent behavior in the last two days, he might send me abroad once I turn fifteen.

He hopes I can help him run the community, as he calls it, since he doesn't have an heir.

I hate him with all my guts, but for freedom, I have to pretend and use any weapon available in my arsenal. "Kids, wash your hands. Dinner is ready," Aunt Jessica calls from the kitchen, and Anna's eyes widen while she whispers dramatically to me, placing her hand on her chest. "Finish it!"

Laughing, I resume playing with one hand, while hugging her close to me, and she rests her head on my chest. This little munchkin is the one thing that gives me the drive to move forward. I'm a dirty sinner anyway.

But her? She is an angel who deserves to live in a bright world where evils of this world do not touch her. Thankfully, her father died of a stroke three years ago, and I didn't have to worry about that asshole touching his own daughter when I was not around.

Enjoy heaven, you fucking asshole.

Life at home has been nothing but bliss, and I'm glad for all the useful stuff like a washing machine we have due to me being one of the selected ones. Aunt Jessie has already worked hard on the plantation, taking care of plants and leaves to use for medication. She didn't need to worry about dishes and stuff.

I finish on the high note and Anna claps loudly, and that's when I feel Aunt coming close to me and putting her hands on my shoulder. "Your talent becomes better and better with each year. You will do such great things. I'll make sure of that." She hiccups and tears roll down her cheeks, and my brows furrow at this.

What the hell? What did she do? She's never cried, always keeping her wide, bright smile intact.

But before I can question her, a loud thump comes at the front door, but then it's kicked open, and Pastor enters with his armed enforcers behind him.

I also see people panicking outside, their voices becoming louder and louder, almost bordering on hysterical, but I can't check it since the enforcers are blocking the view.

"You fucking bitch," he bellows, slapping her hard, and she lands on the floor from the blow.

My eyes widen and I act on impulse, darting after him, but he does the same with me and my back hits the wall. I grunt in pain; it's still sensitive from the last guest who liked to use a flogger on a daily basis.

Anna runs to me, and I hug her close while Pastor looms over Aunt Jessica and practically spits the words. "You told that agent who always wanders along the borders, didn't you? The fucking FBI is coming here now." What? What's

FBI? We are constantly told strangers sometimes come to town to try to find someone on the borders to talk, and question us about our faith.

But no one talks, because the punishment for betraying your own is death. That's the most absolute law around here.

She holds her cheek, although she looks at him with hatred, as she screams, "Yes, I did. What you are doing to these kids is disgusting and sick. I won't allow anyone else to suffer." She then shifts her gaze to me, her eyes filling with tears, and I hang my head in shame, because I never wanted her to know how dirty I am. "If only I knew...." Regret fills her voice, and I take a step toward her when he grabs her hard by the neck, bringing her up.

"You ruined everything!" Without taking his eyes away from her, he orders, "Lachlan, pack your stuff. We are leaving now." Then he addresses his men. "Is everything ready?"

They nod, although he can't see them. "The car will take you from the other end to the plane. But you have to go now. The fire has already started." Fire? What fire?

He lets go of Aunt, and Anna quickly runs to her. She picks her up in her arms, rocking her and murmuring, "Shh, sweetie, everything is going to be all right."

Pastor chuckles at that, and it sends shivers through me. "You think I'll run away like a rat and you'll get your happily ever after? Move, Lachlan."

"No," I finally find my voice and stand near my family. "I'm not going anywhere with you."

That's when another man glances inside, saying, "Sprayed it all over the house, and everything else is burning down, Pastor. You gotta leave. Cops are on the way too."

Pastor motions for me again. "Lachlan, don't make it difficult."

I step in front of my family and shake my head, ready to fight for it. He always covers his ass. He will run away. "No."

"Very well." Rage unlike anything I've seen before crosses his face, and he takes a gun in his hands while ordering, "Hold the boy."

"No!"

But as always, the word no means nothing around here. They each grab my arms while Pastor points a gun to Aunt Jessica's forehead, and says, "You are finally going to heaven, Jessica. Welcome it." And he shoots her while I scream, "Noooo!" but he doesn't stop. Instead, he quickly moves his gun to trembling Anna and fires again, and both of them fall down on the floor, dead.

In an instant, gone, because he decided so.

I pull at my hands and wrists until finally they let go, and I fall to my knees next to them. I run my hands over their warm, lifeless bodies and tears roll down my cheeks.

I promised myself not to cry, but I do. Because they are forever gone.

"You chose wrong, boy," he informs me, and I cry out, picking up a nearby vase from the table and aiming it at him. He kicks me in the stomach and I land on my back, groaning in pain as the vase shatters around me, small pieces scratching me and barely missing my eyes. "You should have gone with me. Now you will burn in here." With that, he leaves as the fire spreads around me, but all I can do is lie there next to my family and vow.

Vow to someday take revenge on the man who destroyed everything I ever loved and had.

*N*ew York, New York
January 2018

*V*alencia

Wrapping my hands around the steaming mug, I inhale the smell of chamomile tea, hoping it can calm me down, although I'm not sure it's possible after the truth that has been dropped on me.

Lachlan dragged me outside, on the way barking something to the blue-haired guy while we passed his room, and the man just shrugged, even grinning widely as if it was no big deal.

Well, I guess not everyone is scared of Lachlan.

I was still in a haze and shocked from the information Lachlan revealed that I barely paid attention to anyone. He brought me to the kitchen and muttered something about cold and underground, and poured me tea.

Pushing the mug back, I glare at him. His brows rise as he leans on the counter, crossing his arms, and that's when Levi enters, his eyes moving from me to Lachlan and then back to me. "If you're hungry—"

he starts, but shuts up at my frown. What's up with this guy? He always offers me food. Who can think about food in the current circumstances?

"Do you know why I'm here?" I figure someone has to have answers for me, right?

He blinks, glances at Lachlan, but I click my fingers to bring his attention back to me. "Well, do you?"

He shakes his head, fidgets with his fingers, and shifts uncomfortably.

What a lie. He knows I can read it in the accusing look he throws Lachlan's way. But even if he doesn't agree with his ways, why does he follow them?

Might as well ask, I guess. "Lachlan is a serial killer. Why do you help him?" This time, he blinks rapidly, placing his hand on his chest, and his mouth drops. "I mean, I understand you feel sorry for me and all, but really. Are you guys related?"

"That's really complicated—"

Complicated, my ass. "No, it's not. You help him and think what he does is right. Why? Did he save you too? Why?" I push. As he swallows loudly under my pressure, I pour all my frustration on him, because isn't he like sixty or more?

Where is his compassion?

"That's enough. Valencia, watch your mouth when you talk to Levi." The protectiveness in his voice surprises me, and with a nod, Levi exits the kitchen while I hear Lachlan's knuckles crack in his palm. His blue orbs drill into me as something dangerous flashes in them. "Levi is family. You don't get to put him in this situation. Understood?"

"Rich coming from you, considering I didn't see much respect from your side."

"You know nothing, Valencia, so I'd advise you to be careful."

I slap the table and get up, facing him. That's all I do lately it seems. "Why does he help you?"

"A man wronged him in the past. Long story short, he had a wife and two beautiful sons. And a ranch," he says each word carefully, watching my reaction, but I have none for him. Is that supposed to mean something to me? A brief memory of visiting a ranch with Dad pops into my mind, but it's quickly gone. Probably due to so many similarities. "A pastor promised him a better life."

"Pastor?" The P letter above the question mark.

Pastor, as in my father? But I quickly shake away the thought. No, it can't be him. Lachlan wouldn't have waited this long for such revenge and probably would have inflicted the same pain on me.

But maybe the pastor is one of the people who know me? "Uncle Aidan?" I whisper, praying it's not true and sigh in relief as Lachlan shakes his head.

"Doesn't matter who right now, Valencia. Anyway, he lost two sons and a wife and basically his own life, because of *him*. And I was the only one who helped him, and he helped me. So Levi is off limits in your dramatics and hysterics." We stare at one another for a moment, and then he clears his throat. "Want to go play soccer?"

"Excuse me?"

"Since you are in the mood to drill me even further, how about we just play ball while you do that? For every scored goal, you will get an answer to a question." I open my mouth, but he presses his fingers against my lips, and the zap of electricity makes his eyes darker. I step back as he continues. "Just not the one you seek the most. It's a good trade."

Crossing my arms, I ask, "Why such generosity all of a sudden?"

"You are acting like a spoiled brat, and for what I want to do, I need you sane, so...." He arrogantly shrugs, and I can practically feel the smoke coming through my ears as fury zips through my body.

What choice do I have but to agree though?

I'm a puppet that he plays easily, but at the same time, any information is valuable. At this point, I have no hope of getting away from him, but I don't intend to give up.

He motions for me to follow him, and we go out through the kitchen door into the snow-covered grass. I see Chance chasing something and then plunging into the pile of snow, rubbing his back on it. "You have a nice dog."

"He likes you."

"At least his affection is honest."

He doesn't react to my jab and reaches for the ball in a bin while pointing at two ends of the spacious grounds, which have two water fountains on each side. "Let these be the goals. If the ball gets near it, you score, and vise versa."

"Fine." This is beyond stupid. If someone told me Lachlan would kidnap me, and then we would play soccer together, I'd laugh in their face.

This guy can easily give me whiplash.

He drops the ball on his foot and then pushes it up before it ends up on the snow. Then he kicks it hard, but I manage to block it and maneuver it to the side. He quickly snatches it from me and is about to run, when Chance gets to it first and darts to the other side with it, and the ball slides to the fountain on Lachlan's side.

"Goal!" I shout, and Chance hangs his tongue, clearly pleased with himself.

"So it's two against one, huh?" He whistles to the dog, and Chance brings it back, pushing it with his muzzle.

"You don't play fair, so why should I?"

His lips pull into a grin and then he nods. "Very well. Ask your question." He puts his foot on the ball, awaiting my words, and even though there are thousands in my head, I blurt the most unexpected one to me. "Do you hate faith? You always react weirdly when people mention the word heaven or... generally any faith word. You also never joined us at church when Victor invited you." Then it dawns on me. "Pastor is not just a nickname, right? So were you..." It's still hard to say out loud, so I decide not to. "Were you hurt by someone who was religious?"

"No. I was hurt by a religious fanatic, by people who hid their darkness with faith." A beat, and then he says, "I detest the word heaven for multiple reasons. None of them has to do with God."

"So you believe in God?" But how can that be?

He chuckles, although it lacks any humor. "I believe in a higher power, yes. What I don't believe in are people who justify everything they do with faith, claiming it's the only right way."

"People who truly have faith come from the place of love, not hate," I say, because as much as I felt guilt over my dad, that's not the only reason I held on to my faith. I truly believe in those things.

"Right. And a place of love allows freedom to live as one wishes. The idea of how people lock themselves into their beliefs doesn't sit well with me, and then they preach to everyone and their mother what they think is the right way. Churches, praying, hoping have no meaning to me. But I do believe in God." In other words, he accepts that there are things he can't explain, but at the same time, he finds it useless to follow the rules.

He kicks the ball again, so we start fighting for the ball. I thank Bella for her freaking love for soccer, as she dragged me to her practices, so I know a few tricks and turns.

The ball ends up on my goal and I raise my brows. "I suppose we continue playing? You already know everything about me." The huge-ass board on his wall proves it.

"Do you regret sleeping with me?"

I blink in surprise at this, facing him as frigid air hits me in the face, but I don't notice it through the burn spreading over my skin, remembering all our times together.

I used to think they were the most passionate nights of my life, as he gave me things no one did—or rather, I never allowed anyone to give to me.

Regret.

Do I? After knowing the truth? Try as I might, I can't will the emotion to come and settle in my heart. Or strong hate.

It's awful what he is and what he does. But he is the product of vile people taking advantage of kids. He says it was his choice to be bad, and it's true.

But at the same time, it doesn't change the fact that no one taught him how to be good either. As weird as it is, he doesn't strike me as a man who loathes everyone and everything. Rather as a man who knows what he wants and what he despises, and he doesn't seek redemption for his actions.

Hating him in light of his past is almost impossible, but even without those things, I wouldn't have regretted being with him.

Weak and pathetic probably, I don't hide from this knowledge, but accept it.

So I reply, "No."

He tenses, his knuckles becoming white as he squeezes his hand, but then he whistles again and Chance is fetching the ball. He brings it to me, and I pat him on the back while he nuzzles into my touch. "Don't spoil him," Lachlan orders, although there isn't much command present in the voice.

"Simple kindness can do that?"

He kicks the ball again, but this time I decide on a full attack and manage to kick it far enough to reach the fountain before he even gets closer. "Score!" I cry out, and then point my finger at him. "Pay up." He crosses his arms, lifting his chin, and I add, "Do you have any family?"

His face completely closes off, but not before agony shadows it as he masks it under indifference. "No. Everyone is dead."

My heart pangs painfully in my chest; everything in me longs to soothe him, because it's such a tragedy to be completely alone. Losing my dad was devastating, but I can't imagine not having Mom or Victor or Braden. "I'm so sorry."

He returns his attention to the ball and we play for a few minutes, my legs aching from so much exercise in the last twenty-four hours, when finally Chance scores another goal for me. "Your protégés. Do they lead normal lives? Are they your best friends?"

"That's technically two questions."

"Second one is the extension of the first one."

"No, they are not my friends. Most of them are assigned to Arson, like I said, and he teaches them at another place. I personally pick a few to show my technique, but that's it. The original seven that you've seen, I trust them. But I can't call them my friends."

Well, he might as well have told me he loved them. I imagine trust is a big thing for a man like him. In a world where so many people probably have failed him, it takes a tremendous amount of loyalty for people to prove their trust.

"As to a normal life, it's all in the eye of the beholder. Sociopath and

Shon do have women. Although they fucked up, the situations they got themselves and their women into were hilarious."

"Like you did with me?" I cover my mouth with a gasp, because isn't it admitting out loud that I'm his despite all this mess?

His blue eyes drill into me as he agrees. "Yes, like I did and will do with you. Although there will be nothing hilarious about it."

I wish he'd stop warning and just get on with his plan, instead of having this imaginary ax looming over my head.

He continues though. "I had only one best friend, Logan. We lived the nightmare together. He chose a different path. He blocked out our past. Became a legendary rock star." He smiles, although I detect traces of worry in it. "But I guess, all things considered, he didn't manage to escape from it as much as he wanted."

Logan the rock star. As in... "You're not talking about Logan Davis are you?" He nods and my eyes widen, because holy shit.

His story is tragic anyway, but adding this truth... no wonder he fell from grace.

He lightly touches me on the arm, tracing the goose bumps on my skin. "You're getting cold. One more goal and we are done." He aims for the ball again, but I try to get it first. Then he tackles me and I lose my balance, dropping to the snow, but since my legs are tangled with his, he follows. We both stay silent for a moment, and then a bubble of laughter erupts from me as I look up at the bright sunlight.

For a brief moment, the monster and the angel have made a truce, and he shared his secrets with me, but unfortunately the secrets accomplished only one thing.

I can't hate him anymore.

And this will be my ultimate downfall.

*L*achlan

She is so beautiful, like a fairy lying spread under me on the snow while mischief plays in her eyes. Her face lights up from her laughter while Chance looms over us, creating a peaceful picture of a couple enjoying themselves on a snowy day.

It's almost perfect.

Except it's a lie.

I roll to the side, getting up as she sits in the snow. Chance plops on her legs as she pats him lightly while the familiar look of dreams shadows her eyes. "Do you ever wonder what would have happened if we'd met under different circumstances?" she asks, hiding her gaze from me as I dust my knees.

Wondering about what-ifs has no point; this is the conclusion I've come to through my entire life. It doesn't help you, only sends you deeper into a spiral of regret and wanting impossible things.

Love is an emotion that only few of us can experience, those who are not damaged by their past or drowned in dirt. It's not so much about the pain that envelops us, but by the choices we make.

Marcus Aurelius once said, "The best revenge is to be unlike him who performed the injury."

That's true. The biggest challenge is to not become the monster like the person who made you one. I lost in this game, because my revenge is not for my sake. Nothing can save my soul.

But for others not to be like me, so they can win. Sometimes we think there is a higher mission and fight so much for justice that we become the very thing we hate, and while I didn't become a pastor in that sense of the word... I am a monster.

And I don't hide from this truth.

The burning in my chest and the tenderness that shows itself when Valencia is around is the only indication I'm alive, besides the beating heart that pumps blood through my system.

She doesn't deserve any of this, but we are the product of our choices.

Deep down, she loves me, even if she doesn't say it out loud. And she hopes she can change me or find a straw she can hold on to, even without realizing it.

Hope is a fickle thing. Sometimes it gives an illusion of a different reality when in fact nothing of the sort exists.

Jason wasn't the bad boy who broke the perfect good girl.

That will be me.

She grabs my hand, squeezing it between hers, and I close my eyes, wincing, hating the weakness that slowly spreads inside me.

I've trained myself not to flinch from touches, to forget about the boy who got victimized only a daily basis, who was afraid of his own shadow sometimes, even if he had to show the world otherwise.

Even during sex, I was always in a state where I could concentrate only on pleasure, for the light reprieve it gave me.

With Valencia, I don't have to do any of these things. Her smell, her presence, the softness of her skin, and her raspy breath bring me reprieve, yes, but I want to forget myself in it with her.

Be with her all the way, calmness that never comes if she's not around.

I feel her hands on my chest as they travel to my neck and slide up to palm my face, and I meet her gaze, as she whispers, "We would have been a romantic couple who met in Italy and fell in love at first sight." Her fingers gently rub my cheeks, while the puff of our breaths fills the space between us.

"Such things don't exist," I reply, inwardly begging her to let me go and stop searching for something that doesn't exist.

A part of me, small part, wishes of giving her that.

But I can't.

She is mine, and because she is mine, she has to suffer. No part of me can live without it for long.

"I wish it were true," she says, and then she places a soft kiss on my lips and slowly opens her mouth, asking permission.

I remove myself from her arms and step back. "You are a prisoner here. Did you forget?" She jumps at my harsh voice while turning to the side. "For both our sakes, let's stay in our color zones. Black and white."

I move in the direction of the house, when her voice from behind stops me. "No place for gray?"

Willing all my self-control into my fist, I walk away from the garden, hating every step that takes me away from her.

For the first time, two words play in my mind, despite my iron belief to never use them.

What if?

*V*alencia

Shifting on the bed, I roll onto my side and huff loudly. No matter what position I take, I can't get comfortable or let my mind rest.

Considering all the circumstances, this is heaven on earth and I should be seeing pink dreams while resting on the silky sheets.

Instead, my mind is occupied with his last words and the music coming from downstairs that sounds oddly familiar, even though I can't place it.

You think only your truth has merit. Isn't that ignorance?

He said this to me back in Italy when I argued about Greek history with him, but these words can be applied here as well. "Why do I care?" I murmur, hiding under the pillow, hoping to evade his voice in my head, but it doesn't work.

After the game, he told me to stay put in either my room or the living room and threw several folders at me, which had different floor plans and ideas.

Turns out, they were renovations he has planned for Patricia's studio and reports showing that it's a wonder the place hasn't blown up with how old all the systems are. In a way, he has helped these kids and it warms my heart.

Confuses it too.

Levi and Maria were nowhere to be found as I studied his house, noticing his *everything* is about mystery and luxury, as if he is showing off to someone.

And all the security, why does he need it?

After strolling through the mansion where various cameras located on the ceiling probably traced my every move, I grabbed a bite and locked myself inside the room.

Which brings me to now, where I try to sleep, because it seems way easier than having all these thoughts swirling in my mind, but it isn't working.

I still hear the music and finally recognize the Mozart tune.

Giving up on sleep all together, I throw away the blankets and curl my toes into the carpet. The heat is on full force in the mansion, so I remove the sweater, leaving me only in a nightgown. Rolling my eyes at the stupid silk that sticks to my skin, I pad softly into the hallway and follow the sound, ending up in the common room where I danced yesterday.

Lachlan sits by the piano, drumming on one of the keys with his finger as he sips from his whiskey glass and music plays in the background. It's pitch dark, the only source of light coming from the ceiling, giving Lachlan an even more dangerous vibe.

"Go to bed, Valencia," he orders, not even looking at me, his voice void of any emotion.

"I can't." What's the point of lying or pretending?

Dwelling on it for hours, I came to the conclusion there is no greater agenda for having me here. He probably kidnapped me for himself but can't admit to this weakness he feels for me.

It's easier for him to hide behind the façade of indifference and this scary individual who wishes me harm, but the truth is he didn't do anything personally to me, aside from psychological torture. He is punishing me for what I don't know, but that is also keeping him from truly allowing himself to want me.

And instead, he has created this scary reality around me to explore him and me without lies.

I don't care if he kills someone who deserves it. Maybe I should, but I don't, or that's the conclusion I came to.

Maybe if I gave us a chance all those months ago, everything would have been different. He wouldn't get obsessed to get me, because I'd be by his side. "Have you slept with anyone in the last six months?" The question is out of my mouth before I can stop it, and I have no business asking it, since I went right back to Max. Granted, nothing ever happened between us, but still.

I just want to know.

His fingers pause midair right before he is about to hit the key again and he looks at me, while I do the same, not hiding anything from him. "Question time is over, Valencia." But I push it, because beneath it says something else.

A storm that needs an outcome.

"I didn't know you play."

"You don't know a lot of things. Get back to your room."

"No. Your family played?" This explains his love for classical music that is almost part of the design of this place. He shuts the piano with a loud thud, gets up facing me as liquid spills on the floor from his glass, but he doesn't care.

His hollow laughter echoes in the room, as he replies, "Since you insist. I have my aunt to thank for that." I think he wants to pass by me, but I stand in his way, so he huffs in frustration and says, "If I just had the chance to tell her goodbye... I would have done so with a song. She loved how I played. Told me it soothed her soul. I wish I could have done it after he told her the truth. It was the only way I could have shown her what fire raged inside me and calmed her storm."

He? The bad man who hurt him?

But he doesn't let me dwell on it much as he laces his hands around my head, pulling me so close to him there is barely any space left between us, his lips inches away from mine as he growls in my face. "You fucking stubborn woman, you want me to lose control, don't you? Are you sure you are ready to see what's beneath it?"

"No, I'm not." It might burn and destroy me, but I've spent so much time running away from myself and my life, and I no longer wish to do so. "But I need to for both our sakes."

We hold each other's stare for a moment. The only thing I can hear is the buzzing in my ears while my whole body stills, awaiting his next action.

With a groan, he finally kisses me with all the frustration and passion brewing inside us. With a gasp, I open up to him, grabbing him by his shirt.

He demands entrance to my mouth by biting my lower lip hard before licking it and then pushing his tongue inside, and I surrender, allowing him to savor me in lazy strokes that are filled with so much pain yet softness that I forget to breathe, urgently seeking his every touch.

Pulling at my hair roughly, he lets go as we both catch our breath, and he murmurs before slapping his mouth back on mine, "No one. There has been no one."

Relief along with lust envelops me, and I press against him harder, melting in his arms. I want to forever stay here with him, where my head doesn't think and I only concentrate on my heart that wants only him despite how wrong it all seems.

But I can still feel the fight in his rigid muscles, filled with tension, and even though everything in me protests against it, I step back. The tips of my fingers rub my swollen lips as his eyes trail my movement.

This time, I don't want to rush.

Extending my hand to him, I wait for him to pick it up, and he waits a beat before taking it. I turn around, dragging him after me as I go back to my room, not wanting to go to his, as it's coated with previous lovemaking.

Where honesty wasn't present between us.

But with our wounds out in the open without the masks we can hide behind, I long to give myself to him freely in a different place where memories or reality don't exist.

There is just the present moment that no one can take away from us.

Finally, we reach the door, and I stop in front of it, his heat surrounding me while his hand wraps around my waist, his lips skimming over the skin of my nape. "We are pretending?" he murmurs, as he shifts his lips to the crook between my shoulder and neck while his hand slides lower, tearing a low moan from me. "As if we are different people with different circumstances?" Disgust coats his voice, showing me he hates just the idea of it.

Shaking my head, I enter the room while pulling him after me and whirl around to face him. My fingers immediately start to unbutton his shirt. "No. I don't want to forget or pretend. I want just once for us to be... us. With all the sins and good deeds."

An unfamiliar emotion crosses his face, but he doesn't say anything else. He allows me to push back his shirt as he gets out of it, and I walk around him, remembering something.

Back in Italy when we made love, I noticed barely visible almost white scars on his back, but I never paid much attention to them, thinking he got them during one of his adrenaline rushes. But now, even though he didn't tell me anything about them, I suspect they come from far darker memories.

His back tenses as I trace my fingers over them, asking, "Did it hurt?" His soul probably harbors the same faded scars that have stayed there, no matter what.

Nothing ever can cure them, no matter how much you pour on a person.

They stay forever.

"No. These are from my uncle. They stopped quickly." He doesn't elaborate and my brows furrow that someone could be this cruel to their family member, but I shake my head, because this is not about pain.

This is about us.

His breath hitches as I drop a few soft kisses on them. My hands unzip his jeans, and I rise on my tiptoes to place one final kiss behind his ear before I go back in front of him. Kneeling, I tug his pants down and his erection springs free. His hand at once laces in my hair, yanking me closer.

I slowly drag my tongue around the head, tasting the precum before closing my mouth around him, sucking him in as much as I can, and he groans as he fists my hair and pulls me closer. "Deeper, Valencia. You can take it deeper." He rocks forward, and I tip my head slightly back as I listen to him, sucking harder and working over his length. I wrap my hand around the base of his cock, squeezing it and earning me another groan as he tugs my hair harder, almost to the point of tears.

I focus on nothing but his taste, smell, power, and stripping this man of his iron control, and then I raise my eyes to catch his as he watches every move. His eyes are shadowed with desire, and it fires the blood inside me, zipping hot lava through me while my core drips with wetness coating my thighs. My fingers travel to cup his balls. As I let go of him, I lick him from head to base, tasting the soft skin on the underside of his cock, and then my hand slides up and down.

My body aches, my nipples pucker, and I moan around the head before sucking on it lightly. What I'm doing must send vibrations through him, because I'm roughly hauled up, and without giving me a chance to take a breath, he tears the nightgown away. I only have time to blink as he throws me on the bed where I bounce, ending up on my back.

My heart stills and then gallops again as I see the expression on his face when he removes the strands of hair that fell over my face.

I think the gentle part has ended and I'm about to be fucked hard.

$\mathcal{L}$ achlan

This woman is my undoing.

I can't think through the buzzing in my ears and the raging beast inside me that chants one thing only.

Mine. Mine. Mine.

I tried to stay away, leave her alone until my plan came to fruition, so we both wouldn't suffer more, which is inevitable at this point. But she had to come to me and demand this.

How could I have refused? I'm powerless against her, and when she gives me this mouth of hers that...

No.

I can't use this word.

That drags on me as if nothing and no one in this world exist but her for me, there is just no way to resist her.

Just remembering her hot, wet mouth sucking off my cock makes me almost come on the spot, but I focus on her body splayed in front of me, flushed and needy as she stretches on the bed, showing me every graceful part of her.

Hooking my hands on her knees, I yank her closer as I kneel on the carpet, my breath fanning her dripping pussy as she pants loudly, her fingers skimming over her stomach. I put her feet flat on the bed so nothing will be between us.

A man has to be comfortable before he feeds on his woman.

Nuzzling into her heat, I swipe my tongue from bottom to top, spreading the wetness all over her as her hips rise, seeking my touch, but I still her, ordering, "Patience, darling." Breathing in her unique smell, I taste her sweetness on my tongue and dive back in, probing deep inside her and swirling it against her walls as her pussy clenches tight, her thighs almost squeezing the breath out of me.

My fingers rub her ass cheeks, settling her down as I continue to push my tongue back and forth, mimicking the act of fucking, preparing this pussy of hers for deeper penetration. My thumb presses against her clit, massaging it.

"I want—" Her hips roll into me as I lick her again, from one lower lip to the other, filling her emptiness with two fingers, giving her all my attention.

Her scream can probably be heard downstairs, and that fills me with male pride and possessiveness. I want to beat my chest and let everyone know this beautiful woman belongs to me and no one can make her feel this but me.

Sucking her clit into my mouth, I play with it, dragging it from side to side until she moves relentlessly and her pussy almost swallows my fingers whole. She is close to coming and finding the one sensation she so desperately yet gorgeously seeks.

I pull back, then continue again with soft licks before diving back again, using my touches to bring her to the edge, only to slow down and repeat the process all over again.

Her wetness coats my mouth and I love it. I want to rub her scent on my skin so her smell is forever imprinted on me.

She presses my face closer to her pussy, demanding I finish, but instead of listening, I slide my tongue up her stomach, dipping it into her belly button, and graze the soft skin with my tongue. I move up and bite the underside of her breast, quickly soothing it with long licks. "Lachlan, please," she begs, her nails raking my back, but I merely rock against her, touching her wetness with the tip of my cock but then focus back on her breast.

Not so fast.

Tweaking her nipple, I bring it closer to my mouth and then suck on it hard, flattening my tongue against it and then swirling around it while she bucks against me. I hold her steady, continuing to pleasure her as my fingers pay attention to the other breast, and I slide my mouth there, repeating the action, biting on sensitive flesh, causing her to groan.

I can taste her for hours, enjoying every second of it, but I can't wait anymore. The roaring need will drive us both insane if I don't get inside her right fucking now.

Sucking her neck, I make sure to leave my mark on it so she'll always fucking remember who makes her body ache, and before she knows what's happening, I enter her with one swift move, digging my fingers into her ass, adjusting her for a better angle.

Fuck, she is tight, so fucking tight I almost lose it right there. I catch my breath as she cries out and wraps her legs around me, pushing into my ass. "Move, Lachlan."

"You are not in charge, darling," I say, thrusting deep as her breath hitches. "I am." Despite all my talk though, I pull out only to slide back in again, groaning as she tightens around me more and more with each thrust.

"Please, Lachlan. I want—" she rasps, hugging me closer while squeezing me inside her as I rock back and forth, giving yet denying us at the same time.

I continue this for some time, enjoying her every hitch, smell, and skin coated in sweat and a blush. I know there is no one but us in her head.

As it always should be in an ideal world, but life is not that kind to us after all.

Her pussy clenches around me, her mouth hangs open, and her eyes fill with pleasure. A cry tears out of her throat and she falls back on the pillow, her chest rising and falling, my cock still drilling inside her, deeper, deeper, and deeper, finding solace in her heat and seeking the calmness only she can give me.

Then I feel it. The tingling of my spine, my balls draw closer, and finally I spill into her as pleasure unlike anything I've experienced before washes over me, almost knocking me out completely.

For the first time in my life, I've made love to a woman, leaving myself completely exposed and bare, and I hate Valencia for it as much as I need her.

She leaves me hollow without her. How will I ever hurt her?

Breathing heavily, I blanket her body as she shudders under me and clenches around me once again. Wrapping her arms around me, we lock in a tight embrace that blocks out the world that will never accept this as anything but bad.

Not that this will ever have a chance to flourish.

Valencia
What if...

Lachlan
Gripping the banister of the balcony, I breathe the frigid air into my lungs and will all the bad memories to come back. To build armor around my heart that is used to pump my blood, not to feel anything aside from loyalty or praise.

But the strong pounding in my chest right now is only for her, and I don't know what to make of that.

In a short amount of time, she's gotten under my skin and found the darkest secrets, cravings, desires.

Challenged my self-control in ways I never expected. Blinded me with her beauty that leaves me speechless and powerless against her.

But the strength and courage she shows me is what truly bonds me to her.

All those years ago, when I chose her as my means to revenge, I always believed the plan had formed in my head because it was the perfect solution. Now I see that the perfection of it had nothing to do with it.

It's her.

I wanted her for myself from the first glance. That's why other women wouldn't do and why I stalked her in Italy, even though it was never part of my plan.

In normal circumstances, people would call it love at first sight, but I don't know what that is, and I can't give it.

So for me, it's an obsession bordering on insanity. If she has the power to do this to me now, what will happen in the future?

For now, she is experiencing Stockholm Syndrome, because

accepting and seeing goodness in her captor is better than facing the devastating truth.

But maybe I should do it for both our sakes.

We've already sunk deep.

I should crush this connection before living without each other becomes unbearable.

The end of this plan has always had only one outcome for us.

And it doesn't include us ending up together.

Let what I'm about to do be my gift to her. Before, I looked at this part of the plan as the culmination of my show that would bring me the most satisfaction.

Now I dread it and use it as a necessary evil to accomplish my goal.

She needs to hate me, because right now she loves me.

Her hate is better for her sanity to survive it all. But her love... her love will forever stay in this moment with me, reminding me that for a moment in time an angel gave herself to the monster freely, allowing him to feel emotions he thought he was incapable of.

Not every story has a happy ending.

CHAPTER EIGHTEEN

Lachlan, 12 years old

"*H*ere you go, Lachlan," the nice lady wearing the blue uniform says as she gives me the bottle of water. I accept it, burrowing deeper into the blanket thrown over me, although it doesn't give me warmth.

Nothing can warm the cold in my heart.

She does the same to Logan, who sits numbly next to me, gazing into space as we share the same pain.

His little sister Chloe got lost in the fire, but he tried to save her, and as he rushed back into the house, he couldn't find her. Finally, his father pulled him back, claiming there was nothing they could do.

He begged paramedics until his voice was hoarse to search for her, but they just gave their condolences as everything burned to the ground.

A lot of people died, most were injured, and few just sat not knowing what to do. Red lights surrounded the place with reporters wanting to enter the area, but the FBI—that's what those people called themselves—kept them away because of some kind of privacy.

"She is gone," he murmurs, his raspy voice barely audible in the space between us. "He killed her." My hands fist on my knee, because I want to offer reassurance and hug him, do something to numb his anger, but can't.

Because deep down, guilt nips on my skin, slowly destroying my insides. All this is my fault.

If Aunt Jessica hadn't tried to save me, she wouldn't have gone against Pastor Mark and none of this would have happened.

"My family is gone too." That's the only reply I can muster, and at least Logan has his parents. They might be fucked-up and in love with this cult or what the fuck ever, but at least he has someone.

I have no one.

His bitter laugh kills me as he grabs my shoulders and forcefully makes me face him. His face and any bare skin has soot smeared on it, probably just like mine, and several fresh bruises are on his face. Licks of fire touched us both as each of us tried to do something.

Something that failed anyway. "My parents mean nothing to me. They knew what he did. They just didn't care as long as they supplied them with 'gifts,'" he spits, throwing the empty bottle in the trash can. "I'm sorry for your family. They didn't deserve it."

He wraps his arm around me, and although my body stays unmovable, I lean a little on him, seeking at least some small comfort in this nightmare.

Pray and everything will get better.

Hysterical laughter bursts out of me as tears appear in my eyes, and a second later, Logan joins me as we laugh and laugh at everything as he croaks through it. "Pray, right?"

I nod and we laugh again, because it's so fucking hilarious.

The more we prayed, the worse shit became.

Faith has brought nothing but pain and loss, and we have scars on our bodies and souls forever to prove it.

We still chuckle as a man with a notepad in his hand comes closer to us, and we shut up quickly, reflexively scooting back.

You never know who hides behind the masks of good people.

"I'm so sorry for your loss," he says, and we just blink, not really knowing how to react.

Rarely has anyone said those words to us.

"Would you like to give statements of what happened here?"

We share a look, because what are we supposed to do? For so long, our lives have been directed by specific rules that it's hard to do something on a whim.

"We've seen the scars and found torture places. Who else was subjected to it?"

I open my mouth to explain, when Logan beats me to it. "They just punished us if we performed badly at school. We couldn't go beyond borders. Had to ask for permission. We don't know where the pastor is," he says, and my brows furrow. This has to be the shortest fucking version of events ever! Why does he hide the other truths?

The agent writes it down, but then shifts his attention to me. "Do you have anything to add?"

Logan kicks my leg and words still inside my mouth. As much as I want to spill more, we made a pact a long time ago. Unity. So I reply, "No, that's it."

He nods again and then smiles sadly at us. "Social workers are on the way. Hold on, kids." With that, he walks off to other officers as they murmur something amongst themselves.

"What was that?"

Logan shrugs, adjusting the blanket. "I want a peaceful life. The fucker got away. We won't be able to track him, but with all we know? We will be held in either witness protection or with these people. I have a chance for a foster home and to build a life. Imagine. We can create music."

What he says is so weird it takes me a moment to make sense of it all. What the hell? "What music and foster care, Logan? You have parents!"

Anger flashes in his silver eyes. "They will be charged. Me and you will go to foster care. It won't break us after this. We will build a new life, forgetting this nightmare."

Forget? I won't ever do that.

Revenge, that's what I want. How can I live in the world where Pastor is alive? Where he freely might harm someone else?

And besides... I want blood. No, need it.

As long as someone suffers, I'm good.

Normal is not for me.

In this exact moment, a shadow looms over us and I raise my eyes, only to almost choke on my spit.

The man standing in front of me has come to Pastor countless times, and although he never touched kids, he approved of everything going on. Based on what I heard, he owned a shady business that brought tons of money, but Pastor never liked him much, as he claimed the guy had specific sinful preferences that he didn't approve of.

Which was rich coming from Pastor.

"Lachlan," he addresses me, gracing me with a sinister smile that sends chills down my spine. "Let's talk, shall we?"

And what he says changes the direction of my life forever.

*N*ew York, New York
January 2018

*V*alencia

Padding barefoot to the kitchen, I find Levi gazing through the terrace door at Lachlan throwing the ball to Chance who chases after it eagerly and then repeats the action, each jerky movement only emphasizing his muscles.

Levi's back is to me as he exhales heavily and turns around only to blink in surprise when he notices me. "Valencia," he says, and I grin at him, enjoying the happiness spreading through me.

Last night with Lachlan was... magical. In his arms, he showed me softness, gentleness, and passion, making me feel like his most cherished possession.

There is goodness in him, overshadowed by darkness, of course, but he doesn't know any better. How can a person have compassion or want a relationship if his childhood and everything else was nothing but a constant nightmare? He does bad things, but he punishes those who in his mind deserve it. Which doesn't make it all right on the grand scheme of things, but is it important?

If he doesn't harm innocent people and saves someone from experiencing the same nightmare, does it matter that he continues to do so?

Happiness diminishes in me as those thoughts swirl in my head, because deep down, I know it does.

I won't be able to live or be with a man who continues to do what he does, but how can he ever stop? Serial killers experience the same cravings as addicts, needing victims like crack to inflict their desires on them. They want blood and gore. How is it possible to build a life with one if he surrounds himself only with darkness?

My mind travels to Sociopath and Shon, as he calls them. Do they continue to do what they did? He said they both have women. Does this mean that their women accept everything easily?

I wish I had the chance to talk to someone about it, to someone who has experienced something like me to give me advice.

Pressing the button on the electric pot, I'm rising on my toes for a cup when Levi's voice stops my movements, and my hand pauses midair. "Whatever he makes you do, please remember there is goodness in him. It's buried under the pain, but there is light."

"Levi—"

He shakes his head, flattening his palm to me, so I shut my mouth, awaiting his next words. He never spoke to me directly without Lachlan's presence, so this is weird to say the least.

"I raised him in a way. I know him better than anyone. He will punish you." Regret laces his voice as my brow furrows, a heavy stone settling in my chest. "For that smile you had that I spotted when you entered, you probably shared something beautiful with him. And this is killing him," he whispers, as I just stand there numbly, wishing to scream at him to shut up and not burst my bubble, but I don't. "Any kind of emotion besides anger or fury or satisfaction is killing him, because he doesn't know how to handle them. He will bring you so much pain, Valencia." He comes closer, cupping my cheek as a single tear slides down it, and he wipes it away, his eyes wrinkling even more as they fill with remorse, while he pleads, "Please hold on to him, because there *is* goodness."

Like the traits he had shown me during the soccer game. But small cracks of light are not enough to build a life, no matter how much you want it or love a man.

Love.

This is what it is... no?

Love should never hurt, but obsession and devotion? That sure fits our story. Does a beautiful thing flourish under rough passion?

I finally find my voice. "Hope is a dangerous thing. Sometimes goodness is buried too deep to dig for it, Levi."

He opens his mouth to add something, but that's when Lachlan comes in, his face hard as granite and void of any emotion. He reminds me nothing of the man who spent the night with me; instead, he is again this cold stranger who greeted me all that time ago when I woke up in the cage.

Deadly.

That's the right word for the vibes he is sending my way. "Come with me," he orders, roughly grabbing my hand, and I try to wiggle free, but his grip is so tight it bruises my skin.

"Let go of me, Lachlan," I shout, at the same time as Levi says, "Lachlan, maybe—"

He turns to him, barking, "Shut the fuck up, Levi. Do not interfere."

Levi bites his lip, resting on the kitchen counter, shaking his head, and looking down, but Lachlan is already dragging me to his torture rooms. Although I stumble and halt his movements, he doesn't care.

"What is going on with you? Ouch!" I bump into the small table's corner, and that stops him at once, as he swiftly spins around and his eyes roam over me, searching for the source of discomfort. "Careful," he snaps, and my jaw drops at his arrogance. I slap his chest as anger burns strong inside me, because I don't understand him.

What happened between our night and this morning that makes him act insane? "Why do you care? You drag me like potatoes!"

Regret flashes in his blue pools as he presses cold metal to my temple. Removing the safety from his gun, our gazes clash as my breath tightens and he steps closer, our chests almost brushing against each other. "You forgot you are the captive, Valencia. The time has come for you to learn why you are really here. Follow me or your brain will be splattered on the fucking wall." For a second, I don't know how to breathe or even think, my shock freezing everything inside me. "Is that clear?"

This is the man I allowed to touch me last night?

He holds the gun to my head, and for the first time ever threatens to kill me, and by the looks of it, he will do it with no remorse.

I know in normal circumstances, I probably should panic or run away, but I just numbly nod, too shocked with anything to fit any norm. His weird behavior lowered my guard, and I allowed myself to think that there was more to him than meets the eye.

But it was all part of the game, probably in preparation for the final introduction, for the point of all this.

"Crystal."

He proceeds to drag me to his office again as he presses the code, and the door to the torture hall opens. He takes us down, aiming for torture room number seven, and enters it in a quick move, shutting the door behind him and punching in a code on it.

A code so I can't escape?

A shiver from the cold in the space runs through me as I study the environment. There is only dim light above the table that has knives, guns, and other weapons spread on it with bleach and gloves.

Several bats and chains along with—is that gasoline?—are on the counter next to it. Basically, it's like the mix of all his previous rooms based on what he said.

Why did he bring me here? The place reeks of devastation and doom, coated in a permanent depressing atmosphere that grates on one's nerves.

"Let's get you all the answers you're looking for," he says to me and clicks with his fingers. Immediately, the bulb in the circle a few feet away from us lights up, and my eyes widen as a shocked gasp slips out when I see a man attached to some kind of bar right in the middle. His hands and legs are tied with ropes, while silver cloth is wrapped around his mouth as he mumbles something. He is almost in the same position as the Church placed women who they considered witches back in the day.

"Oh my God." He is only wearing pants, and for now, he is completely unharmed, which means he is a freshly brought victim.

Lachlan chuckles sadistically at my horror. "Too soon for those words, darling. You ain't seen anything yet."

The man sends his pleading gaze toward me.

"Lachlan, don't do that. Please, I don't want—"

"I don't care. Life doesn't revolve around your wants." He picks up folders from the table and throws them at me, and I manage to catch one while the rest fall to the ground. "Let's meet the creator of all this, shall we? The great and mighty Pastor."

With trembling hands, I open it up, but I already suspect the truth, which will devastate me.

"No," I whisper, placing my palm over my mouth as photos of my father come into view with details on his whereabouts and a place called Peaceful Heaven. Back when we did a history research project on cults in class, this story came up, saying that the entire community burned down and there were almost no witnesses, and those who were left all thought the apocalypse had happened and they didn't want help.

Next to each of the photos taken of him and me is written the year and what Dad did in that community. The number of boys he had essentially sold, how the place grew and grew, and finally the grand fire that ended it all. He never wanted outside power, just enough resources to keep his place growing, his little kingdom where he was a king.

I scoop up the rest, and these are files on the people who died in that fire, how they had houses, and he took them away promising a better life.

Better life that seemed more like a prison.

With each new piece of information, my heart breaks and breaks until it doesn't have places left to do that. My dad, who was a loving man, doesn't add up in my head with this... picture of a... lunatic. Of a man who did this to innocent people. Part of him runs in my veins. This truth is the one I won't ever be able to outrun.

"Perfect daddy. Because of him, you stayed good and proper, and he did all those vile things. How do you feel about him now, Valencia? Does he still wear a halo above his head?" he asks, stepping closer and then grabbing my chin painfully as I shift my head to the side. But he forcefully brings it back. "You don't get to hide from it. I am who I am because of your father. We were the collateral damage in building his empire." His constant anger, the way his eyes flashed when Patricia mentioned heaven.

No wonder he despises anything that has to do with faith.

His hands get wet from the tears flowing from my eyes. "He killed

my aunt and cousin right in front of me. Because she called the cops."
I hiccup but he shakes me, and my teeth snap against each other.
"Revenge is the only thing that has kept me alive."

"You wanted to sleep with me and hurt me because of him?" This
makes so much more sense than Victor. Did he get some kind of high
knowing that he managed to sleep with Mark Moore's daughter?

"No. Sex with you had nothing to do with him and everything with
us." For a second, he cups my cheek and we forget each other as I see
remorse written all over him.

Closing my eyes, I rest my forehead against him, needing his
strength in this time when everything I knew about my father crum-
bles at my feet. Where there is deeper understanding for the crimes he
has committed, or rather what he did to me.

Why he can never let go, because the source of his anger died
before he could punish him for it. He just needs me to be scared while
delivering this information and—

He roughly pushes me away, and I gaze at him in shock, as he tells
me, "I wanted to taint his beautiful princess in darkness so she would
join hell despite how much he hated it." He goes to the table and
wraps a leather belt around his wrists. "The princess he spoke so highly
about, claiming she would always stay his little angel. Even though
back then you were only two years old."

"By touching me?"

He laughs, and the bitterness of it all chills my bones. "No. By you
committing the greatest of sins." He waits a beat and then delivers a
blow I never expected. "You will become my protégée, Valencia."

*I consider them mine if they will kill under my instructions. Because then
they know how to do it right.*

Murderer.

He wants me to be a murderer!

My heart sinks, but his granite face lets me know he is serious.

I had no idea what fear tasted like until he told me the true reason
he captured me.

*L*achlan

By the hope shining on her face, I know she doesn't want to believe me, yet she doesn't find anything in me that convinces her otherwise.

Sex. Desire. Mind games.

All this was about us and the passion I've experienced with her. This was for Valencia, my brave one.

However, killing a person and forever smearing blood on her hands that she won't be able to wash off? That's my punishment and satisfaction for Mark Moore.

"Sins of our fathers," I say. One way or the other, the next generation always pays for them.

Debts are collected, and in this case... she is one.

I ignore the voice inside me that roars and tells me to stop, to not put her through this; she doesn't deserve it.

To not show her the side of me that will forever strip her love from me, a feeling I've discovered I need, even if I can't do anything with it.

Damned from the very beginning, our pasts don't allow us to ever form a future.

So I might as well follow through.

*V*alencia

The man screams his lungs out as the drill enters his shoulder with a bolt, sticking him to the wall. Lachlan unlocked him an hour ago after he'd had enough of whipping him and using electroshock devices.

I cover my ears with my hands, hoping to evade the sound, but it doesn't help. I begged him not to do it, to let the man go, because neither he nor I was the one he wanted to hurt.

Lachlan just told me to stay put or the man would be in even greater pain, and I didn't want that.

The smells of sweat, urine, and blood coat the place, and I sit on the cold floor, praying for it all to stop.

"What's that?" Lachlan asks and swiftly removes the tape from the man's mouth, and he groans again. I can see traces of his skin on the tape, and bile rises in my throat. "The trash bin is next to the table if you want to barf, Valencia," he says, as if it's no big deal.

He studies me. "You are too pale. We should bring life to those cheeks of yours." My stomach flips as I still, afraid to breathe, wondering about his next move.

So far, he's dished out all the horrible things, but his promise constantly swirls in my head. I hope he said it only to scare me. "Come here, Valencia," he orders, but I shake my head.

"Don't," I plead, but he cocks his head and extends his blood-covered glove to me.

"Come here," he repeats, as the drill in his hand comes dangerously close to the man's temple. I jump to my feet, stepping toward him. "Pick up blade number three." He points at his steel collection to the long one with sharp ends that reminds me of one of the knives butchers use to cut meat. He clucks a few times. "Hurry up, Valencia." With my heart beating rapidly, I snatch it up and walk back to him as he motions to the place next to him, facing the victim.

I do that, not looking at him, because it's too hard. Gaping is as bad as the crime itself, because you either wait and don't do anything or participate in the downfall of the person.

I offer it to him, but he shakes his head and points at the artery that's pulsing under his finger on the man's neck. "Stab him here and end his misery," he tells me, and I hold my breath, just staring at him and not comprehending his words.

"What?" Surely, I'm mistaken.

"Stab him. For an hour now, I showed you all the different skills. You can handle stabbing him."

The man whimpers, kicking with his feet, not that it's much use, as they're nailed to the wall too. Just the slightest of movement is possible in this position. He moans and moans with his eyes begging me not to do it.

"I won't." I push the blade at Lachlan, but he doesn't budge, still holding the drill to the man's temple. "Let me rephrase it. Either you will stab him and he will die relatively easy. Or I will drill a hole in his head, and all this time, he'll be screaming. Since it's your first kill, you get to choose."

"Don't do this to me, Lachlan. Don't," I say, but his face stays hard as granite, and I understand I've lost him.

In the battle between revenge and love, I've lost him.

Because he chose the former.

"Do it and put a stop to all this." To us, he means. Forever smear myself in his dirt so the sins of my father won't escape me and I will pay for them with my soul.

How is it possible to kill and not carry this through your entire life?

He turns on the drill again, and it buzzes loudly as the man speaks. He barely has the energy, but I hear it nevertheless. "Please." He prefers a quick death rather than the drill.

Lachlan plays it very well. He doesn't make me kill someone, no.

He puts me in the position where I can sacrifice myself once again or be selfish. But I've spent an hour with the live torture; how much more can I take? If I don't do this, the man is dead anyway.

But Lachlan's prison will last forever.

This way we can end it all once and for all, even if it forever shatters us.

"I'm so sorry," I whisper as, with a shaking hand, I raise it up and close my eyes while Lachlan wraps his around mine, and with all his power stabs the man. He gives one last gasp before silence falls over the place.

The blade drops to the floor with blood oozing from the wound, and I look at my hands.

The monster has won.

The angel became a permanent resident of hell.

CHAPTER NINETEEN

Lachlan, 15 years old

I fall on the floor with a loud thud, stifling a groan of pain, as my back still holds bruises from yesterday's beatings. I breathe heavily, trying to steady my heart when Rodrigues' voice from above says, "And you are dead." And then kicks me lightly. "The minute you end up on the floor, you are giving advantage to your enemies to kill you. You spent seven seconds and shifted your attention to your pain. That's five seconds too long," he proclaims, and then motions with his hand, so I jump up, standing opposite him in a fight stance. "Never show your enemies it hurts, Lachlan. That's one of the most important rules."

He punches forward, but I block it. My arm throbs and my bruised knuckles can barely bend due to the lacerated and swollen skin, but I place an indifferent mask on my face and step back.

He advances, and I repeat the action and then move forward, delivering a hit to his chin, but he quickly bends and grabs my chest, rapidly beating and beating with his fists while I stand, having him securely in my grip so I won't fall down.

The minute I feel him slow, I roar and push him back and then punch him *in the face. He stumbles back as I spin around and kick him in the chest, watching as he falls on the mattress.*

I jump on him, pressing the knife to his throat while his pulse beats against my finger, and say, "Now you are dead." Blood from my mouth and nose, the one he broke just five minutes ago, seeps onto his face while I gulp as much air as possible. I learn to adjust to the pain and block it away until it's safe to loosen my guard.

Which means never.

A loud clapping snaps my attention from my mentor to see Angus MacAlister standing near the door, watching us fight. "See, Jaxon? That's how you fight." The guy looks around my age and gives me a bored expression, although I don't miss the fury brewing in his gaze.

The son doesn't like his daddy it seems.

I get up, wincing at the dizziness, but quickly grab the towel to cover it up. Angus looks around while addressing Rodrigues. "Where is the boss?"

"Upstairs." My fists clench, because I know what it means.

He is having sex with one of his women, who he fucking kidnapped from the streets. Most of them love him though and see him as kind of a savior, because he provided them a life with food and clothes and luxuries. They don't understand it's a prison and they have no free will.

And anytime it happens, I hate myself for continuing to live here and accept all that bullshit. One of the reasons is I religiously follow the training and soak up as much information as I can.

Knowledge is power that many people underestimate, preferring stupidity and ignorance.

Dmitri assigned me a mentor from his assassins; he's also making sure I learn a few languages and everything there is to know about torture.

He took me in three years ago, because he didn't have an heir and he saw potential in me. He hated Pastor for something, so it was doubly amusing for him to get the boy he so wanted for himself.

I hate him with a passion, but he is my key for revenge, and that's why I can never leave him.

At least for now.

He claims I'll be good as an interrogator. I love to inflict pain with fists; there is a thrill seeing skin turn purple from pain.

An art form.

I shake my head from the thoughts, because on most days they confuse me. I heard that, at my age, teenagers dream about fucking all the time, but my nights are filled with images in the killing rooms. The way blood slips from victims, their cries, and my fingers tingle imagining this high.

What is it like to take a life that you know has no meaning anyway? A kill is a kill, doesn't matter if the killer is a fucking piece of dirt who doesn't deserve to live.

Some killers even have morals. They won't hurt women or the elderly or whatever.

If I'm ever going to be there though, I will never exclude anyone. If you help in child trafficking, fuck you, you are dead.

Angus's voice brings me back to the situation at hand. "Call him. We need to discuss business." He pushes his son toward me. "Go with him, Jaxon. A friendship with my friend's son will do you good." My brow lifts at the word son, and I barely hold back the laughter that is about to spill from my lips, because he knows the truth. But like everyone else, he pretends.

They deserve nothing but death too.

Someday, someday.

And in time, Jaxon and I become strong allies who help each other eliminate the evil men in our lives, which in turn helps us build our empires.

But it comes with a high price for both of us.

*N*ew York, New York
January 2018

*L*achlan

Valencia rocks as she sits on the floor, her gaze completely void of any emotion as she stares in front of her with shock covering her features. Her palms are swollen from digging her nails painfully into the soft skin, bruising herself in the process. "I killed him. I killed him," she keeps murmuring, and each word is filled with self-hatred and fear.

Remorse.

Although I've accomplished my ultimate goal, tainted the beautiful angel in a way she'll never be able to escape, inside I weep for the beauty I've destroyed.

She didn't deserve it.

Sins of our fathers.

Valencia was punished for something she had no control over—she was a means to an end. And God knows I've done a lot of vile things in this fucked-up life of mine, but turning her to the dark side was the worst.

I shouldn't have touched my angel.

In the span of time where she fought so hard to escape and pushed her ideals on me, where desire between us was so strong neither of us could resist it, where we shared with each other stuff neither of us knew... somewhere along the way, she got under my skin.

Is this thing called love? The speed of the pulse, the constant want to be near her and not want to hurt her, even though my dark nature demands it?

But how can it live inside with the constant need to punish and control her, to remind her she is dealing with a monster who will never change?

She is my prisoner, but along the way, she became my obsession and possession.

However, the truth is simple.

She never wanted any of those things.

"If it helps, he was a bad person, Valencia," I say, but she doesn't react to my words, just continues her motions. I don't feel the need to add that the fucking guy raped women on a daily basis as an enforcer in one of the mafia houses. There is nothing to mourn about his death.

If I had to do it all over again, I would.

"Valencia," I bark, harsher than usual, and she finally snaps her eyes to me, and instantly anger clouds her chocolate eyes.

She gets up swiftly, swaying slightly to the side, and I step forward to steady her, but she pushes my hand away, laughing hysterically. The sound reverberates through the walls. "I just killed a person, and all you can say is he deserved it?" she asks, and then screams, "I don't care about his crimes! I shouldn't have done it. I shouldn't have to choose between the drill and blade. I shouldn't have been placed in a position where I had to kill him!" She paces the room back and forth, running her fingers through her brown locks while I rest my back against the wall, staying silent.

Anything is better than her catatonic state earlier. "Because of you, I became a murderer." She dashes toward me, her hand raised to slap me, but I stop it midair as she breathes heavily. "I hate you," she whispers, and then all bravado leaves her as she punches my chest with her fists while tears stream down her cheeks. "You made me just like you." She fists my shirt and sobs harder into my shirt, and I close my eyes, because I can't see her like this.

Slowly, you will get used to it, Lachlan. You will.

As her father's words ring in my ears, I come to a decision, and with that, I scoop her up in my arms. Although she tries to get free, hitting any kind of flesh she gets her hands on, I don't budge.

Taking two steps at a time, I take her upstairs to her room and dump her on the bed. She lands on her back, but quickly sits up. Her eyes shine brightly from the tears, and her mascara-smeared cheeks give her a haunted look.

Not for long.

The game has come to an end.

Checkmate.

Valencia

Breathing heavily, I watch Lachlan as he rests his forearm on the door, his back to me, and I can see every rigid muscle strained tight as if he is preparing for a battle and doesn't know where to start.

I notice several bloody scratches across his back that I probably put there while in search of bringing him pain after what he put me through. I glance at my hands as they tremble, and I can still remember the knife that dripped blood on the floor after I killed the man.

Fury and hatred come back overwhelmingly, along with a deep desire to bring him more pain for making me a killer. But this is also mingled with love that knows why this man does what he does.

However, nothing excuses it. Understanding and accepting are two different things.

Also, he never lets go for the hell of it. What will he want from me now? Maybe the time has come to kill me instead?

The ultimate goal has been accomplished, after all. Mark Moore's daughter became a murderer and can no longer qualify for heaven.

"Get ready. John will take you home." His words freeze me on the spot, shocking me to the core, because I never ever expected him to speak those words to me.

The minute he disappears behind the door, I rush toward the bathroom to wash my face and quickly study my reflection in the mirror. I open up the foundation, applying it to my neck and collarbone to mask the bruises so no one will ask me any questions. I also make sure to look presentable enough to not scare anyone considering he fed them the bullshit that I went to Russia to better understand *Swan Lake* and study with a ballet master for a few weeks there.

Once I'm done, I exit the bathroom and put on the ballerina flats, the only shoes present in the room, and then it dawns on me.

My reaction was so strong to his words that I spun into action without even stopping to think what it would mean.

Lachlan is letting me go, as in he no longer wishes for me to be part of his life.

The man who told me I'd die by his side before ever seeing my family again.

I drop onto the bed, resting my elbows on my knees and blink a few times, hoping for my mind to get clarity, but no matter how much I try, it doesn't come to me.

Why would he do something like that? Didn't he say he doesn't follow the rules? That once he lured his victim, there is no escape?

Why is he allowing this?

Glancing one last time at the room that has become my sanctuary, I grab my scarf and step outside, and that's when the music floating through the space echoes in my mind.

The instrumental piece from *Braveheart*.

I follow it all the way downstairs, almost mesmerized by the

perfection and beauty of each note as if I listened to it through speakers. Not one single wrong note.

When reaching the last step, I freeze as I see Lachlan sitting at the
piano and playing with his back to me on the dark-as-night instrument
that, thanks to the round ceiling, allows the music to spread through
the entire mansion, probably one of his plans when building it.

A conversation from yesterday plays in my head, while a tear
threatens to slide down the bridge of my nose, but I hold it back.

*If I just had the chance to tell her goodbye... I would have done so with a
song. She loved how I played. Told me it soothed her soul. I wish I could have
done it after he told her the truth. It was the only way I could have shown her
what fire raged inside me and calmed her storm.*

Before I can stop myself, my feet move toward him as I try to
concentrate on all the good parts we have experienced and memories
that prove to me he has a heart. That deep down, there is the man I
fell in love with, even though it was stupid.

That deep down there lives a boy who just never knew what peace
was, who had his innocence taken away from him in a way I wouldn't
wish for anyone. That he didn't have a choice back then, and he ended
up on this road. Maybe he needed to do all this stuff to Mark's
daughter so he could let go of all his demons.

But as I'm about to touch him, I pause. His back tenses, even
though he continues to play. No matter how much I can imagine all
those excuses, it doesn't change the fact of who he is.

A serial killer who teaches other serial killers to kill people, even if
they are evil people. How can I ever be with a man who accepts it?
Who thrills in such a life? I once heard a saying that a fish and bird can
fall in love... but where will they build their nest? What future do I
have with him?

Love is supposed to win every argument, but what if love is the one
thing that destroys you the most?

"I'm sorry," I whisper, and then with one last glance, I turn around
and run to the door, because I'm afraid if I stay for just one second
longer, I will change my mind. I will stay forever with him silencing the
voice inside me and ultimately killing myself.

Jumping into the car, I cover my face with my hands while sobbing loudly, and John quietly shuts the door. With that, the music dies.

And so do we.

Once upon a time, an angel and a monster fell in love.

And both of them paid dearly for it.

CHAPTER TWENTY

Lachlan, 21 years old

Padding naked to the bathroom, I wipe my face while rolling my eyes at the heavy sigh coming from the room. "Lachlan," one of the females murmurs, and I barely contain myself from choking the fuck out of her.

Women tend to be annoying after sex, which means most of the time.

I get back and see two women still lounging on the bed, breathing heavily, but it inspires nothing but disgust in me.

Grabbing my pants from the floor, I zip them, and then bark, "Get the fuck out." They quickly jump into action, their hazy gazes gone as they scramble into their clothes and leave me alone. They know better than to question my orders.

My reputation precedes me after all.

Pouring myself a glass of whiskey, I take a large gulp while placing the cigarette in my mouth and lighting it up. Stepping onto the balcony, I take a deep pull and close my eyes, enjoying the thrill that rushes me as I gaze on my empire... as I like to call it.

For the last six years, life has turned into bliss.

Serial killer bliss at that.

Old Dmitri wasn't lying when he said he didn't have much time to live and needed an heir. He died—well, not without a little help from me and Jax—when I was sixteen and left all his businesses to me, including the killer-training one.

I quickly shut everything down and let his advisors handle the business side of things. Instead, I'm studying a lot. I enrolled for a medical degree, majoring in surgery, and I decided to get a minor in psychology. In my spare time, I've studied ancient torture methods and explored different cultures with their input into such stuff so I can have one hundred percent knowledge on the subject.

And thanks to all this, I outgrew this place, my mansion as I call it, but in truth... my university.

I'm about to take another sip when a loud commotion from behind me grabs my attention, while loud voices shout, "Are you insane? He doesn't—"

Whatever Levi wants to say dies on his lips apparently as someone pushes into the room, almost breaking the door, and looks at me, breathing heavily. "Lachlan Scott?" he asks. Authority laces his voice, and my brow rises at this.

He is around eighteen years old, bulky, and has several scars on his hands. Scars I'm painfully familiar with.

But he must have escaped his kind of hell, judging by the expensive clothes he is wearing.

"I tried to stop him, Lachlan, but he—" My raised index finger shuts Levi up, and I wave him off. A beat passes, and then the door closes after him quietly while I still hold the teen's stare.

"And you are?" I fire back as he straightens. He has the fire, but no actual skills to defend himself against men like me.

I put on my hoodie that's lying nearby, as he replies, "You can call me Sociopath."

It means nothing to me. "And real name?" What is this? We will introduce each other by nicknames now?

He shakes his head, and says, "It doesn't matter." I can't help but chuckle at this, because the guy seriously has a fucking nerve coming here and talking to me like that.

"I want to be your student."

"You don't say?" I exhale smoke. "Last time I checked, the admissions office was closed."

He fists his hands, as stubbornness enters his expression and he puffs his chest. "I know about you. Just teach me. That's all you need."

Sipping my drink, I ask, "Why would I waste my time on you?" He must have expected my question, as he takes out papers from his jacket and extends them to me.

Grabbing them, I quickly scan through them, and then it dawns on me.

He is an heir to Eugene Harrison, and fuck, the story of that man was brutal. But he also has assets that are valued around one hundred million. "It's yours if you teach me."

Throwing it on the floor, I smirk. "I'm rich. And I don't teach random people. Look, Sociopath, or whatever the fuck your name is," I start and notice his teeth grit. "Don't know how you found this place, nor do I fucking care. But I don't work with teenagers. Find something better to do and move on." I finish and spin around, done with this conversation, because I raise murderers and killers.

I teach an art form. And I'm not going to waste it on a dumb teen who seeks peace he'll never find. "I know his real name," he says, and my glass pauses midway to my mouth, my breath freezing as coldness slips into my bones. "Where he lives. What he does. Everything." With each word, the ringing in my ears increases as images of the past assault my memory, vivid, as if they happened yesterday.

Pastor. I can't locate him no matter how hard I try, and I wasn't able to crack Dmitri about it either. One of the reasons keeping him alive had no point.

I still stay silent, while he clears his throat then throws his ultimatum at me. "I will tell you, once you make me as skillful as you in torture."

It will take years.

Glancing at him over my shoulder, I see something I haven't paid attention to before. Resolve and deep sorrow that knows no end, a raging inferno that won't be gone until all the scores are settled. If it's not me, then someone else will introduce the kid to this. He chose this path and nothing will sway him from it. And I don't doubt he knows Pastor, because his father had quite the connections all over the place. Probably Luke, one of his most trusted men, had the information I need, but he won't ever share it with me without Eugene's son's permission. Luke was probably the one who dug deep enough to find my past.

I might as well teach him and get what I so desire.

One way or another, he will know that once you step into this life there is no going back. And no matter how many people you kill, it will never be enough.

Because whenever you gaze into the mirror, you will see the same tortured soul looking back at you.

*N*ew York, New York
January 2018

*L*achlan

"Where is she?" I roar, while the police along with Levi hold me back. I'm about to choke the living shit out of the one who just told me there has been a car accident.

"Sir, I'm sorry, but she is dead, along with your—"

I grab him by the collar, shaking the life out of him while his eyes fill with fear, and other men have no power to snatch him away from me.

"She is not dead. Search the fucking cliff!"

"Lachlan, that's enough." Levi's stern voice brings me back to the present as he finally manages to unlock my hands from the police officer and gives him an apologetic look. "I'm sorry. He is very emotional. His fiancée was there after all."

The officer nods, adjusting his clothes. "I understand. It doesn't change the truth though." He shakes hands with Levi and walks off to the crime scene while I pace like a raging beast trapped in a cage.

"Lachlan, you need calm down. John is dead."

"You found his body. Not hers. He has her, Levi. He got to her," I shout in his face, while he stands there stoically, not even a muscle twitching on his face.

"Wasn't that what you wanted?" he asks, and I still, while he huffs in disapproval. "I warned you time and time again not to play with her. You didn't listen."

"I sent her home." I emphasize each word, almost spitting them, and he nods.

"Yes, you sent her home after taunting him. You should have known better."

I growl, fisting my hair and glaring at the sky.

Not for one second do I believe in this carefully staged act of Valencia's death.

My creator got my angel.

Where did he take her?

"Lachlan, focus—" But he might as well speak to a stranger, because the ringing in my ears deafens me to anything else.

He got his hands on Valencia when I wasn't looking.

My trap for him had a trophy after all, but not for him.

As he won once again.

The roar that erupts from my throat can probably be heard miles away.

CHAPTER TWENTY-ONE

Somewhere in the world...
Fall 2018

Valencia

As I roll to my side on the bed, my brows furrow and I wince at the uncomfortable sensation down my back that woke me several times during the night.

I place my palm on my stomach and my eyes widen, because it's slightly flatter than usual, and when the wetness around my thighs registers, I gasp in shock.

My water broke, which means all this discomfort is labor.

I'm only eight months pregnant; he is probably not fully developed yet.

No, no, no.

"No, darling," I say, sitting up and crying out in pain as a contraction shakes me. My skin is coated in sweat and I can barely move. I hear my heart buzzing in my ear while unimaginable fear along with a lot of other emotions travel through me.

Soon, it's too soon. I can't give birth here when I'm alone, when he is so small.

When he has no chance of surviving this. I've fought for us for so long; we can't lose now. "Come on, darling, please stop," I beg, although it's useless, as nothing can stop his birth now. "Someone help me," I scream, grabbing the sheets tightly in my hands and placing my legs in a more comfortable position. I do my best to breathe evenly as my baby tries to push out, but he can't do that when there is no one to meet him. "Someone!" I try again, although only a miracle at this point will save us with these soundproof walls. "Please!" An anguished cry scratches my throat as pain rips through every part of me, and for a second I feel like I'm sliding into oblivion, my strength and control slipping away, but then a voice from the past whispers in my ears.

"*She never knew nightmares. Until she became mine.*" And that voice soothes me in a way that brings me peace and I will myself to hold on for the sake of our baby.

Lachlan, he was supposed to be here. How could he have left me with him?

I imagine his teasing smile, as he whispers, "*Is that all you are capable of, angel?*"

"I can't, Lachlan," I rasp, licking my dry lips. But then I know I will, because I have to save our son.

Even if he doesn't know about him.

Another cry tears from me, and this time the door opens, as the nurse's voice says, "What is this—" The sound of shattered glass bounces off the walls, as she shouts, "Help! She is giving birth! Help!" I rest on my elbows, breathing evenly, trying to hold on until they bring someone to help.

And then he rushes inside, muttering, "No!" He runs his fingers through his hair as his golden rings glisten in the light. "I cannot lose this boy," he says as if in a trance, and I want to weep.

Because the monster who put me through my greatest nightmare wasn't my captor turned lover.

No, it was my father.

A father who is very much alive.

ew York, New York
Fall 2018

Lachlan

I sip the last drop from the whiskey bottle and with a loud roar throw it over the banister, and seconds later, it crashes loudly on the concrete, the sound of shattered glass echoing through the silent night.

I should have never let her go; then she wouldn't have gotten in the car accident and been vulnerable to that fucking father of hers.

But then again, he is not a monster to her; he is a monster to everyone else. And between the two of us, he is her safest bet.

That's just the way of the world.

But she is *mine*.

And he doesn't get to have anything of mine anymore.

I've been going insane all these months, searching and searching, finding missing links, but none of them had any information for me, no matter what I dished out on them. I haven't slept, haven't properly eaten, my mind always with my angel. He fucking abducted her and took her to a place even I couldn't track. I don't trust that fucker to be kind to her, even if he loves her.

My phone vibrates in my pocket and I press the Accept button on the fourth ring. At once, Sociopath's voice speaks in my ear. "Lachlan." I don't reply, because I haven't heard a question, and with him, it's always coming. He doesn't contact me for the fuck of it. "I think I found something."

Everything inside me stills, and the air leaves my lungs as I squeeze the phone in my hand so tight I think I might crush it. "Get ready." I don't wait for his reply as I throw the phone on the floor and spin around to quickly grab my gun and everything else in preparation of the specific plan.

I need my best men on this mission, and I only have four people in this world I trust, my best students.

I gave Valencia the choice, but that choice only led to destruction and pain.

No more fucking choices. She is going to stay my captive forever.

It's easier to concentrate on the anger and fury at the man who destroyed my life than the fear and destruction at the prospect of forever losing Valencia. Whatever happened to her is my fault, because I wanted to use her as a decoy.

However, when I let her go, I gave up on luring Mark away from his shadows and wanted to do it differently. But like the coward he is, he attacked when no one expected him.

Time to remind him he's no longer dealing with a small boy, but a man on a mission to get back what belongs to him.

No one takes away what's mine.

Especially not Pastor Moore.

CHAPTER TWENTY-TWO

Lachlan

The clock is ticking loudly, *tick tock tick tock,* and I drum on the table to the beat of it while four of my most trusted men sit at the round table with me, pondering my last words. I just explained the situation to them and await their answers. Although back in the day I helped them all out, I never asked for anything.

Only loyalty.

It's one thing to teach a serial killer an art form.

It's another to trust one.

Jaxon speaks first, leaning his elbows on the table. "How do you know his location?"

My mouth lifts in a half smile, because if he asks for details, it means yes.

But then again, Jaxon MacAlister's loyalty to his family is legendary. And oddly enough, I know he considers me one for what we did a few years ago. Spit that loyalty in his face though and he will be dangerous.

Fucking lethal.

He is the head of the mafia, after all.

That's another story though, so I reply, "I know someone who knows it." My finger presses the remote and the TV slides up from the middle of the table. On the screen is room number two, where a man is chained to the chair, tugging on his restraints and mumbling something through the tape on his mouth.

Arson rubs his chin as his eyes light up with excitement. "Ah, torture? What are you going to do to him?"

Shon gives me a sideways glance, clearly questioning my sanity in bringing Arson here. They are close in age but never liked each other. Shon considered him too wild to tame and hated his ways of inflicting pain.

They are not for the faint of heart, that's for sure, but then what Shon has experienced is nothing compared to Arson. Even I shudder at just the idea of it, and how fucked-up is that?

"Let's focus on the situation," Sociopath says, opening up the folder. "He has kept her all this time with him. We don't know where, but you are sure she is with him?" It doesn't surprise me he is the one to take the reins in this case; he has an aura about him that no one ever threatens his leadership.

"That was my plan," I reply, and silence falls over the table as they shift uncomfortably. None of them says it, but I know the thought is running through their minds.

My plan.

Valencia was supposed to be my protégée and sink into the gritty world while her father watched, probably going crazy that filthy fucks like us touched his daughter. I wanted her to be forever smeared with our past and darkness, so what her father did she experienced firsthand. So many people lost lives.

He took out my family. Didn't I deserve to show him an eye for an eye? And I knew for her, he would come from hiding, because in his fucked-up head, she was his little princess.

And then I'd have delivered my revenge.

Someday, Lachlan, she will give me grandkids and they will be my heirs. Pure blood, as no one will ever diminish her light.

His one weak spot that could have served as a decoy.

It sounds so fucking stupid and useless after everything we've been through. The fire and anger to punish him for days and days, so living will become worse than death, still rides hard inside me, but if it costs me her?

I need to save her. Choosing between my revenge and the woman who is mine is impossible.

To sustain my sanity, I need both, and I can't live in the world where he continues to do whatever the fuck he pleases. He won't hurt her; that, I'm sure of.

But his words about perfect grandchildren didn't escape me, and I've been replaying them over and over through all these months. Knowing his sick ways, and since perfect Max died, he can find some perfect religious fanatic for her and make her have his baby.

Or worse, just do it through the doctors. He lost everything in the fire all those years ago, and although he built his system back, it's not as strong as before.

Which means common sense no longer resides in that fucking creature. The idea of my Valencia pregnant doesn't sit well with me, but I don't give a fuck.

She just needs to be alive, and everything else we will handle. She won't want me, but it doesn't matter anyway. She can live happily wherever, but I will save her from her father and kill him.

Fulfill my promise to my family.

"If the dramatic pause is over, how about we go 'talk'"—Shon quotes with his fingers—"with our guest downstairs and figure out the plan from there? It's impossible to discuss anything without the location."

"You don't have to say yes," I say, and they all freeze, probably not expecting it. They might not agree with my methods, but if they feel like they owe me one, they will go.

Each one of them has someone to go back to. They've built a life in the ashes of their nightmares.

As much as I want to, I cannot bark an order and drag them into this without their consent.

Jaxon sweeps his gaze through the men, and although none of them even as much as lifts a brow, he turns his attention to me and nods. "We're in. Let's get her back."

*V*alencia
       Gazing into the space, I watch numbly at how the small golden fish swims in the round aquarium, seeming perfectly content with the boundaries placed on her.

Because she doesn't know better, or that there's an entire ocean where she could have had complete freedom in the world. That small, glassed space is the only thing she knows, so no wonder she feels safe.

But if someone comes to destroy her perfect little world, she'll probably die, because she has no means to get to the ocean.

No one taught her.

The metaphor seems fitting in my current situation. My father, with Victor, created a cocoon around me. A small little world where I knew no nightmares, because I lived by their rules.

Lachlan destroyed the glass, and then I was like a fish out of water before he threw me into the ocean, not warning me that in the ocean, you have to be careful who to trust and everyone is only responsible for themselves.

And I ended up in the ocean only to be swallowed by the whale.

"Valencia." His voice brings nothing but disgust, but I don't react, not acknowledging his presence, and he speaks again, this time coldness slipping into his tone. "Valencia, if you are going to be difficult, you are not going to see her." Although he tries to sound regretful, he is merely bothered by my silence.

He wanted a grandson, an heir to an empire. Ever since the doctor showed him on ultrasound that it was a boy, he became obsessed with my pregnancy, claiming it was divine intervention from God.

That he was finally getting what he deserved. Even though the father of the baby was an evil spawn, his grandson would only have his blood.

After orchestrating my accident eight months ago, he brought me to this place, claiming that I can no longer live freely, as Lachlan and my mother completely ruined my faith. He told me I should accept my new home and live by his rules, and laughed a lot at the stupidity of Lachlan's plan. He said he left me for my sake, so that I would understand the consequences of my actions and leave Jason, which in turn allowed me to see clearly and not be tempted by the demons.

He also told me no one would come looking for me, as everyone thinks I'm dead. My heart hurt for my mom, imagining what it was like for her to hear the news about her child.

Father is fucking insane, but I had no idea how deep it ran until he showed me with his cruel actions.

Beatings, interrogation chairs, knives—all opportunities to kill the baby naturally, as he called it.

He didn't want to abort it, as it's a sin. Killing me in the process hardly can be considered that, I imagine.

But my little warrior held on; she probably got it from Lachlan, and when the doctor told him it was a boy?

Everything changed.

He didn't punish me anymore unless I tried to escape, but at least the beatings and kickings stopped.

Ultimately, it didn't matter, because he took my baby from me. The minute he knew it was a girl, she became a bargaining chip in his twisted, sick game.

And I blamed Lachlan for becoming a serial killer? It's a wonder he possesses any good qualities at all.

"Get out," I finally reply, still focusing my stare on the aquarium, complete numbness overpowering me. I can feel him not moving, his shadow looming over me, so I pick up the glass from my nightstand and throw it at him, but he manages to dip his head as it shatters into tiny little pieces all over the floor. "Get out!" I scream, and the mask of evilness crosses his face.

He snarls, "You will learn obedience. And the minute this little girl is healed enough, I'm going to sell her to the highest bidder. She is a bad seed." I freeze, air stilling in my lungs as my eyes widen, and for a moment, I can't breathe from the implications of his words. "And then you will get pregnant again from someone worthy to give me a grandson."

"You won't do this." His sadistic chuckle only proves he has every intention of doing it as he waves me off and goes to the door, not caring in the least about my turmoil. "Lachlan will save her." I don't care what happens to me, as long as my baby girl is okay.

He steps outside, but not before sneering over his shoulder, "Lachlan will not do anything. That boy was never anything but a useless piece of shit. He couldn't even properly punish you." And with that, he closes the door, while I sit there horrified to my core.

Grabbing my hair and pulling it to the point my skull throbs, I rock back and forth while insanity threatens to destroy my mind completely.

Father finally did what Lachlan started.

Destroyed my spirit.

The angel is gone.

The monster has come and killed her.

*L*achlan

Sipping his whiskey, Shon gazes with a bored expression at the one-way mirror as Arson lights the match, grazing the skin of his victim with it as the man convulses in fear. "Show off," he mutters, and on instinct, I slap the back of his head. He rubs it, spilling the drink. "The fuck? We are wasting time, Lachlan. Tell him to speed up. You know if you let him, he can play for hours."

All in good time, we don't need just a name. He is saving him for a different kind of information that we write down as Sociopath types furiously on his computer, searching for the location and everything else using FBI databases.

"Bingo!" Sociopath mutters, picking up the laptop and showing the screen to me. "It's seven hours away from New York, in a deserted location in the woods. The land belongs to some guy who is presumed dead and the man accrued the right to build shelters for abused women. They actually live there as a place of new hope or something." Indeed, the center is advertised as such and has a bunch of stupid reviews about it.

Even the approval of a social worker, but then it doesn't surprise me. Pastor knows how to be convincing.

"Kids," I mutter, fisting my hands. "Most of them probably have kids. He continues to do his fucked-up shit." And all these years, he has been under my radar. I throw the chair and it bounces off the wall, but no one says anything as they feel the same. "Shon, order a plane. Jaxon—"

"Yeah, my brothers will be there with us. But listen, the FBI—" he starts, and I nod. He takes a beat and quickly sends a message to someone on his phone while I bark into the microphone. "Arson, enough with the bullshit. Kill him already." He is of no use to us anyway. Arson looks at the wall and shrugs.

Then pours gas on his victim and lights up the match simultaneously, stepping aside as the man screams and thrashes on the chair, and the smell of burning flesh can be sensed even here. Arson jogs to a hose, splashing water over him. The room is designed security wise for this kind of torture, since fire is one of the first things I taught.

After all, I'd learned the hard way how to fight with it.

"On the plane, we can adjust the plan. Let's get moving." They spring into action as I go to my room to get a specific folder to give to Levi before I go, when Sociopath's hand stops me, bumping my shoulder.

"Is this a suicide mission for you?" he asks, and I smile, although it lacks any humor.

My friend knows everything. Instead of answering his question, I grip his shoulder tight, and confide, "Valencia is entrusted to you."

We both know that if I want to destroy Pastor, I have to die with him. This revenge has been twenty-three years in the making, and I never envisioned a different future. This path always leads to death one way or another, and the only reason I valued my life was because I had to kill him.

Valencia will be forever free from the evils that destroyed her life. I'll make sure of it.

Once upon a time, there was an angel.
Who made the monster's heart bleed.

*V*alencia

A knock sounds on the door, and then a young girl enters; she is probably in her twenties. She holds a tray of food and gives me a tentative smile. "Pastor says you need to eat."

I blink and then erupt in laughter, which turns quickly into tears as the pain crushes my soul and sucker punches me when I try to move a little. She speeds up her steps, placing the tray on the bedside table, and wants to adjust the pillow, but I slap her away and she freezes. "Don't touch me. I don't need your help," I snarl, and she casts her eyes down, defeated.

No matter how brainwashed you are, you can't possibly think this is the way to treat a woman. She has seen my condition from the very beginning, and she follows my father's commands blindly. And yes, I shouldn't blame the victim, but they took away my baby.

I don't owe anyone understanding.

"I'm sorry," she whispers, fumbling with her fingers.

"If you are sorry, then let me go." The request is irrational, because I can't move; my body is too weak from the birth, but the implication is all the same. She can call for help or do something. Instead of standing there like a freaking lamb ready for slaughter.

"I can't." She jumps at my strained chuckle, but I just shake my head, exhausted by it all.

"Leave. I don't want food." Extending my arm, I throw it on the floor, making everything tumble and splash around us, and she quickly moves to the side. "Get out!"

"He is doing it for the greater good. For us," she says, and I catch her gaze, my eyes widening.

"This is not a greater good for me. Do you even have any idea what he does to the kids here?" I suppose a leopard doesn't change his spots with years, and I know all these women have kids here. He wears expensive watches and rings; they don't come from a side business, especially since he keeps this place for his own ego and power, and for the kids.

How many poor women fall into his trap? Thinking they are getting away from whatever they are running from and getting their kids into a nightmare? My father is a born actor. He probably never touches an adult, providing them with the best care and lots of promises.

But the kids?

"You are mistaken. He takes care of everyone. He never touches any of them, just teaches them at Sunday school. It's your illness speaking." She places her hand on my chest, but I push it away, yet she stubbornly holds it there. "Your heart is broken. But it can be mended with faith."

"This is not faith," I hiss in her face and shake her as she steps back, shocked. "Get the hell out of here."

"Forgive my daughter, Chloe. She is sick."

Chloe nods, scoops up the tray, and, with a bow, leaves us alone. Chloe.

Logan's sister was just three years old. Chloe. We doted on her. He lost her. Because of your father.

Lachlan shared a lot of random stuff while inflicting pain on that man in room number seven. Among it all, he mentioned how Logan's self-destruction always had to do with his sister.

Can it be her?

Dad chuckles, rubbing his beard. "It's still so easy to read your mind, Valencia, after all these years. You were always a smart child. Yes, it's her." Not allowing me to dwell on it, he sits on the edge of my bed, cupping my cheek, and I try to jerk from his hold, but he doesn't budge, almost bruising my skin. "This stubbornness has to end, my child. You have things waiting for you."

"You are crazy!" How does this kind of craziness escape everyone's radar? He was just a regular dad who always supported me and never, ever shouted at me. Are people like him born with such masks that hide their evil from good people?

But more importantly, do I hold any of those traits if he is the one who sired me? Lachlan blamed me, claiming I had to answer for the sins done by my father.

I didn't believe him back then, but I should have.

Out of the two of them, he ended up being more honest. "I built a community here."

"On the bones of innocent children?"

He huffs, while I fight his hold on my chin and wince. "I give them a new home, new meaning. They love their rules that keep them ready for heaven. They are happy. And kids... they pay a small price for our peace here. Besides, most of them grow up quite well. Last time I checked, Logan became a rock legend. And Lachlan... he is a piece of shit, but he built an empire. Look what my teachings gave them!" It's impossible to reason with him; clearly, he is in crazy land for good. "No empire or country is built without losses."

"You ruined their lives, Father. You are not God, and what you do is not faith or religion. It's one man's insanity."

He flicks something in his other hand, and then cold metal presses against my throat as he clucks with his tongue. "Maybe it's better to kill you, because you will bring nothing but trouble."

"And you will commit a sin?"

"It's not a sin if the child doesn't see the right way." I should be afraid, but there is this calmness in me that surprises even me.

He won't do it, because he needs his pure bloodline or whatever he mumbled about during my torture. I just need my child and to hold on.

Lachlan will never leave us to him. I know it. He doesn't know what love is; I'm not delusional enough to believe that. But he considered me his and my father stole me from him.

Dad might think he is invincible, but he is not. And my Lachlan will rescue his angel.

His phone vibrates and he slides it open, and whatever he reads there changes everything.

CHAPTER TWENTY-THREE

Arson

Whistling loudly, I walk nonchalantly to the edge of the town, dragging an open gunpowder bag.

Two men notice me and startle. "What the he—" I fire at them with my silenced gun and they fall to the ground with a loud thud. I shake my head.

This quick death is an embarrassment for me, but oh well, no time to play. Too bad I can't light their bodies as well so they will burn to the ground and their ashes would forever stay in the fucked-up prison they so carefully guarded.

Finally, the powder runs out. I kick the bag to the side and take out matches as Shon's voice annoys me through the earpiece. "For fuck's sake, light it!" If he were here, I'd flip him off. What a fucking jealous prick.

Sighing heavily, I'm about to do that when I notice a woman standing in front of me, her mouth hanging open as her eyes roam around everywhere, and she whispers, "No intruders." She is probably going to scream and call for help, and this is not part of our plan.

Jaxon will handle the security guys while I need to create panic, but it has to be unexpected. In this play, each one of us has a specific role, and we cannot allow the audience to leave before the grand finale.

Before she can spin around, I grab her by the nape, and she struggles in my arms as I wrap my hands tightly around her neck, choking her when I press on her artery with enough force for her to faint but not die.

As she gulps for breath but can't do it, I study her unmistaken beauty. Lake-green eyes that hold so much fear and pain, a perfect combination, blonde locks that fly around with the wind, and pale skin that shows every vein.

Her full mouth with pink lips, which call out to draw blood from them, are another form of art though, making her almost a living porcelain doll.

What a magnificent creature, like a wounded bird that can never find a nest.

Finally, she slumps in my arms, and I place her on the ground outside the fence boards.

I chuckle, looking at the silent town with around twenty houses, and one huge-ass church that sits in the center of it.

Pastor Mark will soon learn that yet another empire of his has burned to the ground. What a grand punishment indeed! At the same time though, it's sad to use fire, my oldest and best friend, on such an imbecile.

The match lights and I drop it to the ground, letting the fire rapidly spread, burning the powder like in a chain, moving and moving where I spread it, and surrounding the town in the flames. It won't harm anyone but will be enough so that they will start running around, and it'll be easy to call the feds.

As long as it keeps burning, and I made sure of that.

For a moment, I'm mesmerized by the orange flames and the power they represent. Thrill penetrates my bones and I inhale deeply, basking in the smell of burned ground.

It's quickly gone though and the voices come back.

Screams, and screams, and screams.

And just like that, my five-second reprieve is over and I have to come back to reality.

Until the next time.

Clicking the call button on my phone, I inform Jax, "I'm done. Your turn." I hang up, not waiting for a reply, as it's time for me to go.

My eyes land on the beauty still lying on the ground, and I tip my head to the side, drinking her in, and imagine what it would be like to show her different kinds of fires.

Would it inspire more fear on her doll-like face? As she really shines then.

Without dwelling on it much, I kneel down and scoop her up in my arms, propping her more firmly on my chest, and disappear into the night with a trophy.

No one said I couldn't leave with a little souvenir from this trip.

Valencia

Standing up, I fall back on the bed as my knees wobble. Groaning into the pillow, I pull at the sheets and lift myself up again, breathing heavily as I glance at the door, which is still wide open as noises come from outside.

Father left in haste; the message on his phone seemed important enough that he didn't even remember to lock me up. That's unusual to say the least.

But I'm not going to look a gift horse in the mouth, and accept it as divine intervention. Although at this point, I think I've accepted that it not always comes on time.

Sometimes it waits to teach you a lesson.

Grabbing the rail at the end of the bed, I move slowly, and each step brings more pain but relief as my muscles learn anew the action after being kept on the bed for so long.

I rest by the headboard, gulping breath while groaning loudly. It would be so easy to lie back down and gaze at the ceiling; this escape probably won't bring anything much anyway.

They will hunt me down with one of their cameras and punish me even more, bringing agony with them and probably stripping my desire to live for good. Is the fight really worth it?

But all this lasts for only a second as the cry of my baby echoes in my ear.

My baby.

They didn't even let me hold her, just took her away as if she belonged to them.

As if she wasn't mine.

She doesn't have anyone but me. I can't give up.

"Mommy will find you," I whisper, and fist my hands while turning and letting go of the wood. I move toward the door, each step surer than the previous one as I ignore everything else but the deep understanding that it's now or never.

And that's when a man shows up in the doorway, reminding me of an angel with his long, black hair and hazel eyes that are devoid of any emotion. His powerful presence almost wills my energy to listen to him

Angel of death.

"Fuck," he mutters, scanning my appearance from head to toe, and I step back, franticly searching for any kind of weapon and failing, because Father wouldn't have left any objects here.

But then something glistens in the night, and I realize it's the knife Father dropped on the floor when they messaged him. I rapidly stoop and pick it up, pressing it against my neck, right on the artery. I guess my adrenaline is running high, allowing me to do the impossible even with my body functioning in half measures. "You come any closer, and I will kill myself." Despite all the things he put me through, Father keeps me alive.

So his dogs won't touch me with that threat looming over their heads.

The stranger raises his hands, but he still holds the gun and speaks softly with a slightly rough tone as if his throat is permanently bruised. "Valencia, I'm not going to hurt you. Just—"

My bitter laughter interrupts him as he thins his lips, clearly displeased with it.

Yeah, well. Fuck him.

But then it dawns on me, and I scream, "Just be compliant, right? No way! Take me to her or I will kill myself." He doesn't look like a guy who is someone's bitch, and if he holds a higher position in Dad's prostitution and trafficking chain or whatever the hell this place is, he must know where my child is.

His brows furrow, as he asks gently, "To who?"

"To my daughter. Take me to her."

His eyes widen in shock as strange emotions cross his face and he speaks into the radio that he takes from his back pocket. "Jaxon, you here?"

There is a buzzing sound, and the man on the other end of the line replies, "Yeah, what's up?"

"You found the kids?"

Found them? Why would they do that? Based on what I understood, Father kept these women with the kids freely roaming in the town until they came of a certain age. Last time he talked about it, he claimed, because of Lachlan, he now has only three boys for the taking.

How on earth he is still alive surprises me. I'd say he deserves death, but it would be an easy out for him.

"Yeah. Why?"

"Was there an infant?"

A longer pause, and then, "Several actually. But there is one that is in the basket with an elderly woman watching over her. A little girl."

I cover my mouth with my hand as tears roll down my cheek, because it means she is alive.

I almost fall to the ground as relief brings so much happiness. He didn't sell her; she is here! All I need to do is get to her and manage to call someone so they will know to come here and do something.

My eyes blur, but I slap myself, searching for clarity. No time for weakness when I'm so close to winning.

The big man exhales, rubbing his chin. "Thank God. Keep an eye on her. She's Lachlan's."

Lachlan's.

Oh my God.

My tortured monster came after me, and this guy must be his protégé.

Sociopath, Shon, Arson, Jaxon, Isabella, and Amalia.

And he sent Sociopath after me, because those hazel eyes of his are hard to miss. I don't have to be strong anymore. My daughter is in safe hands, Lachlan is here, and the man standing in front of me will protect me from any harm.

The knife drops from my hand with a loud clank as I sway to the edge of the bed behind me, and he quickly crushes me to his chest, cursing. "My baby is alive?" I ask, and he winces but nods, barking into the radio. "We're coming, man." With that, he puts it back into his pocket and picks me up, and I have nothing else to do but rest my head on his chest.

But before I let the oblivion consume me, one bright thought nags my mind. If all of them are here saving other kids and disabling the security system, then where is the man behind all this?

Where is my Lachlan?

*L*achlan

"I knew you would come after her." The voice from my childhood greets me as I enter the grand hall. Lights and candles flicker, creating an almost religious and fairytale like atmosphere. "To find me."

That fucking man is all about appearances and luxury after all.

No wonder the biggest house made out of the finest wood and steel belongs to him. This entire fucking place is almost an exact replica of the house where he selected us to entertain his guests.

It probably serves the same purpose with the customers; he just doesn't have a good system in place right now.

And he never will.

He sits on the stage, on his golden throne, sipping wine while smirking at me, and I don't miss the guards surrounding us who all have their guns aimed at me, ready to shoot at his command. "Sometimes she made it so difficult with her belief in you. You poisoned her mind, but I did my best to clean her up after your mess. She will be cured from a disease like you soon."

I barely control the desire to walk up to him and snap his neck with my bare hands. Just the idea that his filthy, sick desires touched my Valencia unsettles me.

No one but me has the right to do anything to her. "Well here I am, then."

His sadistic laugh bounces off the walls as he nods. "True. Your stubbornness will become your ultimate downfall," he informs me, raising his glass to me and then drinking as if wine will help his situation.

Let him enjoy his small victory while he can.

"Last time we saw each other, you promised me revenge." He spreads his arms wide, wine spilling to the ground like droplets of blood. "Did you envision it like this?"

"Pretty much," I reply, and then cut to the chase. "Where is Valencia?" I should remember to act like an obsessed fool who came here, controlled by emotions.

To an extent, it's true, but not the way he wants it.

"You won't kill me until you know." I expect him to send his soldiers at me, but he manages to surprise even me. He waves them off, ordering dismissively. "Get out. Do not disturb us unless I call for you." They frown but follow the command, leaving one by one, while I wonder if it's possible for my guys to kill them in the process.

They do not deserve mercy. A grown-ass man should know better than to support this fucked-up shit. The women had no choice, as they probably saw it as a sanctuary. Most of them will be crushed to realize they brought their kids from one hell to another.

But they will survive, because that's what survivors do.

That's what I was trying to do with Valencia too. Transform her into a survivor when she knew no nightmares, thinking it was only fair, since so many suffered because of her father. I shouldn't have done it; no one should apologize for the sins of their father or for being happy.

Happiness shouldn't be considered something for which people should be punished, and isn't it ultimately what serial killers do?

Search their whole life for the happiness and euphoria that killing brings them, because they know no other way to achieve it.

"When I saw you for the first time with your aunt all these years ago in the selection process—"

"Don't mention her," I snap, but he doesn't listen.

"I'll say whatever I want. I suggest not interrupting me if you want to see my daughter."

I grit my teeth, willing all my self-control in my fists to keep the show going.

"I thought... this is my future heir. A fighter. What your uncle did to you didn't break you. What I did... never. You just learned more, got more skills. With a son like you, this empire could have become so much bigger. So much stronger. We could have raised generations with our values. In time, I would have even given you Valencia as my gift." I barely contain myself from laughing in his face, because this man is delusional.

Laughing, I taunt him. "Even if Peaceful Heaven stayed untouched, I'd never have been by your side."

He squeezes the glass in his hand, fury crossing his face. "Arrogant. Always so arrogant. You would have, because then the devil wouldn't have tarnished your soul."

"The devil owns it, I think. So it's a lost cause," I inform him, and he clearly has enough.

Fucking finally.

He flashes the gun out of his lap, aiming it at me. "Did you really think this would end with you and me? I will never give you my daughter. You shouldn't have touched her. She is pure, and you are—"

"What you made me," I tell him, but he shakes his head. Of course he won't agree with it. He thinks I became a monster due to the fire. Losing my faith and all that jazz.

What an idiot.

"You lost again, Lachlan. But this time I won't leave any loose ends." With that, he fires the gun, and simultaneously the light on my watch beeps red.

Hiding my grin, I pretend to evade the bullets, turning to the specific side, while inside there is nothing but satisfaction.

Showtime.

*V*alencia

Sociopath places me in the church's main hall, and I rest my back against the bench, gulping fresh air and scrunching my eyes under the harsh light.

People sit around us with crying kids and women soothing them gently. Several men are tied in ropes, their guns lying on the ground. If this is the entire community, then Father didn't have enough time to build it into something big.

Thank God.

"They weren't cooperating. The FBI should be here soon, so we really need to move before they show up." He puts his hand on my shoulder, giving me a reassuring smile. "You can tell them everything, and then they will take you home." I read the meaning between the lines easily; they can't be around for the feds. So it will be up to me to explain everything as believably as possible without mentioning any of their names.

But in this moment, all this has secondary meaning to me. "My daughter?" He lifts a chin to his right, and I follow his gaze to see a dark-haired man walking toward us, holding a bundle in his arms.

He gives me a weird look and then puts her in my open arms, and for the first time ever, I hug my little bean close. She is sleeping, munching on the pacifier so peacefully it breaks and mends my heart at the same time. Running my finger over her gentle face, I can't stop the tears falling on her, as I murmur, "Hi, baby girl." She shifts a little, and I lift her up, pressing my cheek against hers, rocking her from side to side, empowering love flowing from me as everything else ceases to exist in this moment.

There is only me, and her smell, her breath, and just her. I never imagined meeting my child for the first time under the current circumstances, but at the same time, it's a dream come true. All the pain, all the suffering, even the psychological torture experienced back in the mansion is worth it, because it gave me her.

I always heard women say that you fall in love with your baby fast, but I never believed it. But how can I feel anything but love for her when she has been under my heart for eight long months, the scariest months of my life?

"I wouldn't have survived without you," I murmur into her ear, giving her a light peck on the forehead. "I'm so happy no one hurt you." I hiccup, sending a prayer to God, thanking him for keeping her safe despite all the odds.

She is a fighter, just like her dad.

"Lachlan?" I address the man, who is Jaxon, I assume. "If you are all here, where is he?"

They share a long stare and then sigh heavily, while Jaxon motions for Sociopath to speak. "He is a bit busy right now."

"Busy?" Disbelief laces my voice, as I rock my daughter in my arms. "He's not here with me in all this madness… because he's busy?" What kind of bullshit is this? He would have never allowed other men, even his most trusted students to…

No.

Licking my chapped lips, I say without any hint of question in my tone. "He went after my father, didn't he."

They stay silent, but that is enough.

Feds.

If they want to leave before they show up, it means they had a specific plan in motion, a plan orchestrated by Lachlan.

Till my and his death.

He didn't go to my father with the hope of finding me with him or obtaining revenge.

He went after him to finish everything where it all started.

In Pastor's mansion.

*L*achlan

Blood is slipping through my fingers as I hold my side where the bullet entered my liver, bringing pulsing pain from it along with the bullet in my thigh. I sway back a little as Pastor continues to laugh, standing up from his throne and crashing the glass against the wall, crunching it even more under his leather shoes.

"All your reputation is nothing compared to my power." His footsteps are exceptionally loud, as I can't stand straight anymore and fall on my knees, breathing heavily, hanging my head as blood soaks my sweater. "The power is not in torture skills," he shouts in disgust, "but in knowing the weaknesses of your opponent. You were always stupid.

Egocentric. Had no chance for anything. Valencia was supposed to be what?" He reaches me, stepping on my hand, and I stifle a groan. "Your weapon against me. A decoy that would catch the hunter. And how did that work for you?" he asks, kicking me in my wounded side, and I breathe in, not giving him the satisfaction of the burning that consumes me. "I killed your aunt and cousin." He kneels down, fisting my hair and bringing it up so our eyes meet, his wildly excited and mine void of any emotion. "And I will kill you too. So my daughter can be free from the dirt you smeared her in and start her life anew. With the right man picked by me. My empire will thrive, and you'll be forgotten like the piece of trash that you are," he says, putting the gun to my heart, and that's when my mouth spreads in a wide smile.

Sliding my hands from my wound, I swiftly snatch the knife from the side of my boot and stab him right in the back, between his fifth and sixth vertebrae, and his screams fill the room.

Ah, now this is more like it. That theater of one actor started to bore me.

He huffs as I stab again between fourth and fifth, and then again between third and fourth. "Did you really think I would come to you begging?" I mutter, maintaining a tight grip on his neck, squeezing the life out of him as he becomes redder with each tightening of my hand. "Everything is a careful plan with me. You think I'd want to kill you? Death is a reward to you. No, you will suffer with paralysis in prison. Where everyone will know what you did." Fear shades his eyes as I smirk. "And you know what they do there to those who hurt kids, don't you?"

I've never had it in my plans to end his suffering. I wanted to find him so he wouldn't touch other kids, but for him I always had a specific ending. One that will put him in the lowest spot on the chain and will make him suffer every single day. "And the fire will crumble this empire too."

He struggles to say something, but I push him aside as he coughs, gulping air but at the same time groaning in agony as blood smears his shirt.

Whoever comes to his aid will be too late. His spine is damaged and nothing, not even the golden hands of surgery, will save him.

He won't ever walk again.

Inhaling air, I close my eyes as I finally allow myself to feel the tremendous pain, but he didn't do any important damage as I dipped, giving him only those places to shoot where I knew I could survive.

But as I concentrate on my breathing, I don't notice him reaching for his gun, and before I can react, he fires it at me, shooting me right in the heart. And everything stills.

Quite an iconic moment we have now.

He truly ended it where it all began.

Ah, how fucking dramatic.

"Lachlan!" A shout from behind me snaps my attention as I swing my head to the side to see Valencia running toward me barefoot, in her white nightgown that is smeared in dirt. She drops on her knees, touching my wounds. "No, no. We need to call for help."

My beautiful angel, ready for the rescue.

"Shh," I say, cupping her face as my blood marks her skin, and I bring her closer. We are in our respective colors, black and white, and when it mixes it doesn't end up being gray.

It becomes red.

If the bullet hit the artery, I have a maximum fiv minutes to live. I'm not spending them on dwelling on the fucker. "My Valencia." I kiss her hard on the mouth, demanding entrance, and she answers, but I'm too weak to continue it and I slide to the side and roll on my back. I cough on the blood spilling from my mouth.

Five minutes come all too soon. "Lachlan," she cries out, but it's late.

Too late.

My eyelids drop and I count in my head, oddly welcoming this freedom and sensation, because I did what I came here for.

Killed my creator.

And freed my angel.

Maybe I came into the world to accomplish this, and what a life it has been.

"Lachlan," her voice comes from far away as I count.

Five. Four. Three. Two. One.

And here comes the all too familiar darkness.

EPILOGUE

Paris, France
  Six years later

*V*alencia
        The birds chirp loudly, flying around the emerald green
trees while the air is filled with the smell of freshly cut grass as we walk
on the narrow concrete path to the local cemetery.

MacKenzie bounces in front of me, huffing loudly, and then stops,
propping the flowers in her hands higher, and resumes her walk as her
chocolate hair sways from side to side. Her pink sandals that go with
her flowery dress slap against the concrete, sending small rocks flying.

"Do your feet hurt, darling?"

She shakes her head, giving me a toothless smile. She had her first
ballet class a few days ago, and I watched her carefully, making sure she
didn't overdo it and her teachers treated her well.

Finally, we reach the silver headstone, and she squeals, "Look,
Mommy! They bloomed!" Indeed, the tulips we put in the soil gave
fruit and now the entire stone has yellow flowers all over it. She shifts

to me and gives me the bouquet as she runs toward the hose, a stubborn expression on her face. She always acts like they have a fight going on and she wins every single time.

MacKenzie generally enters competitions only if she can win, as defeat doesn't work well for her.

We quickly water the flowers, and then I kneel in front of the stone and take a deep breath, closing my eyes. "Hi, there," I say, wondering if he can hear us up there. In exactly the same moment, the chapel bells ring and a soft smile spreads on my mouth.

I think I can consider it a sign he does.

Dusting away the headstone with my white-glove-covered hand, I place ten red roses on the grave while MacKenzie scatters a few candies on it, and I exhale in exasperation. She gives me a look while batting her eyelashes at me. "Mommy, I'm sure they take sweets to heaven." Then she leans to my ear, and whispers, "They always disappear from here." More like birds snag them once we leave.

Her sky blue orbs practically drill into my soul, reminding me so much of Lachlan that it takes me a moment to snap out of my stupor and shake my head. "No matter how much I explain, it won't help, huh?" I pinch her nose, and she giggles, kneeling next to me while wrapping her hands around my neck, and I hug her close. "I miss him, Mommy," she murmurs, and my heart painfully pangs as I pat her back. "Me too." She wiggles out of my hold and hops to pick a few dandelions that are scattered over the place on this beautiful August day.

"MacKenzie is almost six now. She has a birthday party tomorrow." I stop as a tear slides down my cheek, and I quickly wipe it away before she notices it. Clearing my throat, I continue. "I wish you were here to see it. She constantly runs around with your picture when we are in the house." Rubbing the stone again, I whisper, "Miss you." And then I get up and call for my daughter. "Mac, come on. We will be late for your practice." She hops to me, throwing a few dandelions on the grave and then blowing one in my direction. As the white things fly around us, I wink at her.

She locks her hand with mine and we slowly walk back to the car as she keeps telling me about the new move Mistress Julia promised to teach her. As she babbles away, I wonder how fast the time has passed and about all the changes that have happened in my life.

The FBI were quickly on the scene, not even shocked with what they found. I suspected my father was on their radar for a long time, but without proof, they couldn't do anything about it. They helped to get most of the kids back to their homes, and they asked me tons of questions, but I couldn't concentrate on any of them.

Not after how it all ended.

They took my statement about my captivity and what led to me being in the mansion. It was self-defense, so no one had any more questions for me, although they had plenty for everyone who worked for my dad. Surprisingly, all those fucked-up people truly believed he had the right to behave like that.

I had to spend nearly a month with Mac in the hospital until we were discharged, and Mom met us at the gate, crying her heart out. Victor told us everything would be different, and in a way, it was. She always knew the truth about him, but couldn't do anything, because he threatened my safety.

At that point, the information didn't surprise me. Dad couldn't walk and was sentenced to prison for life with no chance for parole or appeal. His lawyer tried to get him into a facility, but it didn't help.

Last time I heard, Lachlan's friends made his life there a living hell. I thought it would bother me more, but in truth, I've accepted that he is my father and someday MacKenzie will know the story too.

Accepting it though and dwelling on the past that I can never change are two different things, and I've learned to let go.

After everything, I couldn't stay in New York anymore, as the city brought nothing but bad memories to me, and I needed to escape it for just a little while. We found a house on the outskirts of Paris that opened up to a beautiful view of the outdoors, and the nearby town was so small that literally everyone knew everyone.

With time, Bella introduced me to dance gurus in France, and I staged a few dances with my experience and then opened up my own studio that thrived under my touch, and parents brought their kids from all over the city. Mackenzie and I explored the city, danced together, and learned to be happy without feeling guilty about it.

A few months ago, I opened a studio in New York, so we travelled between countries, living life to the fullest.

"Daddy!" MacKenzie screams and lets go of me, her little feet pounding loudly as she darts toward the man in jeans and a T-shirt, who leans on the black Mercedes. He kneels down, opens his arms wide, and she jumps into them as he locks them tight around her, breathing in her scent.

She leans back, palming his face. "Did you bring me anything?" The man tenses a little, but nods and gives her the box in his hand, and she claps her hands. "Yay! A tutu?" His gaze catches mine and I just shrug.

It was his idea to introduce her to ballet. I preferred something else for her.

He moves the loose strands of her hair to behind her ear, and finally replies, "Whatever you want, MacKenzie. It's a box of wishes." Her mouth drops open, and then she turns to me, saying, "Daddy is the best, Mommy!" And she presses her cheeks against his. "I love you, Daddy." He doesn't reply, but she doesn't expect it. She knows he never says it back. Lachlan shows his love with his actions, but he never speaks of it.

"We visited Levi. It's bad he decided to leave three year ago. He didn't see me dance." She pouts, and I imagine he would have loved to know his little grandkid missed him.

Levi enjoyed his role until the sudden heart attack took him away from us, and his last wish was to be buried near this chapel, because he found peace here.

Lachlan never visits, because just stepping on any soil that has to do with church... yeah, it never ends well for him. So MacKenzie and I come here every month alone.

"Now let's go!" she tells him, and he wiggles his brow at me. "The adventures await!" She raises her hand high and Lachlan rolls his eyes.

He puts her inside the car and then nods at me, even though his stare drills into me. Everything in me longs to join them, but I know I can't.

It's the choice we made a long time ago. I go to Chapel every Sunday, but he can't, nor does he allow MacKenzie to go inside. When she grows older, she might do it if she wants to, but for now... it's impossible to reason with him. That's why they usually have their father-daughter time while I spend some quality time here.

MacKenzie waves at me as my husband joins her in the car and they drive away, leaving me behind while all I can do is watch them in the dust that springs up in the air.

* * *

*C*losing the door behind me after MacKenzie finally fell asleep, I remove my scarf and pad downstairs to my studio that we built in case I needed to practice, and I grab my pointe shoes on the way.

Putting everything on, I turn on the music, and Lana Del Rey's "Religion" softly starts playing. My eyes close, letting it wash over me, as this song speaks the truth about my emotions.

Slowly, I dance, giving myself to the music and the words, my hands moving in synchronization with my legs as the black skirt swirls around me and my shoes slap against the wood.

For a moment, the music quiets and I freeze in place, gulping for breath, and then it picks up again, but that's when strong arms wrap around me, and the hair on my neck prickles as the man brings me flush against him.

He pulls on my hair, opening up my neck for his mouth, and my eyes close the minute his lips touch my heated skin. His hand slides down my waist before squeezing my hip harshly, and a moan of pained pleasure slips past me. "Lachlan," I whisper, and he spins me around, holding me tight in his arms.

Placing my palms on his chest, I kiss his heart before raising my eyes to him as he hikes me up, leaving me no choice but to circle my legs around him. "You shouldn't do this."

He chuckles against my mouth, biting on my chin, and I throw my head back as his lips slide down my neck, leaving little flashes of desire everywhere. "There are a lot of things I shouldn't do. When did it stop me?" His mouth lands on mine, taking it prisoner as his tongue probes deep, and I just press against him harder.

My safe harbor.

He didn't receive a shot to his heart as he initially thought, but instead the bullet grazed his shoulder. He felt the pain in his chest and combined with the wound in his liver, it all kind of bundled into one pain for him. Thankfully, medics arrived along with feds and they took him in a helicopter to the hospital where he had surgery.

My back hits the wall as he rips my shirt open and my thighs squeeze him tightly as both of us groan. "Those trips to New York will kill me. You better move there permanently," he growls, biting my lips while his fingers slip past my skirt, reaching the naked skin, and a tremor runs through me.

He has been away on some business deal for the past seven days; he always has one when it's this time of the year. I think the loss of Levi is too great for him, but he never talks about it.

He didn't transform into the perfect husband who has a nine to five job while he comes to enjoy his time with the family. He is still dark and broody, ruling his protégés with an iron fist.

Once the nightmare was over, I understood with clarity that I couldn't live without him, nor did I want to. For all the dark stuff he does, maybe he is the balance this world needs. And maybe it's better to teach all those lost souls how to control their desires and concentrate them on specific targets, instead of roaming around the world, chasing everyone who stands in their way.

He is still very much a serial killer who enjoys torture, although he keeps this life hidden from us.

Lachlan is no prince and never will be.

But he is the man I love, and that's enough for me.

All this may end quickly, and suddenly, he could die any minute and I wouldn't even know why. But while he is here with me, life is bliss.

I lived perfection, and it brought nothing but sorrow. His darkness, though, opened up the doors to happiness for me.

How can I turn my back on it?

"Valencia," he murmurs against my mouth, and our eyes meet as he tangles his hand in my hair, bringing us even closer to the point of us sharing a breath. "You are my symphony."

I smile softly, hugging him close as we freeze in this moment that cements everything between us.

That's why I stay and will never leave.

The End

ACKNOWLEDGMENTS

First, I want to thank God and my family for allowing me to write and make this dream possible. The support means so much to me, and I understand that sometimes it drives you crazy, especially when I try to meet my deadlines and seem unavailable to you. But I love you guys and appreciate everything you do for me.

Lachlan was one of the first heroes who popped in my head back in 2016. I had a prologue and chapter one ready along with the plot...but I couldn't write the book. I would come back to the manuscript several times a year, but something wouldn't click. Finally while writing Psychopath's Prey, I knew he was ready to tell his story. I hope you enjoyed reading it.

Huge thank you to Hot Tree Editing team for helping me with my editing process. Especially Becky, Donna, Peggy, Kayla and Mandy. Plus beta readers and final eyes, who gave me valuable feedback and made sure I covered any plot holes I had.

Thank you to Sommer Stein, Wander Aguiar and Colton Benson for the fabulous cover.

Heather Roberts and Lauren Rosa, thank you for being with me during this release every step of the way.

L. Woods PR thank you for hosting my cover reveal and release blitz.

Thank you to Ena and Amanda from Enticing Journey Book Promotions for hosting my release blitz as well. It's always a pleasure working with you, ladies!

Thank you to my V's Sapphires, ladies you are amazing!

Thank you to all the bloggers for spreading the word about Lachlan's Protégé and leaving reviews.

And finally to all the readers who took a chance on this journey of love between Lachlan and Valencia. Thank you to each one of you.

ALSO BY V. F. MASON

Dark Romance

Sociopath's Obsession

Sociopath's Revenge

Psychopath's Prey

Mafia Romance

Pakhan's Rose

Pakhan's Salvation

Sovietnik's Fury

Brigadier's Game

Contemporary Romance

Shane's Truth

Coming Soon

Kaznachei's Pain

Forbidden Jaxon

CONNECT

Website: http://vfmason.com
Newsletter: http://eepurl.com/bTq66n
Reader group - V's Sapphires: http://bit.ly/2iXZdol

Made in the USA
Coppell, TX
26 October 2020